D1409844

# THE
# EVERYTHING
# GIRL

## L. MALEKI

*with Holly Lörincz*

Skyhorse Publishing

Copyright © 2018 by L. Maleki

All rights reserved. No part of this book may be reproduced in any manner without the express written consent of the publisher, except in the case of brief excerpts in critical reviews or articles. All inquiries should be addressed to Skyhorse Publishing, 307 West 36th Street, 11th Floor, New York, NY 10018.

Skyhorse Publishing books may be purchased in bulk at special discounts for sales promotion, corporate gifts, fund-raising, or educational purposes. Special editions can also be created to specifications. For details, contact the Special Sales Department, Skyhorse Publishing, 307 West 36th Street, 11th Floor, New York, NY 10018 or info@skyhorsepublishing.com.

Skyhorse® and Skyhorse Publishing® are registered trademarks of Skyhorse Publishing, Inc.®, a Delaware corporation.

Visit our website at www.skyhorsepublishing.com.

10 9 8 7 6 5 4 3 2 1

Library of Congress Cataloging-in-Publication Data is available on file.

Cover design by Erin Seaward-Hiatt

Print ISBN: 978-1-5107-3126-4
Ebook ISBN: 978-1-5107-3127-1

Printed in the United States of America

If two wrongs don't make a right,
try three.
—*Laurence J. Peter*

# Prologue

"How much do you charge?" I asked.

The woman smiled, her teeth snow-white. Expensive high-lights and lowlights in her long hair glistened against a slinky black jumpsuit. Her shoulders were bared and New York pale. "It depends—"

A horn from Park Avenue's never-ending traffic drowned out the last of her words. The woman, maybe ten years older than me, paused, unwilling to raise her voice. Instead, she drew me across the threshold, the ornate doors ringing shut behind us.

I tried unsuccessfully to hide my trembling. With a tilted eyebrow and posh accent, the woman said, "I'm Madame Elena. Do you know where you are?"

Staring at a handful of men in suits moving between the negligee-clad women lounging on velvet couches in the dim lobby of a private theater in Midtown, I had a damn good idea. The muffled burlesque music from behind a set of double doors did not entirely mask the groans coming from the writhing shadows in the dark corners. According to Frank, the floors above housed suites furnished by Armani Casa. Suites you could rent by the hour. Decadent, gilded apartments meant for boinking strangers.

*I should be back at Galli's with my friends, laughing and drinking cheap wine, or, since my friends currently hate me,* in my tiny apartment eating Spicy Doritos I bought from the Bodega guy who doubles as my therapist. I should be watching a marathon of Friends and trying to tune out the endless horns and sirens and shouting and the voice in my head asking why in the hell am I still here.

"Um, there's these clients . . . my boss . . ." My neck hurt from locking my head into one position to avoid accidentally looking around. I, in no way, wanted to cross glances with a rich dude rubbing his crotch.

I want to die.

"Ah, yes. Of course. There's always a boss." Madame Elena's sleek stilettos tapped across the marble floor to the leather bar that apparently doubled as a reception desk. Over her shoulder, she asked, "Are you a secretary?"

My voice climbed as I said, "I am an executive assistant to the CEO. I have a degree in finance!" I ended on a high c.

She ignored my lame, operatic attempt at justifying my existence. "Did he give you a passcode?"

"Jump Street 1987." Back to a whispering tenor, I felt stupid saying it aloud. Then again, I felt stupid being there, gawky and unkempt amongst the languishing herd of exotic women.

"Ah, so he's a big gun, then. When does he require our services? How many women does he want? Did he give you any names in particular?"

The heat prickled across my cheeks and over my scalp. Instead of answering, I fumbled out a bundle of one hundred dollar bills—$10,000 in total—from my tote bag and handed it over. I was unwilling to repeat Frank's instructions aloud, but his words were seared into my brain: *"Jordy prefers Asians. Chris will be happy if she has a vagina. Me, I prefer a Bubbles over a Jasmine. And when I say 'Bubbles,' I mean a natural blonde with big tits."*

I couldn't say that, not to this woman. I sucked in a lungful of air and tried not to cry. "Frank wants three women. May I . . . look over . . . who's available right now?"

She gracefully gestured to the room. "If you don't see anything you like here, I have a catalog."

I shut my eyes. *She said see anything. Not anyone. Are they okay with that?* But I didn't keep my eyes closed to reality for long. Surveying the room, I saw my expression reflected over and over in the faces of the women around me, calm and pleasant masks with a banked fire sparking deep in the eyes. Were they angry? Afraid? Feeling trapped, powerless? Or was I projecting myself onto them? Maybe they were completely empowered and just really tired after a long shift of putting up with sweaty men.

Pointing to a blonde, a redhead, and an Asian woman, as if I were choosing dim sum from a cart, I felt my soul try to leave my body. "I will take those three, please." I spasmed, hearing the words. *If my mom were alive, if she knew I was renting women at the command of my male boss . . . well.*

I made a strange gurgling sound. And this is how I came to know that a top-shelf escort was well worth the money: Madame Elena took one look at my splotching skin and stroked my hair as my face crumpled. She made soothing, maternal noises, leading me away from the humping masses. She knew how to handle distraught girls.

After wiping streaks of mascara off my cheeks, the beautiful lady of the house gently placed her fingertips under my chin and tilted up my face. "You look so young; everyone must think you're a teenager." Then, untangling long dark strands of hair from my gold hoop earring, she said, "You know, with those big brown eyes, that dusky skin, you should consider working for me. I always like to have the Middle Eastern look on tap."

A bray of laughter shot out of me. A symphony of shifting satin and silk filled the room as women swiveled around in search of the jackass. I spied the heavy, closed doors and boiled with an urgent need to escape to the other side.

A gob of spit dropped onto my shirt before I could mash my lips back together.

The women watched as I wiped the saliva away, leaving a smear of wet across my chest. *Just trying to make sure I don't leave with* any *dignity intact.*

# Chapter 1

*Six Months Earlier* . . .

If I closed my eyes, I could picture Darien in front of me, cupping his balls. After I kicked them. Really hard. But when I opened my eyes, the fantasy faded. The white picket fence and surrounding suburbia were still there, and, as far as I knew, so were his man parts.

And I could still feel: The splinters from the porch swing poking at the back of my bare legs. The damp of the Pacific in the breeze. The cell phone in my hand, laden with weighty text messages.

*Really, Darien? Her?*

*What are you talking about?*

*I saw you. She's one of my clients. Douchebag.*

*Listen, she's Jewish. You know that's important to me. It's time to move on, Paris.*

*You dick. You didn't say it was over, you said we were on a break. So, now, you break up in a text. How Millennial of you.*

My dad stepped onto the porch. "Paris? What are you doing out here?"

I shrugged, pushing off the floorboards to keep the bench swinging. If I told my father about Darien breaking up with me in a text, his irritated-old-man side would kick in, lecturing me about technology and the downfall of humanity, and then how Darien was a simpleton and a snob. And then his patriarchal side would show up.

No, that wasn't fair. My father had never been oppressive. Never.

Ehsan Tehrani had left Iran and his brothers and sisters because he didn't want me to grow up under the same regime that forced my mother, a strong-willed woman, to cover up. After twenty-five hundred years of continuous Persian monarchy and freedom, my young mother and father were surprised when a new Khomeini and his sexually frustrated guerilla leaders barged into power. And, unfortunately, they were extremists with a special hatred for females, who'd been turning up their noses at them since elementary school. So, Persian women abruptly went from being part of everyday life, laughing and talking in the streets, dressed in miniskirts and pantsuits, to second-class citizens pushed into hiding by crazy men who filled their pockets with stones and made themselves little morality police badges.

My mother had eyeballed the long coat and hijab headdress she was supposed to put on over her favorite blue sailor dress and gold hoop earrings, looked at her husband and me—an infant at the time—and made my father promise they would get out as soon as they could.

Before I reached the age I would have to cover my hair, my father brought us to the land of the free. I didn't remember my mother, not really, since she died of cancer when I was only three, but our house in California was covered with photos of a smiling woman who always had a hand on my head or my father's shoulder. Because of my mother and father, I'd spent my teen years daydreaming about dancing in a music video or wearing a sexy cocktail dress to my own showing at an art gallery, instead of learning to sew from under the heat of a black drape.

My father wasn't caught up in being the stereotypical, stern-faced masculine type. Nor was he particularly religious—when I was in high school and wanted to see the inside of a mosque, my dad had to search for the address in a phone book.

I grew up an all-American girl, Iranian traditions folded comfortably into an all-American home run by a single dad who fawned over my report card and was proud of his lawn, grilled hot dogs, and made baklava for my friends before we tromped down to the beach and spied on the lifeguards. He believed wholeheartedly in working toward the American dream with Persian rugs underfoot. The only real throw-down argument we'd ever had was when Dad told me he wouldn't pay for my college if I majored in art.

"How many famous photographers are out there?" he'd said. "I can name two. How many poor, hungry artists? The list begins with last year's art majors."

Though I conceded to his good sense and majored in finance, it rankled.

Still, when my internship at Deutsche Bank turned into a long-term position working with mortgage-backed securities, I stayed. What else was I going to do? I was good at it. I was making money, learning fast, and successfully pretending to be a real adult. I was bored out of my mind and the color drained out of my life, but I was well respected and felt like a functioning part of society. And, occasionally, I met eligible businessmen. That's how I met Darien.

Stupid Darien. I should have known the day he marched up to my desk in the back of the bank that he was not like my dad. I should have known the dark, handsome man would take advantage of my . . . of me.

"Ms. Tehrani?" His darkly fringed eyes had moved across the nameplate on my desk, then to my face, where they'd stayed. "No one else here seems to know what they're talking about. Do you?"

Not the most romantic of beginnings, but over drinks that night, he'd complimented my mother's earrings and asked me questions about my dreams. We discovered we had a number of friends in common. Darien, who was only two years older than me, ran his own import company, and that was pretty damn attractive—especially when the bulk of men I'd dated played World of Warcraft or Halo like it was a job. And he'd treated me as an equal, discussing problems with his business and eliciting my advice. We'd have long, thoughtful discussions on how to grow his business, or about the world of finance in general, and go on expensive wine tours. It felt like an adult relationship.

It didn't hurt that the confident, sleek man was Persian—my dad was thrilled. That is, until Darien wanted me to convert to Judaism. My dad rolled his eyes and shook his shiny bald head in exasperation whenever he saw me studying the Hebrew Bible.

"You cannot acquire a new belief system simply because someone tells you to, Paris. Believe me, I know."

Oddly, once I'd capitulated, Darien became increasingly condescending, when he wasn't being distant. Darien said he was starting to wonder if he needed a "real" Jewish woman in his life. Conversion wasn't enough.

Then, last week, came the worst blow: "You're just too accommodating, Paris. You'll do anything to please anyone. Maybe we should take a break."

I'd spent the last few days crying the ugly cry, off and on, waiting for him to contact me, to break the break. My father said nothing, only handed me a cup of tea occasionally. Nor did he say anything as I planted myself on the couch, eating tubs of ice cream and trying to figure out what being on a "break" meant.

Darien was right. Accommodation was my greatest flaw. While it often opened doors, it sometimes threw me to the floor, a doormat to be stepped on. As evidenced by me joining a religion with which I had no emotional ties, me putting up with tepid orgasms, and me continuing to live at home, helping with the family business, way past the time I should have been buying my own dining set.

And so, here I was, on my father's porch, dealing with a breakup like a middle schooler, hiding my texts from my dad.

"Can I sit with you, *Parisa*, my little fairy?"

I snorted at the endearment, as he knew I would. "Dad, how many times do we have to talk about that?"

He settled next to me on the porch swing, barely disrupting the sway. He'd bought this house because of the swing and the iconic white fence—he claimed because he thought it was so hilariously Americana. But he painted that fence every six months. He kept it clean and sturdy. Looking at it glowing in the sun now, I knew for him it was really a symbol of security and pride. It was a symbol that the Tehrani family belonged in this neighborhood, with a white picket fence just like the rest.

And suddenly, I knew I was about to break Dad's heart and leave him alone, inside this bubble he'd created for us.

I switched off my phone and put it to the side. There was nothing left here for me. Darien had never been worth sticking around for, anyway. We'd only ever had one common interest, business, and that interest was not my passion. He'd just been a handsome excuse for avoiding the unknown in the bigger world.

The only *real* reason I had for not leaving was Dad, who was shorthanded at his accounting office. I was accommodating him, too, but he wasn't taking advantage of me like Darien. He was family, and he needed me to help with clients. These days, however, business was slow, with fewer and fewer people bringing their money to Tehrani Tax Services, probably afraid my sweet father had a terrorist cell hidden under his desk.

He didn't need me like he used to.

"Did you hear, Paris? A local shop caught a man stealing yesterday." Before I could react, Dad grinned. There was a big pause. "He was balanced on the shoulders of two vampires. He was charged with shoplifting on two counts."

I groaned. "Dad, no. Just no." Somehow, his stupid jokes were even more ridiculous when delivered in his stilted, proper English.

"What? Other people are making apocalypse jokes like there is no tomorrow."

"Seriously, Dad, you're killing me."

"Then tell me what is going on, *khoshgeleh*." He called me pretty in Farsi and folded his hands in his lap, waiting.

I said it quickly, not giving myself a chance to change my mind. "I need to move out . . . to move away. I want to build my own life."

Without any hesitation, he clapped his hands once in delight. "It is about time. Go to Wall Street. Make a splash."

"Dad?" I couldn't have been more shocked if my dad had showed up at my favorite bar on karaoke night and busted out some Jay Z.

"I will be fine. It is time you went out on your own."

"I thought . . . I thought I was doing what you wanted."

"I am not an idiot. I am not going to saddle you with my responsibilities. I am not willing to give up just yet, but neither am I going to tie you to a shrinking business. I will miss you, my little flower. But you have been staying because you feel safe, not because of me."

"You know that's not true—"

He put his hand on my shoulder. "Do not get me wrong. I know you are loyal and helpful, and I have been grateful for your help. I have made it an easy decision for you to stay. Now, I am making it an easy decision for you to go."

It was way past time I left our house, went through the gate on our white picket fence, and became a self-sufficient, independent adult. Something inside me leapt and zinged around, joyous, free . . . but something else tugged that joy back down, something akin to guilt and loss and *What the hell do I do now?*

# Chapter 2

The next day, sitting at my desk in the bank, I spotted my client—Darien's "real" Jewish darling—sashaying past the security guard in her tennis whites. She cooed and rubbed noses with the miniature Chihuahua she carried, so I very maturely darted into the break room before she saw me.

Helena, another securities broker, was at the lunch table, eating my yogurt from the refrigerator. She was a sorority sister from University of California, Irvine. Gesturing to me with the container, unashamed, she said, "Figured you wouldn't mind. You had a couple in there."

"Whatever." I sighed and dropped into a chair. "Take the rest. I'm outta here."

"Seriously?"

"I wish. If I could find another job in another state, I'd be on a plane tomorrow. I want California and Darien in my rearview."

"Ah. I see." She slurped up a spoonful of Dannon strawberry thoughtfully. "Have you talked to Gina?"

I stared at her blankly, distracted by the white blob on her chin.

"You know, Gina Romano? She was Sigma Kappa." She pointed at me with a plastic spoon. "She's a headhunter on the east coast now."

"Really? Is she back in New Jersey?"

"I don't think so. I'm pretty sure she's working for Glocap, a Manhattan recruiting firm."

"Huh." New York. It was definitely another state. An entire continent away from Darien. It was also the financial center of the world. If I was going to try to make it in finance, I might as well swing for the fence. It was what my dad wanted. I was good at it. I could do it, but did I want to?

"Paris?" The manager stuck her head in the door. "You have a client waiting for you. She's got a dog with her. Please remind her of our policy about animals."

I bit my thumbnail and stared past the manager. From behind her, a high-pitched yipping bounced off the bank's highly stylized adobe walls. *Oh yeah, I want to do it. I want to go. My boyfriend's new girlfriend wouldn't dare bring her vanity dog into the Federal Reserve Bank of New York.*

......................

Within a week, I was in New York, Gina Romano bent over my shoulder, digging her pointy chin into my neck.

"As much as I appreciate the massage, can you give me some space?" I asked. My friend from university reminded me of a French bulldog. Short and tenacious with cute cheeks you just wanted to pinch. But her chin could be used as a weapon.

When I'd called to see if she knew of any job openings in the Manhattan banks, she had first screamed in delight and then yelled at me to pack up and move across country that very minute. I barely remembered the drive through the states, having distracted myself from the boring, mostly rainy roads by listening to Suze Orman podcasts on managing money and practicing my interviewing skills.

I'd landed at Gina's SoHo apartment three days ago. Gina's roommate, Lucia, hadn't been nearly as thrilled when I showed up with four suitcases and a bag of my dad's sangak bread, exploring the city by day, riding the couch by night.

"Paris, let me help," Gina barked. "This is what I do. I get people jobs. Besides, the faster you get a job, the sooner you can get your own apartment and stop clogging up my shower drain with your ridiculous hair."

Gina and Lucia, Italian American childhood friends, were both hardworking, career-oriented women. They also spent quality time on blowouts and applying hair products, though their hair was much shorter than mine and apparently didn't shed—it definitely was my long, thick strands clogging the drain.

Gina had a trendy chestnut pageboy that went well with her New Jersey accent. Lucia, on the other hand, was a silent, blonde runway model with a shaggy pixie cut and the tendency to sway—when she did speak, her accent was still very Italian. While my old friend Gina was a bulldog, Lucia came off as an underfed minx: skinny, beautiful, and ready to lash out with her sharp claws.

So, what kind of animal was I? I smoothed the dark hairs on my forearms. I decided I was a panther. Maybe I was a little too easygoing for a jungle cat, but I thought with my long, thick tangle of black hair and olive skin, I could pull it off. *Rawr.*

Being silly made me think of Dad. I could easily picture him at his desk, working away as the West Coast sun lit up his office and his bald head . . . while I hunkered down in this cold, shadowed kitchen on a sunless New York afternoon in February.

*Darien is probably on the beach with his new girlfriend right now, rubbing organic oils on her back, discussing schools for their perfect Jewish children.* My stomach clenched. How had I bought into that story for so long?

But his rejection had pushed me into action. Maybe it was for the best. I eyed my stack of luggage in the corner of the living room, ready for a new home. The only other items I'd brought were my laptop and a professional camera, still in the box. The laptop was well used but the camera had been a graduation gift I'd forgotten about, probably because my dad had stashed it in the back of a closet. I figured I could mess around with it while I waited for my callbacks on jobs.

Gina pulled up a chair next to me at the Ikea dining table.

Trying to keep everyone happy, I tapped the computer screen on the table in front of me. "You said to apply for this one, Gina. But I don't see why."

Gina leaned her short, slightly pudgy body back in her chair, folding her hands behind her head. "Loooook, I know you're trying to stick to jobs in banks for now, but you have a degree in finance and a few years in the industry. You want to break onto Wall Street someday, right? So why not try to jump up the ladder?"

"Okay, but this is for an executive assistant."

"You're not looking at the right specs."

"You want me to be an errand girl?"

"What, are you new to this decade? If you can get close to the CEO of a hedge fund—which this is—then you'll be kneeling at the feet of the master. Why start in a cubicle three floors away? Sure, you'll get his coffee and write his reports, but you're going to see how he does what he does. Better, you're going to be in charge of his Rolodex."

"Hmm, okay. I like how you're thinking outside of the box." I wound a pencil in my hair, thinking. "But this position requires over ten years of hedge fund experience. I've never worked with a hedge fund directly."

"Pshh. That doesn't matter. You're smart. Read between the lines. Like, right here, it says, 'Must be able to confidently and professionally manage challenging personalities and high-stress environments.'" She gripped my shoulder and shook me like I wasn't twice her height. "They're saying they need someone who can handle assholes. If you come across as half-way competent with numbers and seem like you're the type to stay calm and say '*namaste*' whenever anyone gives you crap, they're gonna jump at you. Can you ignore a dickhead long enough to get the experience and contacts you need?"

"I don't know—"

"Please. Just tweak your resume to look like you've done this stuff. You *can* do it. Don't be a coward. I need my couch back."

I ducked my head, twisting my mother's gold hoop earring. So far, Gina and her roommate had been pleasant to me. If Lucia was put out, she'd only complained about it in Italian. But her Italian *was* starting to sound increasingly rant-y.

Gina was right; I did have the skills to pull it off and the ability to learn quickly. Besides, the couch was squeaky black leatherette, and I had to sleep on my side like a fetus, afraid to breathe too deeply lest I fall off—but it *had* become my comfort zone, my safe place in this loud, crazy city. Except when my whirling thoughts settled on Darien, and then I'd fixate on how I was never going to find a worthwhile man who liked me for me. Classic, angsty teenager stuff. There was no safe zone from my brain.

Lucia stood in the kitchen doorway. "No offense, Paris, but let's get you out there." The model stepped forward, black dresses and black shirts and black pants draped over one slender arm, and a pack of Benson & Hedges in the other hand. She laid the items, including the cigarettes, in my lap. "You'll need these."

"I *have* nice business clothes! And are you saying I should start *smoking*?"

The model ran her eyes over my purple yoga pants, favorite hoodie, and my non-nicotine stained fingers. "Yes. And everyone smokes. You're not in fucking hippy-land anymore."

Lucia sounded cool even when she was insulting me, with her lilting Italian vowels. She waved a hand over me gracefully. "You go into any interview in the city wearing that yellow skirt you have hanging in the bathroom, they're going to call you a *cafone*. A dork."

I liked her better when she was not talking.

I was skeptical. Skeptical everyone in New York City wore black. Skeptical an entire generation of East Coasters didn't care about lung cancer. Assessing Lucia's clothes, I was skeptical I could fit into a size four—unless, of course, I embraced smoking instead of eating. Mostly, I was skeptical anyone reading my resume would believe I was anything but a rank-and-file kind of girl.

I sighed. *But I can't just sit here and wait for the hand of God to reach down and throw a paycheck at me. Time to get started.*

Gina and Lucia's gazes were heating the back of my head; I opened up the link to the application at Purple Rock Capital Management. *Besides, Lucia probably already has my suitcases in my car.*

# Chapter 3

I sidestepped sidewalk patches of February frost as I made my way to the subway entrance, retching when I put my foot in a bright green glob of phlegm and retching again when I touched something squishy on the underside of the handrail. My gag reflex sat in high gear, thanks to a hangover.

I hated the subway but I was in no shape to negotiate morning traffic in Manhattan; trying to find parking would push me into a stress coma. It's why people who lived in the city didn't drive. I knew with 100 percent certainty, however, that the second I was underground, I was going to get mugged by a middle school gang, or penis-rubbed by a homeless guy, or kidnapped by the mole people and dragged into a dingy, sulfurous underworld.

By the time I spied a map showing the subway routes and had it narrowed down to two lines that might possibly get me to 57th Street, somewhere between Carnegie Hall and Columbus Circle, nervous sweat was pooling in my bra. *Thank God I'm wearing black*, I thought. *Lucia won't be able to see my sweaty boobs outlined on her silk blouse.*

I was on my way to a job interview. I definitely needed the money. The ATM machines heckled me when I walked past. My "life savings" was a joke—when I lived with my father, I'd put my earnings mostly toward paying down my massive student loan debt. Since coming to New York, I'd been trying to maintain what little savings I had so I could afford the deposit on an apartment of my own, but my reserves were dwindling. Despite totally supporting me getting my own place, Lucia and Gina didn't help. They kept trying to get me to go out for drinks and dinner, and never at a Denny's or someplace with a five-dollar special. And they kept dropping not-too-subtle hints that I needed a new wardrobe, but again, not from an affordable source. No, instead, they would use yellow stickies to flag articles on fashion and style in their glamour magazines, with notes like "These would look cute on you" next to a $200 pair of jeans, or "Get rid of your T-shirts" with an arrow pointing to a $150 fitted shirt.

Luckily, I was now able to fit into Lucia's "fat" clothes. Not because of smoking—which she repeatedly suggested—but because of days on the "poverty diet," which consisted of water, carrot sticks, and peanut butter sandwiches on old bread. While saving money, the lack of calories was eating away at my willpower.

Gina had come home from her office in Midtown the night before to find me glassy eyed and depressed after days of sending out queries and resumes to the long list of possibilities she'd put together for me. Over half had already responded with a form letter informing me I was a moron and there was no way they would hire me.

"Let's go out. We need drinks and dicks, stat," Gina said.

"You are so classy." At her look of irritation, I quickly said, "But, yeah, okay, let's go somewhere."

Lucia walked in as I was sliding on a cardigan. "For Christ's sake, Paris. What are you wearing?"

I pinched my pink jersey T-shirt and glared at her. "Listen, this is from Banana Republic. I know how to dress. I don't need an intervention—"

"You look great, Paris," Gina said. "That color is gorgeous against your skin. Lucia simply has lost the ability to dress herself without a manager." She clapped her hands twice, calling us to attention. "Now let's go."

Lucia didn't say anything, just smirked and handed me a fresh pack of cigarettes and the latest edition of *That*, a fashion magazine, before following Gina out the door.

Gina took us to The Rooftop at Viceroy. Her favorite bar was close to Central Park with an amazing view, but it was a twenty-minute taxi ride from SoHo. Once inside, I could feel the base thudding in my chest. As Gina and Lucia yelled over the music with a couple of guys who owned a string of gyms, I wandered around with a Moscow Mule in one hand and an unlit cigarette in the other, drawn to a collection of sepia-toned photos on a back wall. I rolled my eyes when I noticed they were portraits of athletes; this was supposedly a sports bar, but it was packed with suits who likely only spent time on a golf course or were forced to play racquetball with the old guard.

Then the sophistication of the imagery caught and held my gaze. The composition was creative, with fresh angles and perspectives. Each seemed to tell a story about the subject, even the young women, with the focus on different strengths they exuded, not on their thighs or perky breasts.

"So, you like the girls, huh?"

I twisted to my right, ready to lash out at the idiot, but a cute, disheveled guy in jeans and loose button-down shirt held up both hands and laughed. "Wait, don't shoot! I kid! I kid!"

I paused and then said, "Well, to be honest, yeah, I think these are great." I pointed with my drink. "At first glance, I thought they were commercial. But the photographer is pretty amazing. An artist, really."

He smiled, sandy-colored curls swooping across his forehead. Freckles smattered over his nose and cheekbones added a boyishness to his charm. "Eh. He's alright, I guess. At least the chicks are hot."

"Nice." I stepped away, turning to find my friends. *The cute ones are always gay or total jerks.*

"No, wait," he said. I swiveled back to him and he offered a lopsided grin. "I'm sorry. I'm Benji. I took these. See?" He pointed to a name in the corner of one of the photographs. *Benjamin Stark.* "Tonight's the opening for my newest collection. I thought I'd hang out."

"Oh. Okay." I didn't know what else to say.

He laughed again, self-consciously this time. "Alright. I've made this awkward. I'm good at that. Let's start over." He stuck out his hand. "Hi, I'm Benji Stark. What's your name?"

*He really is adorable. And he's got a show in a place like this. How bad can he be?* We chatted for a short while, first about photo lens filters, then about when I thought I might actually smoke the unlit cigarette I'd been holding.

I was disappointed when the owner came by with a couple of art enthusiasts. Paying art enthusiasts.

*Don't leave, okay?* the handsome photographer mouthed behind their backs, which is when I noticed the striking gold-flacked hazel of his eyes. I nodded and made my way over to Gina and Lucia.

"He's not ugly," Gina said.

"And he actually seems to have a brain. Possibly a job." I grinned.

"You can always dream," sighed Lucia. She was ignoring two much older gentlemen who were trying to catch her attention from down the bar. Gina was trying to intercept their gazes, but they weren't budging from the tall blonde throwing them shade.

We tossed down a round of tequila shots, then another.

Soon enough, liquid courage brought one of the older men

into our midst, though he quickly realized Lucia was never going to be interested, or even talk to him. Gina leapt in, using the chance to practice her sharp-tongued banter—Mr. Business called her "feisty" and it was on. Lust was in the air.

I felt my cell phone buzz in my clutch. I took it out, assuming it would be my father with something important to tell me, like "Hey, how come a bike can't stand on its own? 'Cuz it's *two* tired!" followed by a stretch of old-man laughter. But no, it was a number I didn't recognize. A Manhattan number.

"Hello?" I shouted into the phone, ramming my finger in my ear in an attempt to hear over a hundred drunken twenty-somethings and Justin Bieber singing about a woman's vajayjay.

"Is this Ms. Tehrani?"

"Yes . . . ?"

"Good evening. This is Bob from Soloman Page. I'm a recruiter, working with a client of ours, a fifteen billion dollar hedge fund. Do you have a moment?"

Was this guy calling on behalf of Purple Rock Capital? He couldn't be. Yet, that was the only hedge fund I'd applied to.

"Um, yeah, give me a second. I'm going to step outside so I can hear you, if that's okay." I had no idea what he said in response, but I prayed he wouldn't hang up before I could push through a trio of gropers blocking the elevator and then to a quiet corner in the lobby.

"I'm sorry about that. Who did you say this is again?"

"I'm working with a hedge fund anxious to hire someone . . . I know it's late, I hope that's okay."

"No worries." *Should I make him think he's interrupting an important dinner meeting?* I'd heard of a phone app that replicated different background noises. I considered doing a search for "sophisticated dinner party sounds," but decided he'd probably already guessed at the truth.

"Listen," he said. "The woman currently in the executive administration position at Purple Rock Capitol has put in her two-week notice. We need to hire someone now. Can you come in for an interview tomorrow?" I heard him shuffling through papers. "Say, eleven?"

Clearly, my resume had accidentally been put in the "interview" pile instead of the "meh" pile. *This recruiter just lost his commission.*

I turned into a robot. "Yes. That. Will. Be. Fine."

He gave me the address and described a few landmarks, said goodbye in a tired voice, and hung up. He probably had ten way more qualified people to call. By the time Gina and Lucia stumbled out of the elevator behind me, I was in a level-ten state of panic.

"*Mia cara*, you're a mess. Here . . ." Lucia dug a Xanax out of her Hermes handbag. According to Gina, both the pharmaceuticals and the purse were gifts from one of the many women or men who lusted after her.

Gina shooed her away. "She doesn't need to wake up all puffy!" Then she noticed my eyes as I squinted at my friends through tequila and terror. "Puffier. Damn it, Paris, you'll be fine." The New Jersey girl struggled into her heavy peacoat, straightened the trendy bow on the neck of her blouse, and let her homeland come out. "Girl, let's get you home and sobered up. Tomorrow, just go in there with your shoulders thrown back, and be all, 'What's up, bitches,' but Beyoncé-like, not Gordon Ramsay-like. You got this, girl."

I barely remembered the Uber ride home. Why did I love Moscow Mules so much? Thank God, someone set the alarm on my iPhone. Gina had left a note on the table, tucked under a cup of coffee. She'd drawn a picture of a flexing arm. I assumed she was giving me the ol' "Rosie the Riveter did it, so can you."

......................

As I waited for my subway car to stop and the doors to open, I held on to the pole and prayed I was at the right stop. Behind me, a young guy wearing a suit jacket, cargo shorts, and a pair of Crocs repeatedly rolled his bike tire onto the back of my calf. *I'm glad to see narcissistic dudes with a man-bun and zero concept of personal space can be found on public transit anywhere in the US.*

I tried to shift away but the other sardines wouldn't give. Glaring made no difference. My legs were bare and now hosted a red waffle tattoo. *Motherfucker,* I thought, but was too cowardly to say anything. I wasn't up for confrontation so early in the morning, especially when I didn't know if he'd be the kind of guy who apologized, ignored me, or starting screaming about the love of Jesus in my face.

I moved out with the crowd when the doors finally swooshed open, speed walked to the surface, and breathed in great gulps of fresh street air. The carbon monoxide and smell of damp wool coats were mixed with the smells of coffee and curry and the angst of humanity. *Ah, New York.* I desperately wished I was back in California, where the smog was warm and the bums were friendly.

Dodging construction workers and college kids on skateboards, I mentally reviewed what I knew about hedge funds. I felt more confident than maybe I should have but I'd worked in securities for a few years, and I'd aced my classes back in school specific to the strategies and the laws. I'd downloaded the latest *Wall Street Journal* and *Hedge Funds for Dummies* early this morning, brushing up on the buzzwords. I understood the basics just fine; I was way more worried about the people. Information? I could master that. People? *Who knows what these people are going to want from me.*

Approaching the building, I stopped to switch my flats for a pair of heels. I leaned up against the plate glass window of a coffee shop and tugged stilettos from my tote bag. The café looked like the kind of place that massaged the organic coffee plants and then harvested, roasted, and served the coffee with only peace and love in their hearts. Joe's Coffee Shop. I adored it already. I pushed away from the glass and promised myself I'd stop later. Properly attired, I joined the legions of black-suited worker drones marching down the sidewalks.

My feet hurt by the time I stood in front of a newly reno-vated building, PRCM hopefully to be found on the thirty-eighth floor, which is what I had scribbled onto the back of a receipt the night before. I'd used my lip gloss, so it was a little smudgy.

A security guard named Kwan sat on a stool at the front counter. He found my name on a list and handed me a card with a code. "This code will only work for today," he said, before directing me to a private bank of elevators at the back of the lobby.

Inside the teak-paneled elevator, I poked the button for the thirty-eighth floor and then entered the numbers. The ride was silent, the doors sliding open before I even had a chance to straighten my skirt and exhale completely. I stepped into a wood-and-steel Scandinavian-flavored lobby, complete with a blonde receptionist.

An older man, slender and quick-stepped, popped out of an office just past the reception desk and zeroed in on me. I'm pretty sure Hot Secretary hadn't had time to alert anyone to my presence, yet this man was clearly aiming for me. His intense gaze was friendly, though, and his wooly gray eyebrows hovered high above honest eyes. I returned his smile as he approached, my nerves easing a bit.

"Hi, you must be Paris." He held out his hand. "I'm Todd Lindstrom, the Chief Operating Officer."

"Mr. Lindstrom, I'm honored to meet you." I stepped forward, projecting "confident adult," shaking hands calmly and with authority. It felt good, being in a place of business again.

"Call me Todd."

A woman in her thirties appeared next to Todd. "And you can call me Ericka. Briefly. I'm the EA on my way out." Ericka was attractive, though the skin on her face appeared blotchy and there were dark circles under her eyes. "Come on, we're in conference room two."

Once settled, Ericka and Todd took turns politely asking questions. At first, they were normal interview questions, like, *What is your background in finance*, and *As the executive assistant, you'd be overseeing four other assistants. Tell me about your leadership style*, and *How will you react when you're face-to-face with one of our celebrity investors?* I lied and told them I viewed all people equally and had no problem remaining professional when Alex Rodriguez or Brooke Shields needed an Americano or a bowl of blue M&M's.

Todd cleared his throat and said, "Elton John was in here last week and I had to physically remove one of our research assistants. There is to be no wheedling, fawning, or even talking to the investors, unless it is necessary."

"Of course." I nodded and kept my face blank while my inner fangirl jumped around, screaming, *Elton John! Ermygawd! "The Circle of Life"!*

Then Ericka leaned in, intent, and began asking the "real" questions.

"If one of the CEOs asked you to order lunch but then became highly agitated because the food arrived cold, how would you handle it?"

*Show him how the microwave works.* "I would apologize and heat it for him. Better yet, if this is something important to him, I would quality check his food before he gets it."

And: "Do politically incorrect jokes bother you?"

"I assume they bother most people, but I don't let them get to me." I'd had to allow my fair share of sexist and racist "jokes" roll off my back. That didn't mean I'd be thrilled with a racist boss. Was I expected to keep quiet at that kind of thing? And was it such an acceptable habit that they had to work it into the interview?

Then: "One of the CEOs is a mumbler; are you comfortable repeatedly asking him to clarify, though it will bother him?"

"Um. I'm sure I can handle that." *Who is this guy?*

This went on for about twenty minutes. Finally, Todd asked, "Okay, anything you'd like to ask us, Paris?"

I took a deep breath. The crazy questions were jarring, but I wasn't ready to throw in the towel just because the CEO sounded like a nutjob. *It's not like I have to live with him.* I wanted to get this right. They had yet to ask me specifically how long I'd worked with hedge funds, so I hadn't had to lie. Clearly, they were focused on something else.

"I am really good at numbers and have spent my life managing finances. I graduated top of my class, and my past employer made a lot of money because of me. But my greatest asset, I believe, is that I can deal with big, difficult personalities, adapting easily to challenging people or environments. Most of my clients would say I am quick, efficient, and relatable. I make things happen and I do it smoothly, without fuss." I tapped the table with my pencil. "And I can easily see myself here at PRCM."

Todd and Ericka exchanged a glance. Then they had a private tête-à-tête in the hall. Through the wall of plate glass, I could see their heads almost touching, both of them serious. A couple of times they were interrupted by women walking by. *How come they're all so attractive? I hope that's not an imperative.* I twisted my mother's earrings, hoping for luck.

"Okay, Paris," said Todd, coming in with a smile. "You've made it to the next round. We're going to call in a CEO to do the final portion of the interview. I'll be back in a minute." He strode out of the room.

Ericka stayed behind. "Do you need some more coffee?"

"No, I'm good, thanks."

She slid into a seat across from me, gathered papers, and put them in a folder. "You're going to want something. Frank will take forever to get here. He's not exactly perceptive when it comes to time. Or people. And he's the CEO who you'll be working with ninety percent of the time. He's a little . . . needy."

I peered around. We were alone. *Gently, gently.* "So, he's kinda hard to work for?"

She shut her eyes. Nodding to herself, she opened them again but wouldn't look at me straight on. "He's challenging." She cleared her throat. "But you can learn a lot from him, that's for sure. While there are two CEOs here, Frank is the brain of this operation. He's the genius. Andrew, on the other hand, is the voice of reason. Together, they keep fifteen billion in funds afloat."

She finally made eye contact, brushing bangs out of her face. "You're smart. You're easygoing. And you're very pretty. You're going to get this job." Ericka reached across the table and patted my hand, as if she were a grandmother. "When it gets tough, remind yourself: it's just a job, don't take his tantrums personally. Also remind yourself you are extremely lucky. Hundreds of interns and a hundred more finance grads are trying to get a piece of Franklin Coyle. You'll have him, like it or not. Make sure you get something out of it."

"Then why are you leaving?"

The conference room door flew open. I startled, but relief washed over Ericka's face. She stood up and edged away from me. "Okay, Paris, it was nice meeting you! Good luck!"

And she was gone.

In her place, staring at me like I was a strip of bacon, was a man of medium height and medium looks, the bland face and haircut of a high school science teacher—yet some kind of heat boiled off him, a crazy intelligence blazing from his money-green eyes that made me blink. Or it might have been the pink shirt with the darker pink suit jacket and the lime green tie. He was blinding.

"Tehrani . . . are you an Arab?" he asked, beginning to pace.

"Not according to history," I responded, surprised into answering. Was this guy for real? "My family is Persian, not Arab. I was born in Iran, but I've lived in the US my whole—"

"Paris. Your first name is Paris. Ha. How'd the sex video work out for you?"

*Breathe. Control your face.* "Well, I had to ditch the blonde hair and white skin, and the string of hotels, so I guess not so great." This was not the first time I'd heard the Paris Hilton joke. Hilarious, every time.

He stopped pacing. "Good one. I like that—you're spunky. I'm Frank Coyle, a CEO here." He didn't reach out to shake, instead put his hands in his pants pockets and started rocking on his heels. "Are you married?"

"No." I remained pleasant, adopting a nonchalant, slightly amused tone of voice. I could be outraged at the illegal question later. I would also spend some time praying that by answering no, he wouldn't take that as permission to grab my ass.

"Are you willing to work overtime?"

"Absolutely." *Slow down, what are you agreeing to?*

"Do you think hedge funds are shady?"

He'd mumbled the question, just as I had been warned, so I didn't think I heard him correctly. "Umm . . . what?"

"You've been in the game for a while now, Paris. Paris. I

*love* that name. Anyway, you must have had run-ins with the self-righteous fucks who think hedge funds are all about making money off suckers, manipulating the market so others lose, while we gain." He crossed his arms, looming over me.

"Mr. Coyle," I started slowly, "obviously a few traders went rogue and were caught stealing from their investors and now they are household names. But in reality, I know a good hedge fund manager has their own funds tied up in the investments as well and the clients can see what is happening with their money. More than that, hedge fund traders are doing exactly what other investors are doing, they just have more latitude because they take more risk—"

"Okay, fine." He cut me off. Again. He went to the door and yelled out into the hall. "Ericka! Bring me some water!"

I don't know how much I believed in what I was saying, but figured I would find out soon enough, when I had been "in the game for a while" for realsies. Trying to be helpful, I said, "Mr. Coyle, there's a pitcher of water on the table—"

"Ericka!"

A young, redheaded woman came skittering into the room with a bottle of Perrier and a glass. She set them on the table. "Ericka had to leave," she said, turning to me. She had an odd cast to her face. Her voice was friendly but her eyes were cold, a condescending sneer turning up her pale lip.

Frank took a long swig, his Adam's apple working under his pimply, poorly shaven throat. "This is lemon." Frank threw the bottle at the garbage can but missed. It crashed against the wall.

I jumped and so did the assistant, who paled, a sheen developing in her eyes, but she remained in control. "Frank, we are out of lime. I'll have to go to the market. I'll be back in a minute." She picked up the bottle off the floor and marched out the door.

He dropped into a chair. "Ericka should take that one with her," he said, pointing at the redhead's disappearing back. Then, abruptly, he swung his finger to point at me. "Do you have children?"

"No, but I was thinking about getting a puppy . . ." Not my best joke, but he did not even attempt a chuckle. Or seem to hear me.

"Do you live in the City?"

"I'm looking for a place—"

"Good. This job is difficult. You need to be close. You'll create and run my schedule, which changes minute by minute. The junior assistants report to you—you need to make sure they stay on task, and that they're doing it right. It's a lot of work and I have a lot on my plate. I have foundation meetings, I'm on a dozen boards, I donate . . . *you* have to keep track of *everything* at *all* times. My wife has her own business and you might help her from time to time. I have multiple homes, and I have home staff you'll have to talk to: nannies, butler, drivers, a kid. Do you think you can handle it?" He was breathless by the time he was done.

"Yes, I've done this all before." That was a complete lie. I'd tracked investments and managed bank accounts and mortgages, not people. Normally, I would have panicked at his overwhelming list, but I was numb, and disappointed. He had not specified *anything* to do with financial responsibilities. I struggled to put my ego aside. I needed a job. And if I was smart and self-motivated, I'd pay attention to his methods and come out with investing savvy and a good resume. *Just do it.*

I laid my palms gently on the table, leaned toward him, and said, "I like a challenge."

He leaned in as well, dropping his voice. "You are so calm. Are you like this all the time?"

I burst out with a laugh but reeled it in before I contradicted my serene persona. "Well, I don't panic easily, if that's what you mean. I'm driven when it comes to getting things done, and done correctly, but I don't spend a lot of energy freaking out."

Frank snorted. "We'll see. Anyway, do you have any questions for me?"

A rule in interviewing is to always have questions ready for the employer. I should probably have remembered that before sitting down. "Um, yes, the executive assistant who's leaving . . . what do you like about her? Anything she does that you'd change?"

He stood up abruptly and then shrugged, peering off into the distance, like he'd already left the conversation. "I don't know, she just does everything. Everything gets done. She doesn't cry a lot. She doesn't smell like garlic. Why would I change that?"

And then he was gone. He didn't shake my hand or say goodbye, he simply vanished.

I'd tried to say everything I thought he'd wanted to hear. And there he went, with not even a parting glance. I'd somehow turned this guy off, my first real shot at a good job in New York. I was sure I would sink into depression and self-flagellation on the way home, possibly eat a box of Oreos, but, right then, I couldn't quite process what had just happened.

Walking to the conference room door, I noticed a dent in the wall by the garbage can.

*It would suck to work here, anyway.*

# Chapter 4

I'd almost escaped out the lobby doors when Kwan, the security guard I'd met earlier, yelled my name across the wide-open room. Suits everywhere stopped to see what was going on.

"Paris! Paris Tehrani!" The balding gentleman was jogging toward me, his hand on a gun to keep it from flapping against his fleshy hip. At least, I hoped that's what he was doing.

The flush didn't stop on my face; even my arms were blushing. "Yes?" I stammered.

Though he'd run only fifty feet, he bent over and leaned against his knees, wheezing. "Todd," gasp, "Lindstrom," gasp. "He wants," gasp, "you to go back up." The poor man stood up and straightened his collar. "Whew. You walk fast."

"Todd wants me back upstairs? The COO?" I asked, incredulous.

"Yah." He gave me a thumbs-up and lumbered back to his desk, hitching up his pants.

Todd met me at the elevator as I stepped back onto the thirty-eighth floor. "So glad Kwan caught you! Frank approved your hiring. Still interested in the job?"

"I'm sorry?"

The COO grinned. "It might seem like a snap decision, but we need to fill the position right away. If Frank is on board, so are we. I will speak to the recruiter and get the paperwork going and he will present you with a formal offer, but I wanted to let you know."

By the time I was back at the lobby doors, waving goodbye to Kwan, my new best friend, I was loaded down with strategy and market handbooks, office policies, trading regulations and requirements, contact sheets, catalogs, name tags, access cards, and a huge grin.

But by the time I found the correct subway entrance, my arms hurt and my grin had dwindled to a frown. Was I doing the right thing? Could I fake my way through the training?

Franklin Coyle could teach me about hedge funds and provide connections. He couldn't possibly be as douchey as he seemed. Working there gave me a paycheck in the immediate, and a platform on which to build my career. Plus, the pay was three times more than I'd been making at the bank back in California. Yes, PRCM was going to be great.

I had ten days to find an apartment and study up on managing hedge funds—and managing genius hedge fund managers who appeared to be dealing with a cocktail of anger issues and Asperger's.

Todd had wanted me to start immediately but I'd stayed strong, telling him I needed the time to find housing and move my stuff from the West Coast. I promised instead to read every manual he gave me. There was no way I could memorize the appropriate buzzwords, move, and start a new job at the same time.

Plus, I was going to have to deal with my dad. He was going to insist on coming to New York to help me settle into a new place, but really it would be to meet my boss and check out the company. I needed to figure out how to head him off.

My return trip from PRCM to the SoHo apartment did not give me enough time to come to any conclusions. Gina immediately jumped to a decision, however.

"Tonight we drink!" she yelled, twerking around the kitchen.

"Please don't do that to the table. I eat there." I shuddered. "I don't know if I can go out two nights in a row. I had a rough morning."

"Fuhget about it! We are celebrating, and you are paying."

It didn't take much to sway me. "Okay, but I'm bringing my laptop. You're going to help me find an apartment."

"Oh, hell yes I am. Now go put on something slutty."

By the time I'd perfected my cat-eye makeup, decided to stick with my lucky gold hoop earrings, and found a suitable skin-tight black dress balled up in one of my suitcases, Lucia was home. Gina insisted we go to the same bar as last night. She was up for another night of hitting on Mr. Business in the form of harsh sarcasm and taunts.

Lucia shrugged. She found attention no matter where she went and so kindly said, "Whatever you would like, Gina. You should wear that red sheath dress, it makes your chest look *delizioso*." She waggled her eyebrows.

I pretended to be blasé but hoped Benji, the photographer, would be there again. I'd left before I could give him my number. I didn't even tell him my name.

Thinking of him reminded me of my unused camera. While my roommates finished getting ready, I dug through a pile of belongings in the corner of the living room until I found the unopened box. *Shameful*, I thought. *I could have at least taken pictures for fun, no matter what Dad said.* I unwrapped the various pieces. I had no idea what I was looking at—the instructions were created by people from an island country with no written language. *I'm going to have to YouTube the hell out of this.* I hadn't used a "real" camera since I was in high school. After I'd agreed to major in finance, I'd dropped my photography dreams and just snapped pictures with my phone like everyone else. Professional camera technology appeared to have made huge leaps in the past six or seven years.

Putting aside the camera for the night, I soothed my creative urge by posing my friends for a couple of selfies as we headed out the door. I took the time to post them to Instagram from the back seat of the Uber. It couldn't hurt for Darien to see I was hitting the bars, so over him. *And maybe*, a quiet little voice said, *he will want me back*. I mentally punched myself in the head and firmly affixed an image of the cute photographer in my brain. I would love for Darien to be jealous, but the only reason I missed him was because of the companionship. I'd say it was the sex—if it had ever lasted longer than two minutes.

It was too early for the "good" crowd to show up, but at least we were able to find a table. We agreed tonight we would actually eat before we drank. Except for Lucia. She was just going to smell the food, because she had a show in three days and chose to use her daily calorie allotment on liquor. I could respect that. *I guess.*

Good thing I'd remembered to put on the keyboard "condom." My laptop was fed a steady stream of cracker and prosciutto bits as we researched neighborhoods and apartments. Gina proved herself to be useful once again. As a headhunter, she knew of people who were quitting their jobs, meaning they were also likely moving, and she had no problem sending them emails and texts to check on the status of their residences.

*Jackpot.* One of Gina's clients who'd been offered a job in Germany for a year texted back right away. He didn't want to give up his rent-controlled Upper West Side apartment, which was close to his parent company. It was against the building rules to sublet, but he was hoping to find someone willing to evade the building management, pick up the mail, and stay under the radar for the twelve months he'd be gone. In return, the rent would be low. He was glad to hear from Gina, though—he'd been leery of subletting to a stranger. He didn't want to get sued by the owners, or come back to find his place had been used as a meth house.

"Woot woot!" Gina yelled. "What do you think? Can you kick the crack habit and be invisible?"

Before I could answer, Lucia gracefully placed her hand on Gina's phone on the tabletop and slid it to me. "Call him. I know furniture movers, *goombas* from Little Italy."

He answered, but wasn't thrilled when he found out I'd been employed all of one day.

"I'll cosign, don't worry," Gina jumped in.

"Bu, bu, but—" I sputtered. I didn't want to have anyone else responsible for me. It was one of the reasons I had moved so far away from my father. And Darien.

"Paris? You still there?" the apartment owner asked over the speaker.

Lucia pinched my arm and nodded her head with a stern look.

"Alright!" I hissed, yanking my arm away. I knew I should feel more grateful, to both of them.

"We good, then?" the apartment owner asked.

"Yes!" Gina spoke for me again. "This is going to be great."

He promised to have papers ready and meet with us tomorrow. Then he said, "Hey, Gina, do you still have that hot model friend?"

"Actually, she's sitting right here."

"Bring her along."

"Do it!" I whispered to Lucia, pinching her back, hard.

Lucia sniffed, ignoring my counterattack, saying to me, "You must smoke a cigarette tonight. A lit cigarette."

"Oh my God, you are a terrible human being, you know that?" Of course, there I was, selling out another woman in exchange for a place to live.

She smiled evilly, plumped up her cleavage with a confidence in her sexuality that assured me she'd never heard of Gloria Steinem. In a low purr, she spoke into the phone. "We will be there, *bello. Ciao.*"

Gina smiled at me, then at Lucia. "Use what you've got, baby." Maybe Steinem hadn't made it to New Jersey.

We toasted each other in German a few times before I had to get up to use the restroom. I had not seen Benji, but his magnificent photos were there. To the left of the collection, I noticed a small placard. There was a website listed where clients could buy his work or sign up to take a class with him. *A class*, I thought. I studied his tiny bio picture. *So adorable.*

The server came over to me. "Another drink, hun?"

"I shouldn't . . . but okay."

"You like Benji's stuff? He comes in a lot. Usually Thursday nights. That's when his girlfriend"—she pointed to a bartender, a bleached blonde who looked like she taught Pilates in her spare time—"is working."

My heart fluttered and sank. *Just my luck.*

"Thanks. Hey, do you have a light?" I asked, pulling out the Benson & Hedges stick of death.

.....................

I woke up in my underwear and a T-shirt on the living room floor. "Traitor," I whispered to the narrowly cushioned couch.

Lucia came out of the bathroom with a towel on her head and nothing else. Except a cigarette. She pointed the burning tip at me. "*Merda.* You L.A. girls cannot hold your liquor."

"Please, you're killing me over here. Put some clothes on."

"Pshh." She blew a series of smoke rings. "So insecure." She sauntered down the hallway, slowing as she passed Gina's room, where weird noises were coming from behind the door.

Then suddenly we both heard Gina moan, followed by a masculine voice groaning, "Ride me!"

Lucia snorted. "Happy Valentine's Day," she said over her shoulder, before she went into her bedroom and slammed the door.

I closed my eyes and laid my cheek on the carpet. February fourteenth. I'd been so caught up with the job search, I'd forgotten. *You know who probably hasn't forgotten? Darien and New Girl.*

I cried. I cried until I'd emptied my body of liquid, creating a large wet spot on the rug under my face, like a puppy emptying its bladder. Then I wiped my face, stood up, and prepared for my day in the city.

Despite suddenly having a well-paying job and an apartment on the horizon, I was in a foul mood by the time I made it back to Columbus Circle. I was hungover again, and dehydrated, and had no male company on the horizon. I had to drop off a copy of my social security card and driver's license at PRCM—I was going to have to dig deep, act like a normal, functioning human being for a few minutes.

Before I got to the building, I came across Joe's Coffee Shop, the café I'd leaned against yesterday. The pink hearts painted on the glass door tugged at my empty tear ducts but I stayed firm. I went in, searching for a cappuccino and some cool marble to rest my face on.

In a corner booth was Ericka, the woman I was replacing at PRCM. *No way.* I almost rubbed my eyes, but thankfully stopped myself before screwing up my eyeliner. Her eyes widened when she caught sight of me. I couldn't duck back out. After a second, she beckoned me over.

"Wow. Are you following me?" She only half sounded like she was joking. Next to her was a small box. I could see a couple of files, a plant, a framed picture, and random other items you would find on someone's office desk. Her hands were shaky as she took a drink of her hot tea.

"Ha ha, no, I'm not following you," I said weakly, shuffling my feet. "I was just thinking how close this place is to the office, but far enough away I probably wouldn't run into any PRCM people."

"Yeah, well, that's why I come here. No one from work." Ericka shifted in her seat. "And by no one, I mean no Frank."

"Do tell," I said, not sure I wanted to hear what she had to say.

She put down her cup, sloshing tea onto the table. "You're smart. If you can learn to play along with him, it's worth your time there. The money is good. Like I said before, you'll learn a lot." Then she leaned forward aggressively. "But don't get sucked in. Have an exit strategy. You need to know what you're getting into, Paris. I worked for Franklin Coyle for five years. Five fucking long years. He made that place hell. Ninth Circle type hell." She took a deep breath and shook her head, as if to clear it of visions. "I'm sorry. Maybe you're stronger than I am." She pursed her lips. "But you know the girl who I replaced five years ago? She still hasn't been able to go back to work. She's thirty and living with her mom and dad. I know because we share a therapist."

I murmured cooing noises, my head filling with white noise. I didn't want to hear that I was about to make a huge mistake. I wanted her to tell me it was going to be fantastic, that I'd made the right decision and working with Frank would send my career on a trajectory to the moon.

"Oh," I said. "Umm, I need to get going, I'm late, but nice to see you again . . ." I backed away.

"Good luck," Ericka said as I left the table, but then shouted after me. "Protect yourself! Franklin. Coyle. Is. *Lucifer!*"

I forgot to get a drink in my rush to escape. I didn't need

any more buzzing in my veins. My heart couldn't take it. I practically ran through the heart-covered door.

My steps slowed as I approached the PRCM building. Staring at the massive set of doors in the dark gray stone facade, I knew once I entered my life would change. I'd be moving away from regular, clearly outlined banking duties to what sounded like a Hollywood manager's job, making sure the all-powerful moneymaker showed up at meetings and his suits were pressed, his coffee cup filled. *Would* I be able to learn anything useful, maybe even be mentored, so I could walk away with a background in hedge funds, like Gina believed?

It kind of felt like Ericka's version of my future was the more believable.

I'd been warned. I stood on the sidewalk, the clouds low and dark, getting ready to rain down on me and the throng of lovers heading out for a Valentine brunch.

*I deliver this paperwork to PRCM and I'll be joined in holy work matrimony to Frank Coyle.* My feet didn't move. *I don't think I'm going in,* I thought. *Why put myself through the hell Ericka described for an executive assistant position?* I could find another job. It might take a while, but I'd get something. I rubbed my temples.

My cell rang. My father, with his perfect timing.

"Hi, Dad, what's up?"

"Hello! I must wish my special girl a Happy Valentine's Day."

I had missed his soothing voice, his thick Persian accent. "Thank you, Dad. Happy Valentine's Day. I love you."

"I have told everyone about the new job, I could not be more proud. You said in your message you are coming home before you start? Is this today? Are you driving?"

"I'm supposed to go into the office today, drop off some forms." *Oh, and by the way, I'm already here and I'm thinking*

*I might skip it, find a job scooping ice cream, work double shifts in a sticky apron until I can find a bank job. A boring, boring bank job.* "I'm flying out tomorrow, and I've hired movers to drive my furniture and stuff back to New York."

"Movers! I am not sure I can cover that expense right now."

"What do you mean?" I was surprised. "I paid for it—I sold my car. I can't afford parking here anyway. But why couldn't you afford that? Is something going on with the business?"

"No, no, we are fine! I have accounts late on paying their bills, that is all."

"You'd tell me if something was wrong . . ."

"Come now. You have nothing to worry about." His voice was firm but I thought I heard a bit of hesitation. Before I could say anything, he continued. "The business is fine. And you are starting your climb up the American corporate ladder! You are a hard worker, smart and beautiful, you are going to wow them. Everyone has to start somewhere. Did you hear about the young guy who invented Life Savers? They say he made a mint."

I couldn't help but laugh. "I have no idea how you come up with this stuff."

"Just be glad you are not trying to get a job in a shoe recycling factory. It destroys soles."

"You've been sitting on that one for a while, huh?"

I could hear him grin. "I am proud of you, truly. You will take what you have learned from your schooling and from me and become more successful than I ever was."

"Dad—"

"I have to go, I have a client waiting. You will let me know how it goes today?"

"I will call you tonight."

"I would rather you call me Dad." He hung up, laughing loudly.

He'd sounded just a little too upbeat, maybe distracted . . . *He's fine*, I thought. *I'd know if something was wrong.* I didn't have the mental capacity to think about my dad right then. I had to figure out if I was moving forward or going backward.

The PRCM building doors opened from the inside. It was Kwan, the kind security guard, propping open the door for me. "Coming in?"

Just then, a light drizzle descended.

I stepped into the office building to hand over my identification papers.

# Chapter 5

Packing up my old bedroom in Orange County, I realized I could fit everything I owned into a van, especially after I threw away every gift Darien had given me. I did not feel a thing when a giant teddy bear, won at a fair by that slick bastard, went bye-bye. The quilt bed set Darien had bought me was a different matter. It was a hideous shade of old-person blue, and the material stuck to my fingertips, but I'd been held and caressed under that blanket, touched by another human . . .

My heart hardened. Darien wasn't in town. According to friends, he was on a long Valentine weekend trip through Napa Valley with his new girlfriend. A place we used to go together.

Carrying boxes down to the front porch, I was glad I'd decided to hire someone to drive the moving van across country for me. Once was enough. I was flying, and I had no desire to waste any time getting back.

I thought I'd miss my car, but I really didn't. Parking at my new apartment would be impossible anyway. I'd end up paying more to park a vehicle than I would pay in rent. *Besides, I'm a New Yorker now, carless and proud.*

Putting tape on the last of the boxes, I wiped off my hands and then wandered into the living room. I'd miss the tapestries and the grandfather clock and the bright sunlight pouring through the windows.

Passing my father's desk, a stack of envelopes caught my eye. The top one screamed Past Due in bold block letters. "Dad! What's this?"

"That is nothing. I am taking care of it." He plucked the envelopes out of my hand. "We eat now."

"Why are you not paying bills?"

He threw the envelopes into a drawer and guided me to the kitchen. "This is nothing. I have been busy. We are close to tax season, you remember what it is like."

On the kitchen island, he had piled plates with naan bread, feta cheese, and tea. "Eat, my little *Parisa*. You are fading away."

"Yeah, if only that were true, Dad."

"Oh, do not worry, you are perfect. Besides, do you know where they weigh pies?"

"Dad, no . . ."

"That is right, somewhere over the rainbow, *weigh a pie!*"

I groaned. "Are you done now?"

He grinned, his head shiny and perfect. I'd missed him.

"I am thinking you may need me to come to New York with you, to help with the move," he said, handing me a Persian almond cookie shaped like Mickey Mouse.

I had to think quickly. I loved this man but I wasn't ready for days of his jokes and quizzing my new coworkers and neighbors. *Fake outrage.* "Dad, I'm twenty-six years old. Are you saying you don't think I'm mature enough to handle this?! Or because I'm a girl, I can't figure out how to hook up my cable? Stop being sexist, Dad."

He slowly blinked. "No. I think you can call a cable company. Change your own light bulbs, even. What is it? You do not want to spend time with your dad?"

*Oh hell. Set and match.* I sighed. "You know I love spending time with you. But I just want to get this over and done with and start working. I have enough help there, and I know you have a ton of stuff to get done here." I hugged him. "You don't need to worry about me, I'll be fine."

"If you are sure, I guess, okay then. But keep in touch, let me know you are alright." He turned his back to me, moved to the refrigerator to retrieve the almond milk.

*What? That's it?* I eyed him suspiciously. It was not like him to give up so easily. *What gives?*

Later, I watched the movers stuff the last of my boxes and bags in around my mattress, bed, a desk with my high school crush's name carved on the leg, a love seat, and an old Barcalounger my dad joyfully foisted off on me, along with a huge box of mismatched plates and kitchenware. I planned on buying new furniture as soon as I had a couple of paychecks under my belt, but I also liked the idea of meshing the old with the new.

The van left. I wasn't flying back for another day. I wandered down to the local shops along the beachfront, wearing my favorite sundress. *I won't be wearing this in NYC, not for a while, not unless global warming steps it up a notch.* It was a blue sky kinda day. The light February breeze coming off the Pacific tousled my hair and felt good on my sun-warmed skin. I thought about calling up friends for one last hoorah but decided I was too agitated and anxious to be around people. I'd brought my camera for company instead, wanting to capture my last moments here, to bind my emotions to paper.

After a short while, I realized I'd been snapping a number of photos of gates and doors. Some were painted in bright blues, reds, and yellows, some set in mosaic tiles, some layered in posters for sandcastle contests and Chinese restaurants and tattoo artists and wine tours. There were heavily paned French doors and doors that were cracked and peeling . . . It made sense. I was about to walk out one door and through another. *What will it look like on the other side? What will I look like on the other side?*

# Chapter 6

I surveyed my domain with a smile. I was the queen of a box-car. As far as apartments went in the city, I was living the high life. I had a separate bedroom, which made me feel spoiled, and the bed boasted a lovely new down comforter, free of Darien's germs. My bathroom shower was big enough to hold my shampoos, conditioners, soaps, lotions, and most of me. Perfect. I even had two large windows, one in the living room and one in my bedroom. Both had decks—a.k.a. the fire escape.

I slid my furniture around easily and without guilt, since the hardwood floors were scarred and dented from centuries of high heels and dragged bookcases. I loved it, grateful to not have to deal with a shag carpet loaded with cat hair and dead skin cells from previous tenants. Someone had painted the walls a beautiful tawny color, which highlighted the rug my father had given me, a piece he'd brought with him from Iran.

I flirted with eviction, taking it upon myself to paint one wall a deep red. Then I hung assorted gold thrift store picture frames, square but in various sizes. My plan was to fill the empty frames with my own photographs. I'd create my own art.

But first, I had to unpack. Boxes were stacked everywhere. I hadn't been able to find my toothbrush yet. Or clean underwear. I was going to need clean underwear for more reasons than hygiene—my new existence as Carrie Bradshaw from *Sex and the City* was about to kick off.

I had only three more days before I had to report to my new job. I wanted to be totally nested in and comfortable, with an established safe haven to return to each night. Lucia and Gina were each taking a "mental health" absence from work the next day to help me; we were gung ho about using an electric drill and level, mimosas at the ready to ease the callouses and sore muscles. I really looked forward to having them in my new space, playing the hostess and reveling in friendly vibes.

Then I noticed the voicemail notification on my phone.

At first I thought the muffled message was from a dentistry patient, his mouth stuffed with cotton. But then I realized the mumbler was Franklin Coyle.

"Hey, *Paris*—Paris! *Damn, I love that name—I need you to come in tomorrow, first thing. I'm leaving for an extended business trip and you have to do some things for me while I'm gone. Meet me at my office tomorrow morning at nine. Grab a tall butterscotch latte, too, would ya? See you then.*"

I started to hit the call back button then hesitated. *He knows I'm moving right now. It must be important.* I didn't want my first interaction with Frank to be me telling him I wasn't coming in.

Hopefully, Gina and Lucia wouldn't be too bent out of shape if we started later in the day. I wouldn't blame them for being mad. *I'll just make sure the mimosas are stiff and free-flowing, and I won't complain about crooked shelving.*

· · · · · · · · · · · · · · · · · · · ·

I stepped into the building lobby with two lattes and my soft-sided briefcase—a professional black leather Lodis with subtle red piping I'd bought when I started my career, back in L.A. at the Deutsche Bank. My shoes matched. My black pantsuit was ironed. With, like, an iron, and not the dryer. I was adulting the hell out of the morning, despite the short notice.

Facing the elevator, I realized I needed my code. I patted my pockets, then dug through my briefcase. Refusing to be defeated before even starting the day, I marched over to the lobby's front desk.

"Hi, Kwan, do you remember me? Do you happen to have an elevator code for Paris Tehrani listed there? For PRCM's main offices?"

The security guard smiled. "Of course I remember! The fast walker. I don't have anything here for you, though."

"Oh . . . dang it. Todd gave me a card when I was last here but I totally forgot to grab it this morning! I'm sorry. But I did remember this . . ." I trailed off, holding out the badge hanging around my neck.

"That's okay. I know Mr. Lindstrom won't mind me letting you up." He walked with me to the back bank of elevators, hitching up his pants after every few steps. "Make sure to grab that code card, though. I'm not always going to be here for you." He tapped out the numbers, and with a wink, he was out.

On the thirty-eighth floor, the receptionist was on the phone and simply waved me past when she saw me. I wasn't sure where Frank's office was since no one had yet to give me a tour past the lobby and conference rooms. The compliance office, where I'd received the reading material the day I was hired, was two floors down, along with accounts. Todd Lindstrom was on that floor; the older man seemed to be the glue of the company, doing the hiring, the firing, and overseeing accounts. I'd be working closely with him because he also oversaw the personal financial needs of the two CEOs, Andrew and Frank, including their personal taxes. He was the man behind the curtain.

I ambled into a big open room, a modern, clean-lined work space with maybe fifty desks, some clustered together, others off on their own, lit with mostly natural light from a large bank of windows. These were the traders and the analysts. At the very back of the room were two large offices, set apart for the muckety-mucks.

Before I made it two feet, the redheaded, hatchet-faced assistant I met on the day of my interview bounced up from seemingly nowhere. Her tone was sharp when she said, "Paris, right? What are you doing here? I thought you'd told Todd you weren't available until next week."

"Um. Hi. Mr. Coyle called and asked me to come in."

"First, call him Frank. He hates to be called 'mister' anything. Second, Frank left. He's gone for at least a week."

"He called last night, said for me to be here by nine, before he left. Maybe he's still in his office?"

The assistant smirked. "No. No, he's not. His car service just drove away, taking him to the airport." She chortled and shook her head. "Classic Frank."

I shifted back and forth on my high heels. Gina was going to kill me. She'd already taken off work by the time I'd called her to tell her our unpacking party was "pushed back." I couldn't face telling her I'd ditched my friends for nothing.

"Coffee?" I held out one of the paper cups to the redhead. No time like the present to start making new friends.

She laughed a nasty laugh. "Ha. Let me guess . . . butter-scotch latte? Meant for Frank?" She didn't take it, gesturing for me to put it down on the closest desk. "Give it to Michelle. She's the other assistant you'll be working with. She won't mind drinking fatty crap like that." She ran her hand over her twelve-year-old-boy hips.

A voice spoke up behind me. "We don't work *with* her, Nicki. We work *under* her. She is our boss." I turned to find a woman, starkly dressed, her straight blonde hair pulled back in a ponytail, all business in black-rimmed glasses. Her face matched her tone: frosty. I thought at first the coldness was directed at Nicki, thanks to her bitchy comment, but no, it was directed at me. She picked up the full coffee cup from her desk and dropped it in the trashcan, not saying a word.

Nicki, with a twist of her lips and a flip of her red hair, said, "Paris, this is Michelle. Don't mind her. She's bitter because she was passed over for your job." She slid away.

Michelle sighed, her shoulders letting down slightly. For a minute, she simply stared at me. Then, finally, she said, "She's right, Frank is gone. But I can guess at some of what he wants you to do. Let's check his office, see if he left a note."

I followed her through the maze of desks, back to the big offices. "You also applied for this job? I'm sorry."

"Oh, you have no reason to be sorry. Don't take this the wrong way, but you're not going to last long. I'll get another chance." Before I could say anything, she pushed open an opaque glass door to reveal an office with a gorgeous view of Central Park, decorated in rich leathers and mahogany woods. Much of the art was tasteful, subdued. But not all of it.

Michelle followed my line of sight to the huge painting of cartoonish zebra stripes splattered with random red streaks. Next to it was a man-sized ball of pink aluminum foil, crumpled and pierced with a railroad spike. She grinned, which lit up her whole face, transforming her from cold to friendly in an instant. "His wife collects art."

Neither of us said another word, just stared for a minute. Then she said, "Well, there's no note. I might as well get you acquainted with some of our procedures."

"Oh, that'd be great. I have been going over the handbooks Todd gave me, but it would be good to talk it through with you."

"Sure, we can go over company rules and the like, but I'm talking about the real stuff you're going to need to know. About Frank. How to manage him. Nicki and I, and two research assistants, work directly with the traders. We do whatever they, or you, need us to do, while you work directly with the two CEOs."

Michelle showed me my desk, set between Andrew and Frank's offices, a u-shape of blond wood facing out over the rest of the open workspace, where I could watch a bunch of traders and analysts I had yet to meet working their computers and phones. Behind my amazing desk, a veritable fortress, I pictured myself as Donna in *Suits* or Joan Holloway in *Mad Men*, a woman clearly in charge. Minus the sexual harassment and misogyny.

Michelle slid open a drawer, after unlocking it with a gold key, and retrieved a thick binder. "This is the Book of Frank."

Inside were a hundred pages or so of handwritten notes, typed lists, copies of documents, menus, schedules for sporting events and concerts, and phone numbers.

I paused for a second. "Is there a book of Andrew?"

Michelle shook her head, ponytail swinging. "No, he will barely talk to you. Andrew's needs are generally normal and undemanding." She patted the binder. "Frank, on the other hand, comes with an instruction manual. He is about to make your life a living hell."

I flashed on Ericka at the coffee shop, telling me Purple Rock Capital Management was the Ninth Circle of hell and Franklin Coyle was the devil. *So, what, I'm Dante now? Is this me, entering* the Inferno?

"This is confidential. It stays in this room, to be locked up at all times." She handed me the key. "You are in charge of his prescriptions: picking them up, how to talk him into taking them, making sure he takes them. Believe me, you want him on his meds. The info is in here. Also in here"—she flipped to a section toward the end—"is some of his personal banking information. Every few weeks, he expects you to withdraw money at his bank and put it in his office safe. He wants large amounts of cash on hand. We'll get to why later."

She straightened and pushed her glasses higher on her nose while inspecting me for signs of distress. "Never, ever, let Frank see this book. Got me?"

"Yes."

She then left me alone at my new desk with the Book of Frank, reminding me again to lock it up when I was done.

I wanted to call out, "Thank you, Michelle, that'll be all," to her departing back, to establish dominance. She was my assistant but she'd just treated me like she was the superior. I blew my breath out slowly, counting. I wanted to say something, but I also wanted this first day to go smoothly. Like Darien said, I was accommodating.

As I pulled the binder toward me, I noticed a water stain on the surface of my desk, in the corner, about the size of a small potted plant. Much like the one Ericka had been carrying in her box of belongings.

I spent the morning fascinated as the inner workings of a successful millionaire revealed themselves in the form of lists and warnings: Frank's likes, dislikes; his shirt size, pant size, underwear preference (briefs, not boxers); foundations he worked with, foundations he just said he worked with; doctors' names; descriptions and phone numbers of his friends; contact information for useful people, like tailors and personal trainers and concierges from around the world; details on his wife's allowance; important dates and where to buy his wife and son gifts on those important dates; his kid's soccer and school calendar; where Frank liked to eat, favorite foods, how to order his steak, what to keep in his office refrigerator and directions on the sugar-free candies he wanted unwrapped and put in a bowl on his desk; who he refused to talk to and who to put through immediately; how to talk to new investors, how to talk to old investors, how to talk to board members; details for hiring a private plane, what airline he was willing to fly if private wasn't available; hotels he liked and didn't like; the direct line to his psychiatrist; a list of his homes and job descriptions for each one of the house staff; his grandmother's name and her homes and a short list of phrases to use with her when she called . . . and so much more. Like phrases to use on Frank when he was inappropriate, and what to say to the person he'd just insulted.

Also, as Michelle promised, there was the list of his medications, dosages, when and how he was to take them, as well as his bank account numbers so I could withdraw $15,000 in cash monthly. There, on a separate sheet of paper, clearly labeled, were the combinations to his office safe and two of his home safes. It wasn't even in code. *What the hell*, I thought. *He doesn't know me. Now I know the combo to his safe? And that he takes enough Ritalin to calm a silverback gorilla?* I shifted uncomfortably and looked around. *Why does he need so much Ritalin?*

From across the room, Michelle must have noticed me coming up for air. The intercom on my desk buzzed and her tinny voice floated out. "You should make copies of his contact information. It's not confidential. Then you can put the names and numbers in your phone and keep a hard copy. There's a printer and a copier behind you."

So there was. I noticed a flyer in the printer's tray. The banner showed multiple attractive women with the caption stating: *Twelve Places in Toronto Where Gorgeous Women Hang Out.* There was a list of addresses for those who were "lacking female attention."

Franklin Coyle was in Toronto.

I knew way too much about this guy already.

# Chapter 7

I spent a couple of hours at the office every day for the rest of that week, meeting the traders, analysts, research assistants, and everyone else who kept the Purple Rock Capital Management Company knee-deep in trading sheets and bonds. I studied office procedures and operation systems and trading styles, discovering that most of our people were "trigger traders," jumping on trades when Andrew and Frank told them to. I talked to the analysts to hear about the current hot topics in regard to mergers and acquisitions, what they were telling the CEOs to look at, what was good in the market right then and what was not.

Frank was still gone, and I had not heard one word from him. I had no idea what it was he'd wanted me to do before he left. Hopefully he'd forgotten about it. My company email was up and running, and I had a company voicemail accessible on both my desk landline and through my cell phone. But I assumed he didn't need whatever it was that badly, because he did not reach out.

I also spent time trying to win over Michelle and Nicki. It wasn't just Michelle who'd been passed over for my position; Nicki had applied for it, too. I was surprised she was so bent out of shape over it, though, since Michelle had been there much, much longer and clearly was the one with more practical experience, and she was a shit-ton smarter than Nicki, the red-headed harpy.

The more I spent time with Michelle, the more I came to think she was probably the one who had kept Ericka on track for so long. She deserved the job more than I did. She would hunch over her desk without moving for hours, her black glasses perched on the end of her nose, flipping through documents and profiles. She gave off the sexy librarian vibe while working on a mean case of scoliosis, rarely breaking out of her huddle.

She was the one the traders turned to when they needed help. She answered questions and marshaled the troops with a flick of her wrist and a twitch of her blonde ponytail. I was terrified she was going to discover I didn't have experience working with hedge funds. Nor did I want anyone else to figure it out. Whenever I felt a conversation was over my head, I'd put my fingers along my chin, squint, and nod a lot, and then quickly walk back to my computer to research any term or phrase I hadn't recognized.

This worked—until it didn't.

One morning, Andrew, the CEO I had yet to meet (though I often caught him out of the corner of my eye slipping in and out of his office, a tall, dark-haired man in his forties who favored beautifully tailored suits), sent me an email. It said, *I need to leave Teterboro tomorrow morning. Thanks.* That was it. Nothing else.

I wanted to write back, "Alright, good for you," but knew that was not the best play.

When you Google "Teterboro," you will discover it is a town in New Jersey. That was not a surprise to me. Of course it was a town. What else would it be? The name of his lover? I doubted Andrew would email me about that. But it wasn't until the sixteenth Google entry I noticed Teterboro had an airport.

I looked up the website for the private jet company Frank

and Andrew preferred, and voilà, they were based out of the Teterboro Airport. *I'm a genius.* I called the office and spoke with a pilot. He called back in ten minutes, assuring me a plane for Andrew would be ready to go first thing. Some of what he said was garbled by roaring engines in the background, but the plane was scheduled.

The next morning, Andrew was standing next to my desk when I got there. He was composed, stern, his face emotionless.

"You're Paris, I assume. Nice to meet you. Can you tell me the tail number?"

I stared at him blankly. "Umm."

Irritation skittered across his face, then disappeared. "I need the tail number for the plane. Otherwise the helicopter pilot won't know where to take me."

*Helicopter. Did he say helicopter?*

He narrowed his eyes at me. "Do you know what you're doing?"

"Yes, sir, yes, but . . . but maybe not in this case . . . helicopter?"

"Sweet Jesus. You haven't scheduled my helicopter hop? And you don't know what plane I'm flying on?" He slapped his hip, the sound dampened by expensive wool. "If you don't know something, ask questions. If I can't get a heli now, I'm going to miss the departure time. And then I'll miss my meeting. Do you think the president of Coca-Cola is going to care that I'm late because of a new assistant?"

He hovered over me as I found the number for the helicopter service on East 34th, the one PRCM used to get out to Teterboro Airport. By the grace of all that was good and holy, there was a heli and a pilot available.

Andrew visibly relaxed. Picking up his briefcase, he said in a much kinder voice, "Make sure my driver is pulled up around front and that you call the heli service with the tail number of the private plane, so we can find it. And, Paris, know when to ask for help."

His tall frame disappeared down the hall. I jerked my stiff body to the restroom. Quite a few traders gave me weird looks, probably wondering if I was having a seizure. Behind a locked door, I stared at the ceiling, my hands shaking in my lap. *Stupid, stupid, stupid.*

But once I got the lingo, acronyms, and nicknames down, I actually felt like I had a decent shot at pulling it off. I wasn't stupid. I was quite bright at times, I reminded myself, and the basics were not too terribly different than any other job in finance: use money to make money.

By the time Friday rolled around, I was developing a cocky swagger. I'd helped a New York Knicks coach understand basic contract language and I scheduled time for a CNBC news anchor to meet with Frank when he returned. Some of it was overwhelming, but only because there was so much to learn, not because I couldn't do it.

Michelle met me in the break room as I retrieved my left-over hummus and vegetable sticks to take home for the week-end. She took off her suit jacket and sat down, propping up her feet on a gray plastic chair, fanning her face with the newest edition of the *Wall Street Journal*. "Paris. I admit, I had little faith in you."

She undid her ponytail and shook her straight blonde tresses free. With her thick, shiny hair juxtaposed against her black-framed glasses and her white button-down shirt about to bust open, I expected seventies porn music to start playing overhead at any second. She looked at me and offered a slow grin. If I had lesbian tendencies, I would have swooned. I'd always crushed on smart girls. Who didn't?

"But I think I was wrong," she said. "You've got brains, and I'm pretty sure there's a backbone in there somewhere." She rubbed her temples briefly and then re-gathered her hair into a ponytail. "I'm sorry if I've been hard on you. I'm here if you need me. You've got this." She paused. "But don't trust anybody."

Then, Saturday night at 7:04, it all went to hell.

Frank sent me an email from Mt. Vernon, Illinois, where he was at a conference:

*I'm flying back tomorrow morning. Make sure the plane has Sunday's* Wall Street Journal, New York Times, *and* Financial Times. *—FC*

At first blush, that didn't seem so bad. *Thank you, Michelle, for making me put the contact list in my phone.* I knew he was flying on a private jet with the company I'd just called for Andrew—but the pilot had no way of getting the papers.

"Hey, we've got the Saturday editions. You sure that won't work?"

"No, he specifically said Sunday."

The man on the other end let out a gusty sigh then muttered something under his breath. Apparently, they'd been on the receiving end of Frank's wrath before.

"Okay." I rushed my words. "Let me see what I can do from my end. I'll get back to you." And so began my Saturday night sojourn into the bowels of the phone directories for Mt. Vernon. Unfortunately, no one in Mt. Vernon reads newspapers. Not one Barnes & Noble, hotel, gas station, or Laundromat had a copy or even a subscription. After burning through the same sources in Summersville with the same big goose egg, the panic scrabbling at the back of my brain grew stronger.

At eleven o'clock, I wrote an email back to Frank. My first message to my new boss.

*Hi Frank,*
*I have called every place in Mt. Vernon and Springfield that might have these newspapers but nobody carries them.*

*I've also spoken with another plane company, XOJet, but they don't have the papers, either. My only choice, with your approval, is to get a driver to pick them up after midnight tonight in Chicago, which is five hours away, and then drive them to your hotel in Mt. Vernon. A car service from Chicago said it would charge you $900. Okay with the cost?*

*Let me know.*

*Paris*

I figured he would either ignore my email or berate me for such an outlandish idea. He replied within three minutes.

*Yes. –FC*

The first car service I had called—who had given me the initial nine hundred dollar quote—realized I was serious when I called back. But they decided the money wasn't worth it.

Feeling dizzy, I called what seemed to be hundreds of drivers in Chicago, asking if they would drive the five hours to make the 10 a.m. flight—the flight was actually at eleven o'clock, but I didn't want them to be late. Everyone laughed at me, saying the same thing: "Do you know how far of a drive that is? That is going to cost you!" but then inevitably deciding they'd rather go to bed.

I had one last car service to try. The guy who answered was the owner and said they'd do it, but I made him repeat himself since I was having a hard time hearing over the heartbeat in my ears. He didn't have a driver free but said he'd leave by 5 a.m. and drive there himself for the nine hundred dollars, because, "I feel sorry for ya, girl." I thanked him, offering my firstborn child. He declined and promised he wouldn't oversleep. I prayed and knocked on wood.

I did not sleep. I lay in my bed in my new apartment, memorizing the ceiling tile pattern. Outside, the screeching tires, revving engines, honking horns, fire trucks, and screaming drunks made a cacophony of ugly noise. Gina had shrugged when I'd first mentioned the incessant traffic and told me it would eventually turn into white noise and "sound like the ocean." *Well, this particular ocean is as peaceful as a churning, sixty-foot tsunami bearing down on me.*

At 6:10 a.m., I got a text from the driver saying he was on his way. Roaring tsunami or no, I fell asleep with a smile on my face.

At 9:15 a.m., my phone woke me. It was the pilot, letting me know Frank had moved up the flight. I texted the driver and prayed to Mother Earth and the gods of the freeway to turn red lights to green, part the traffic, and let my person through.

Luckily, after I bit off my fingernails and paced a groove into my floor, the driver arrived in time to catch Frank instructing the crew to shut the doors. He sent me a reply, to let me know the deed was done.

*Dropped off the papers with your boss. It was weird, he acted put out. Anyway, thanks for the business and good luck with the new job. Your boss seems like an ass hat.*

I spent the next hour staring out the window, breathing in, breathing out, concentrating on the light rain streaking the glass. I startled when my phone beeped with another text. I assumed it was Gina, wanting to do brunch somewhere laden with hungover Wall Street boys.

It was Darien.

*I hear you made it into the bigs! Congrats! I'm so proud of you. I always knew you were going to be someone. I'm going to be in NYC soon, let's have dinner. I miss you, Paris.*

I turned off my phone. My peaceful moment lay dead at my feet.

. . . . . . . . . . . . . . . . . . . . .

The next morning, I beat Frank to the office. I went to Michelle, handed her an Americano, and told her about the weekend adventure. "The coffee is to thank you for helping me out last week."

"Ah." She sipped from the white paper cup, leaned back in her chair, pushed her glasses up her nose. "He was testing you. He would normally never approve nine hundred dollars for five newspapers. Money is better spent on entertainment. Live entertainment. And he's never early for flights—he's always late. For flights, meetings, everything."

I settled in at my desk, pondering. Was it always going to be like this? Hopefully this shady operation was a one-time deal to see if I could cope under pressure. A grin spread across my face. I'd pulled it off.

# Chapter 8

My back cracked, running pops up my spine, as I levered myself out of the desk chair at the end of my first real day. I wobbled on my gladiator pumps. Six o'clock. Time to punch out.

Then Franklin Coyle walked in. Nine hours late for work.

"Hey, Paris. Right?" He marched through the workspace and past me like he was late for a meeting. He wasn't. "Come on."

He left his office door open behind him. I stood in the doorway. He dropped into his chair and started plunking away on his keyboard. Behind me, there were maybe two or three traders left and one research assistant. They were shutting down and packing up.

I swung my head back and forth a few times. *Day one with the boss and already I'm going to break Rule #1 of Protect Yourself from Sexual Harassment: being alone in an office with this guy.*

He was talking at his screen, as if I were standing beside him taking notes. I hurried over, hoping to understand his mutterings without having to ask him to repeat himself.

"There are a few things I never want to hear about. For instance, refilling the water coolers or stocking the office supplies or crap in the break room, and for God's sake"—he stopped, pierced me with his squinty eyes—"tell that loon down in Compliance to keep her tampon issues to herself!"

"Okay, will do." *What the hell?* "Anything else for tonight? I'm heading out, Mr. . . . . Frank."

"Kind of early, isn't it?"

"Oh. Um, it's after six. But I'm happy to stay if you need something."

*Please, please don't need anything.*

Frank let out a long sigh but said nothing. I stood there awkwardly. After a minute, I crept out and shut the heavy, frosted-glass door, afraid to draw his attention.

*I should have stayed in there. I'm sure I just failed a test.*

Unsure of what to do, I stood at my desk and pressed my fingers against the desktop, swaying back and forth. I closed my eyes for a second, fighting off a headache. I opened them to see an email notification slide across my computer screen. The subject line screamed *TAMPONS!* It was Frank.

I forwarded it to my home email so I could figure out what the tampon debacle was about while in the privacy of my living room, with a bottle of Patrón on hand.

. . . . . . . . . . . . . . . . . . . .

"No way."

"Gina, I cannot make this stuff up."

"Oh my God. Those are some crazy, entitled one-percenters, right there!" Gina guffawed, while Lucia draped her arm gracefully across the back of my couch and smiled, distantly amused.

"I know, right?" I opened up the email to read to them. "Listen to this. The compliance officer sent Frank an email complaining that the receptionist screwed up. She'd stocked their bathroom with tampons made for twelve-year-olds, and the women on the thirty-sixth floor were resorting to using two at a time. It was that or they had to bring their own from home, which is 'simply unacceptable,' she says. 'We are not going to walk down the hall carrying tampons like we are in middle school!' And then she suggests the receptionist be reprimanded because she 'became snotty and told me to use the pads that are in there!' Well, okay, in this woman's defense, those pads look like they've been in there since George Bush was president. The first one."

"Sounds like the *cucchiaio d'argento* is in her *fica*," Lucia said, removing a pack of cigarettes from the bag next to her.

Gina, mid-gulp of white wine, shot clear liquid out her nose. She gasped, tearing up. She finally stuttered, "Oh, no, you didn't just say that!"

"What? What did you say?" I hated to be left out of a joke. "And you know perfectly well you cannot smoke in here, Lucia."

"She said this woman was born with a silver spoon in her vagina." Gina crawled onto the couch next to Lucia, took the cigarette out of her mouth, and hugged her, laughing. "In her chucky! You are my favorite person."

Lucia patted her back awkwardly and then pushed her away. "Give me back my cigarette."

"Gross, Lucia," I said. "In Farsi, we'd just say *jende*. Snobby bitch."

We spent the next ten minutes teaching each other useful Persian and Italian terms, for when we were at a port surrounded by foul-mouthed sailors.

Watching the two of them huddled up companionably on the couch, I became acutely aware of my loneliness. There was a closeness between them that was special, like sisters. They'd both moved from Italy as children and grew up on the same street in Lodi, New Jersey, fending off the same bullies as they learned English together. I was their friend, but they were connected in a way I was not. I was not connected to anybody like that.

"Hey, have you guys been back to The Rooftop? Is it true that photographer Benji has a girlfriend?"

"Are we talking about the chick with abs of steel? And the guy with those adorbs freckles? I saw her stick her tongue down his throat the other day. I don't know if they're going out, but something was going in." Gina waggled her eyebrows, and Lucia smiled a half-smile.

*Oh, woe is me,* I thought, knowing on some level it was stupid to be bitter about anything right now, not when I had a great apartment and a great job. Darien had emailed a few times since his initial text, but there was no way I was letting that guy back into my life, especially not on a long-distance plan, when he'd be out of my supervisory range. *Maybe it's time I start meeting people. But not barflies. I'm too old for hookups.*

Lucia stood and stretched, sensual and skeletal. "I must go sleep. I am on the runway tomorrow."

"Oh, I thought you usually worked the weekend shows."

"I am covering for a friend. It is a sporting goods conference at Javits."

"Yeah, but tell her why the model needed to be replaced," said Gina.

Lucia snorted. "I do not find it as funny as you do. It could happen to any of us." She frowned at some unspoken horror. "She went in for a spray tan this morning. As she stepped out of the booth, her doctor called and told her she has the HPV virus."

"That's keeping her from the show? What in the hell was she going to be modeling?" I asked.

"No, it was not that." Lucia shook her head. "She'd been tested two months before and she did not have the virus then. Her boyfriend must have slept with someone else and then given her a little present. So . . . she started crying. While the spray tan was tacky."

"Ohhh."

"Wide, white streaks . . . she must have cried very hard."

I put my hands to my cheeks, sorry for the girl. "Wow. One more reason to be glad I don't need to tan." *Or have to deal with a boyfriend, I guess.*

Later that night, settled into bed at an unreasonably early hour, I called my dad.

"*Parisa! Khob hasti?*"

"I'm fine, Dad, I just missed you."

"I miss you as well, *koshgelam.*"

I smiled to myself when he called me his beautiful girl, looking down at my ratty college sweatshirt. "It's a good thing you can't see me right now. My face is breaking out like a twelve-year-old's."

"You are always beautiful, do not be silly. Why the acne? Is it stress?"

"Yes, but I'll be okay, Dad. Just learning the ropes, you know."

"Do you need me to come out there?"

"No, no, I'm fine, I promise."

"The purchase of a ticket would be difficult, but I will do it for you, *Parisa*, if you need me."

"Seriously, it's okay . . . Wait, what? You can't afford a plane ticket?" Again with the money comment. This from the guy who put money into a savings account every day of his life. And I mean literally. Even on weekends and holidays, sick days, and Super Bowl Sundays. Quarters, ones, fives, sometimes a twenty. "Dad? Tell me what's going on."

"*Azizam,*" he soothed, calling me his dear, "things are slow, but you already knew that. Before you hear it from anyone else, you should know I am considering getting a second, part-time job, just until things pick up again." He paused at my gasp. "But for now, I am simply tightening the belt. And hey, I've got a new belt—it is made out of a watch."

"Huh?" Last time I was home, he'd told me he was too busy to take care of his bills.

"It has been a total waist of time, though. Get it? *Waist* of time?"

"That doesn't even make sense—"

"W-a-i-s-t—"

"Spelling it out does not make it any funnier."

"Oh, so you are too sophisticated for your father now, hmm?"

I laughed half-heartedly, for his sake. "I don't think that comes as a shock to you."

"You need to relax, *Parisa*. I told you before, I am fine. You are fine. I know you are overwhelmed with the new job, just remember to stop and catch your breath." He'd changed the subject, which he'd been doing a lot lately. I was willing to go along for the moment, not sure what to say to him about our family business. My father's income. His identity.

*My God, what will he do? Should I go home, help him?*

"It is important you work hard but keep balance in your life, Paris. We all need to remember that. There is beauty out there. Do not forget to look at it. Notice the flecks and swirls. The colors. Even a bit of gravel has beauty."

"Okay . . ."

"Even the pimple on your chin."

"Damn it, Dad, there's a line."

He cleared his throat. "I have to tell you something else."

"Oh no. You said—"

"No, stop now. I told you everything is fine and I mean it. I am talking about Darien."

"What about him?" I paused. "No, never mind. I don't care. I've cut him out of my life. I don't want to think about him."

"As much as I am overjoyed to hear you say that, I thought

you might want to know, I ran into Darien's mother at the café . . . Darien is moving to New York City."

It took me a minute to pick my jaw up off the floor. Maybe I should have read his emails instead of deleting them. I controlled my breathing and said, "Okay, I didn't expect that. Luckily, it's a huge city."

"I know you are probably lonely in a new location, but Darien asks too much of you. Keep that in mind."

"I know, Dad. I know."

We spoke for five more minutes, until I had my fill of his dad jokes, but neither of us brought up money or ex-boyfriends again. Both of us silently agreed we would pretend life was fabulicious and that we believed the other one was doing just fine, at least for now.

I couldn't let myself think about Tehrani Tax Services. It was just too big. Too depressing. My breath stopped when I stumbled into a selfish awareness: If my dad was no longer a financial safety net, I was screwed. If I messed up, it was all on me. Suddenly the future didn't just seem shaky, it loomed over me, baring its fangs, hot saliva dripping on the back of my neck, burning, and out of my reach.

*Put it out of your mind, put it out of your mind.*

And Darien. *What the hell?* Why was he moving here? He ran his import business from the West Coast; his family and friends were there. His synagogue.

I'd meant what I said to my father—I did not want to fall back into the Darien hole. I'd tried everything to make him happy and it'd gotten me nothing but heartbreak. Loneliness drowned me in layers some nights, and insecurity stabbed me repeatedly on others, but I couldn't face that kind of roller coaster again. I'd rather stay at the low point for a while.

*Wow.* How had the night gotten so dark, so fast?

I picked up my Mac from the bedside table, but the motion

caused a small square of paper to flutter into the air before settling back to the surface. It was the receipt on which I'd written down the website for a photography class. Benjamin Stark's class.

# Chapter 9

*Paris, read these before you get to work.*

Along with the one-line text, Frank linked ten articles, ranging from global affairs to market trends, to an article on New York private investigators, to articles on stretches for the gluteus maximus and organic snacks to promote weight loss.

He'd sent the text the night before or, more accurately, at two in the morning. I didn't see the message until after stepping out of the shower. Skimming the articles on my short subway ride from the Upper West Side to Midtown, I could only pray I wasn't going to be quizzed on the content, especially the super exciting article regarding the movement of ships in the South China Sea. Why did I need to know about China's version of Battleship? *And is he saying I need to go on a diet?*

At one minute to eight, I stepped into PRCM's elevator, entered the code, and spent the next thirty seconds sucking in my stomach and assessing my black silk shirt in the mirror, trying to adjust the material to fix the X-rated gap between buttons. It hadn't seemed so gap-happy when I put it on this morning. Now I was wishing I'd worn a different shirt, or at the very least one of my lacy Victoria's Secret bras, not the white Target special.

Frank was in his office, though usually he didn't come in until nine. I could see a shape moving behind the frosted glass. I knocked quietly on his door, pen and pad in hand.

"Come in." Or at least that's what I think he said. It was hard to make out the mutter.

"Good morning . . ." I tried not to stare. The nondescript, middle-aged man sat slumped over a stack of spreadsheets, his white dress shirt dirty and missing buttons. He looked like he'd rolled in a mud puddle.

"Frank, can I get you anything?"

"Yes, I need you to contact Jonah at Iron Title and tell him to call me immediately." He held out a business card with the number.

*Easy enough.*

He continued, "The feds released an updated version of the new trading restrictions they're proposing, see if you can find it. Make sure it's from today, not last week. Then, I need you to find me dress shirts—Pronto Uomo, one in every color, especially the green. On your way back, pick up white grapes and Saltine crackers, and check to see we have plenty of Perrier. Do not forget the grapes. Ask Michelle what else I like; you'll need to keep my refrigerator stocked."

I scribbled frantically.

He stood up, unbuttoning his shirt, offering no explanation. As he shrugged out of it, I could see he did not believe in undershirts or exercise. He wasn't fat, but he was flabby, with long, straight hairs circling his nipples.

He tossed me the shirt. "Might as well have that dry-cleaned." He sat back down, shirtless, and picked up his pen. He flicked a glance at me and then down to his pecs and biceps. His jaw went taut as he flexed his muscles. I held in a sigh of exasperation. It was not an impressive show, not physically or maturity-wise.

*This guy controls fifteen billion dollars.*

"When you get back, let's talk over some projects. We'll do it over a late lunch. Bring back some sushi, and I'll get you started collecting and organizing information for the annual reviews. Oh, and let's send out a summary of the decluttering article to the assistants. And the stretches."

I kept my face blank but started backing out of the room, afraid he was going to bring up the other articles, maybe want me to draw a Venn diagram incorporating Asian troop movements and trending US securities. "Well, I better get moving."

I swear he tried to flex his nonexistent stomach muscles. I turned and was almost out the door, glad to no longer have his hairy nipples in my line of vision, when he said, "Oh, could you grab some cash?"

"You want me to stop at the bank for you?" I pivoted, one foot remaining on the threshold.

"No, I mean, I want you to open that safe." He gestured awkwardly to a block outlined in the wall, flexing his bicep while trying to point.

"How much do you need?"

"A stack," he said helpfully. "I have no idea what the combination is. If I'm running low on cash, you'll need to get more."

"What's 'low'?"

"If the stack has gone from big to small."

*Ah, well that clears it up.*

"Okay, I'll be right back. The combination is at my desk."

I'd tried to memorize the combo, but I had too many strings of numbers to remember. I flipped to the right page in the Book of Frank, quickly writing it on my hand before putting the binder back in the locked drawer, just in case Frank wandered out of his office. Next to the combo, Michelle had typed, *Frank is too lazy to memorize this, so you'll have to.*

I returned and did as he asked, withdrawing what I guesstimated to be about three thousand dollars. I figured he'd tell me to put some back, but he didn't.

"Do I have a shirt around here somewhere?" he said as I

piled the bills neatly on his desk. I had no idea if it was too much or not enough, since I had no idea what he was doing with the cash. Taking his son's Little League team out to lunch at Restaurant Haru? A down payment on more of the hideous pink aluminum art his wife loved?

I tried to decide whether I should dash around the room opening cupboards or go out into the cubicles and demand one of the traders hand over his shirt, Hollywood style. Frank finally stared right at me, his squinty eyes money-green, his hair curling moistly on his forehead. I must have looked as bewildered as I felt.

"I know we're getting to know each other, Paris. I don't expect you to have all the answers, not yet. Go ask Michelle. She'd be happy to do your job for you."

My stomach sank. There was no emotion in his voice, or on his face, but I felt a sting on my cheek from the slap. I nodded stiffly and walked out.

Michelle, sitting at her tidy desk, working on three projects at once, peered up in a fog. Pushing her black glasses up her nose, she told me where the last executive assistant stored extra clothes for Frank. I wanted to talk to her, get her advice, but she was distracted and besides, she was my assistant. I was supposed to be establishing my authority.

In a locked closet outside the break room, there were stacks of clothes. And four different pairs of wingtips. Flannel pajamas and a bathrobe, next to a box filled with deodorant, shampoo, toothpaste, and brushes. Another box contained twenty tubs of Lancôme wrinkle cream, three tubes of Tinactin for athlete's foot, and a tube of Lotrimin for ringworm. The only ointment that looked to be opened was a tube of Vagistat for yeast infections; the seal was broken, the tube rolled up like the Colgate in my bathroom.

"What the—" I decided I didn't want to know.

"What are you doing?" Nicki came up beside me, swinging her red hair over her shoulder like she was trying out for the reboot of *Gossip Girl*.

"Getting Frank a clean shirt."

"Make sure you iron it before you give it to him, especially the collar. I have some starch stashed with the extra shirts for the other staff, I'll be right back." The younger assistant flounced off, returning in a second with a spray can. She smirked at my shirt, and then handed me the starch, saying, "Do you know how to use this?"

There was an iron in the closet. I considered hitting her on the head with it. Instead, I used the break room table as an ironing board. Using Nicki as an ironing board would be frowned upon. I speed walked back to Frank's office, trying to control the bounce of my C-cups with my forearms, though creating an even bigger gap between the buttons in the process.

*Note to self: look into lacy sport bras from Victoria's Secret.*

Frank put on the shirt, took off the shirt, and threw it back to me. "Why is the collar stiff?"

"I ironed—"

"If I'd wanted it ironed, I would have said so. Get me another shirt."

Suddenly, his bare skin turned a mottled, tomato red from his chin to his hairy nipples. He laid a palm across his throat, as if feeling for a pulse. "Oh my God, did you use starch?" he shouted, his eyes bugging out.

"Ye-ye-yes . . ."

"Goddamnit! Get me a cold, wet washcloth, now!"

I sprinted into his bathroom and, bunching a hand towel under the running faucet, I vaguely remembered the list of allergies from the Book of Frank. Starch. Yes, it definitely listed starch.

"Do I need to call an ambulance? Do you have an EpiPen?" I made my voice remain calm as I thrust the wet towel at him. "What can I do?"

He glared, wrapping the hand towel around his throat. "Get me another shirt. And an ice pack," he growled. He fumbled a box of Benadryl out of his drawer.

Nicki was waiting for me at the closet. "Oh, didn't he like that one?" she asked in a baby voice.

I refused to be trolled. "Nope," I said, grabbing what I needed and walking away.

Frank looked better by the time I got back to him, more pink than red. He no longer flexed for me. Nor was he talking to me. He just grunted and waved me away.

I had a hard time concentrating after that. Finding the report on the newest federal regulations took some time. Scanning the content, their biggest beef seemed to be that the funds weren't taxed. That, and the managers were asking for a 2-and-20 split, taking 2 percent of the clients' assets and 20 percent of the profits.

I had no idea why that would bother the feds, since clients weren't *forced* into putting their money in hedge funds. They couldn't even be an investor unless they made half a million a year and had at least a million in assets free to trade—which couldn't include their McMansion residence. We weren't working with hobos.

But I knew hedge funds weren't popular when I took this gig. Every trader outside of hedge funds hated hedge funds, since we made money betting against their stocks. Some hedge funds were strong enough to sway the outcome of a stock. I had no idea if PRCM was playing at that level. It might be, but I wasn't sure if I wanted to know. It seemed like there were plenty of reasons to be irritated with Frank outside of his trading practices.

"Paris!" he screamed through his door.

I jumped up and ran in, expecting to see blood weeping from his starch rash. But no, Frank was fine, sitting calmly at his desk, his shirt unbuttoned guido-style, the skin on his chest back to pasty white.

His mouth moved into an unappealing o-shaped rosebud of surprise when I came crashing through his door. He must not have realized his screaming made it sound like someone lit his pants on fire.

He unabashedly watched my girls bouncing under my blouse. I halted, blushing.

"Where are my grapes?" he asked my breasts.

*Is that a metaphor?* The anti-sexual harassment movement was alive and well everywhere else but in his office.

"On my way to run your errands now," I said cheerfully, as if all was right with the world.

Michelle stopped me as I passed her desk. "I heard him yelling. Are you okay?"

"Yes. And so is he, though I did almost kill him. I used starch."

"Ah. I'm guessing this has something to do with Nicki. She's been sauntering around with a smug look on her face."

I sighed. "I won't trust her again, that's for sure. On the flip side, Frank's never going to trust me again, either."

. . . . . . . . . . . . . . . . . . . . .

I clocked out at exactly six o'clock. I was done, figuratively and literally. Stepping onto the damp sidewalk in front of the Purple Rock Capital Management building, I decided to walk at least part way home to shake off some of the day's residue. I'd spent the better part of my afternoon hunting down the elusive lime green Uomo dress shirt, well hidden in the wilds of Manhattan up-scale man boutiques, protected by legions of coiffed salespeople who treated me like Julia Roberts in the *Pretty Woman* shopping spree.

I dug out the pack of Benson & Hedges and stuck one in my mouth. Walking past Joe's Coffee Shop, I caught sight of myself in the window. *I do look cool*, I decided. *New York hip.* At least that's what I told myself.

Then I noticed something more interesting than my reflection; it was Nicki and Ericka, the executive assistant I had replaced. They were sitting together, whispering and giggling. *I thought Ericka wanted nothing more to do with the company? And Nicki?* I would never have pegged those two as friends. But even the bitchy and the crazy need friends.

I kept walking. Ending my day with either of those two didn't sound like fun.

I didn't light the cigarette. The disgusting spongy, acrid filter had begun to grow on me, though, just like how I'd learned to enjoy the bitterness of coffee . . . if coffee caused cancer. Which it probably did. Moving the death stick around with my tongue gave me something to do as I walked. I hoped it made me fit in, look like a secure, sophisticated professional.

*Because I don't feel like a professional. Or an adult. Somehow, I've taken a step backward in my career.*

Dealing with securities at Deutsche Bank, I'd been low on the totem pole, maybe two rungs above the tellers, but at least I'd been working with actual money and numbers, versus . . . this. But I knew, realistically, leaving PRCM not only meant a pay cut, it probably meant living on unemployment and moving back home. The banks were tightening their belts, just like my dad, and jobs were scarce. The truth was, I was lucky to have this job. I was going to have to suck it up.

I wasn't wandering mindlessly. Around Broadway and 72nd Street, I found what I was looking for. A bright red and white door. A storefront window with bold, beautifully framed photographic images fighting for space. A hand-painted sign proclaiming BENJAMIN STARK PHOTOGRAPHY, along with his hours. It was long past time for the photographer to have closed up shop, but I tried the door anyway; his website said he offered evening workshops. A bell chimed as the door swung open. I stuck the soggy cigarette in my coat pocket and stepped in.

There was a small entryway with a wide opening to the left leading into a photo gallery. To the right were three doors, one marked Restroom, one marked Darkroom, and the last marked Classroom. I could hear voices from behind the last, at least five or six people. Then, suddenly, the door flew open. There he was. Benji, the photographer from The Rooftop at Viceroy.

"Hey! It's you!" he said, putting his hands on his hips, a surprised grin creeping across his face, tiny laugh lines crinkling in the corner of his eyes. His thick hair was tousled—*and so sexy*. I could see past him, where a small group sat around a table, peering at me curiously.

"I'm so sorry, I didn't mean to interrupt a class." I twisted my earring back and forth, trying not to scrunch my shoulders.

"No way are you interrupting. Come on in, have a seat. Unless you're here to ask me out? Are you following me, girly?"

"What? No! Of course not." The heat from my blush must have seared his nose hairs. *I wish to God I could control my body.*

"I kid! I kid!" He threw up his hands, as he'd done the first night we met. "I'm sorry, I don't even know your name. What should we call you?" He gestured to the class, the royal *we*. He turned to them. "You know, she left the bar without telling me her name, after promising she'd wait for me. What a heartbreaker, huh?"

Some in the class tittered, but one or two younger women didn't take pains to hide their jealous grimaces. I ignored them, and his witticisms, wanting to get into a chair as soon as possible and sink into the floor.

"Hi. Hi, everyone. I'm Paris."

One of the students started to say, "Oh, like—"

"Yes. Just like Paris Hilton. Minus the hotels and the scandal. And the magazine profiles."

Benji guided me to a seat next to him at the end of the table. "Oh, you're way more photogenic than Paris Hilton," he said with a grin.

The same middle-aged guy who'd tried to crack the Paris joke opened his mouth again. I gazed at him coldly. "Don't say it."

Benji dropped his hands to the tabletop, slapping the wood, and said, "Alright, let's get to it."

I'd planned on stopping for information, maybe asking a few questions about film and processing. To leave now, I'd have to get past everyone while Benji was talking. Also, my leg was next to his under the table.

*I guess I'm taking the class.*

Benji launched into a discussion on finding subjects and then regarding those subjects from multiple angles.

"Don't just look; really *see* how an object changes when you view it from another perspective." Passion and electricity rolled off him as he talked about standing on the bridge over Gill Stream in Central Park and shooting from above, how he would consider the stream's light and shadow and size and place in the world.

He jabbed his finger at the intent faces around the table. "Then I change my perspective in a big way, walking down to the edge of that same stream and lying down. I might look crazy, but man, the things you notice!"

I flashed on him in a pair of swim trunks on a hot summer day, lying on a sandy beach next to the stream, a sheen of sweat on rippling shoulder muscles . . . but refocused as he described, animatedly, holding the lens of the camera inches above the water, first peering straight down into the depths, and then across the surface. "Two more perspectives of the same body of water, but each with a different vibe, and each with its own set of emotions and complexities that change with a simple tilt of your shoulder or twist of your wrist."

*He and my dad would get along so well. Finding joy and beauty in the simple things.*

After class, as the students gathered up loose papers, Benji made his rounds and then sauntered up to me as I made my way to the door. "I can't believe you came in. I have to admit, I'm honored you sought me out."

My hand on the knob, ready to flee, I said shyly, "I really liked your photo collection at Rooftop. I want to take photos like that. I like the idea of telling a story in a single shot." I didn't want him to think I was stalking him for any other reason than to learn from him. But smelling his cologne and watching the way he moved, like one of the athletes he'd photographed, and seeing how he occasionally ran his hand through his sandy-blond hair, a part of me hoped he and his bartender girlfriend were on the rocks. A big part of me.

"Well, good, then I assume that means you're coming back? We're meeting every week for the next two months." He lightly placed his hand on my shoulder, offering something between a squeeze and a caress that sent a shiver down my spine, his hazel eyes intent on mine. Then someone tapped him on the back and his hand slipped away, his attention diverted.

I made my way outside quietly, glad for the chilly air on my face. I immediately called Gina, so I could share my new weekly plans and describe the luscious, full lips of the photographer—while trying not to think of those same lips kissing the hot bartender girlfriend.

Back in the safety of my apartment, facing the red wall, I decided it was time to fill the gold frames. They'd hung empty long enough.

# Chapter 10

The armchairs arranged in front of my desk were meant for investors and advisory clients waiting to meet with Andrew or Frank, but should have been switched out for bar stools.

By mid-March, the office treated my desk as a bar and vomited their fears and hopes out to me, the office bartender. I had yet to sneak in any actual alcohol but that didn't seem to matter. It took about two weeks of working at PRCM for most of the traders, analysts, and researchers to lose the last traces of inhibitions, or pride, when it came to using me as a buffer between them and Frank.

Late one afternoon, Andrea, the head of investor relations, gripped the arms of the chair closest to me, her French manicure digging into the soft leather. "I've got tickets to the Canary Islands. I'm leaving next week," she blurted out.

"That's great!" I said, wondering what was coming next, her face overcome with facial tics.

"Yes, it's great. Great. Greeeeeaaaaat." Andrea's eyes darted around. "Frank doesn't know yet."

"Oh."

"Yeah. Listen, Paris, can you tell him for me, after I leave today? Maybe if he has time to process it over night, he won't yell." There was a vein pulsing in her forehead.

"I thought the COO was in charge of vacations. Did Todd approve it? Why is Frank going to care?"

She groaned. "He hates it when we go on vacation. I've tried explaining to him we have this newfangled thing called the cell phone. Jeez, it's the twenty-first century. I call investors and answer my emails from anywhere—which *he* does all the time—but he wants to be in control. Of when I sleep. Of when I eat. When I pee. Yesterday, during a meeting, I tried to sneak out to go to the bathroom and he told me to sit down and hold it!"

I nodded sympathetically. "I know, he's hard to take sometimes. But don't worry, it's not just you, he does that to everybody. He's from the Donald Trump School of Operation, where urinating is for the weak." I leaned over my desk conspiratorially and whispered, "Yet, he just made me order a $20,000 Toto Toilet for his office bathroom. I don't imagine it will sit unused."

Her eyes went wide. "You're kidding! Does it give you a massage or something?"

I shrugged. "Probably. It has a seat warmer and flushes on voice command. The bidet has six settings, including a warm jet of air. And, for some reason, there's a remote control."

Her shoulders relaxed. She chuckled and then in a much calmer tone said, "So, you'll talk to him for me? He should be in a good mood; he went short on the Inverse stock and made a killing." She got up, not waiting for me to answer. "Thanks, Paris. I think I'll head home right now. By the way," she said quickly, as she began to walk away, "I'll be gone for two weeks." The *tic-tic-tic* of her spike heels performed a double-time tempo as she vacated the area before her bomb went off.

*She's a department head? What a coward*, I thought. But she wasn't acting any different than the other people on the floor, from the assistants to the administrators. I spent a good chunk of most days reassuring the employees that Frank treated everyone "that way" and "no, no one deserved to be so disrespected."

I could see his slumpy outline through the frosted glass. His feet were up. He was reading the paper. *Best to get this over with.* I straightened my spine, tapped on Frank's door, and quietly slipped inside at his grunt. Guns N' Roses was playing low in the background, muzak for the forty-somethings, the generation stuck in the eighties.

"Hey there, what's up, Paris?" he mumbled, his face relaxed, his squint less squinty than usual, his straight brown hair pushed out of his face, no sweat on his cheeks.

"So, a coupla' things. First, I know the yearly report for the investors is due soon, so I've begun collecting and correlating data, if you want to send me your information."

He tented his fingers under his chin, peering at me without saying a word, though his energy remained calm. Which was annoying, since I had been asking him for the material for at least a week.

"Also, I wanted to remind you," I continued, "I'm going to be gone next Monday, for the Persian New Year holiday."

He broke apart his stretched-out legs and re-crossed them. "You're making that up. There's no such holiday. I've never heard of it."

I chuckled nervously, no idea if he was joking or not.

He wasn't.

Slowly, he said, "Seriously, it's March. Who celebrates the new year in March?"

"Persians are celebrating the first day of spring. It's called Norooz. It's a big deal, even for Iranians who aren't religious. Just like how secular families celebrate Christmas."

"So, what, you're a pagan? You're gonna have sex in a green field, like, with a guy wearing horns?"

*What the hell? Is he confusing Persians with Druids?*

How did he make such a crazy leap? Did he spend his free time watching porn and cat videos? For a guy who controlled billions of dollars, globalization hadn't made much of an impact on his understanding of people.

"Um, no, my family is not pagan." I barely managed to keep my voice level. "We celebrate with big family meals, some singing. We exchange presents. There are no fields or fertility rites involved." *He has a son. He's added to the gene pool. Please tell me he's joking.*

Frank picked up his newspaper, shook it out. "Sounds boring. Keep your phone on. I'll text you if we have an emergency."

By "we," he meant him. No one else had emergencies, unless their emergency involved him. Irritated, I forgot to coat my next words in sugar.

"Frank, Andrea is going to be gone on Monday as well. As a matter of fact, she's going to be gone for two weeks. Todd approved her vacation a long time ago but she's been too afraid to tell you."

I should have left that last part out.

"Oh no she isn't! She can't do that! You get her in here right now!" Before I could tell him she'd already left, he started shouting, "Andrea! Andrea! Get in here right now!"

Instead of prolonging the pain, I said, "I'll go find her," and darted out of his office.

"Andrea! You've got five seconds!" he shouted again, his tantrum muffling as I yanked his door shut.

I rested my forehead on the frame for a beat. Then, sighing, I turned and found a woman, maybe in her fifties, possibly in her sixties, leaning against my desk, her eyebrows high on her forehead.

"I'm assuming you're not Andrea?" she asked me.

"No." I couldn't stop a nervous laugh from burbling out.

"Andrea is miles away by now, though she can probably still hear Mr. Coyle. Sorry about that."

The woman—beautiful, slim, and dressed in a classic haute couture white pantsuit—shrugged and said, "I hope you don't let him talk to *you* like that."

Not sure how to answer her, I noticed she held a framed photo from my desk in her hand. She saw me looking and her perfect black hair bobbed smoothly as she shifted around the other framed photos I'd quietly set out a week ago, hoping Frank wouldn't say anything. They were stills from my last day on the boardwalk by my father's house, each focused on a different door, offering a pop of color against a black-and-white background.

"Are these from Newport? Down along the promenade?" Amusement curled her lips into a kind smile.

"Yes! Are you from there?" A flush of homesickness rushed through me. I recognized her vaguely, but I couldn't place from where. I didn't think I knew her from back home. *Maybe a client from my old bank?*

"Yes, I live in L.A. I love Newport." She ran a manicured fingertip over the glass covering an orange-and-red gate in front of a vintage bookstore. "These are fabulous. They make me feel as if I'm there. It's like the heart of the place has been captured."

Heat moved across my face. "Thank you. Really. I feel the same way about them. I'm going to take more, next time I'm home."

She put the picture back with the others and scanned my face, suddenly businesslike. "So you took these? What gallery are you in?"

"Gallery? Oh, no, it's just a hobby—"

"Honey, there's hobbies and then there's art. You've got an eye. Believe me, I know." Her dark brown eyes seared into mine. Then it hit me.

"You . . . you're Tris Jenson . . ." I stuttered stupidly. The uber-famous businesswoman had just complimented my photos. I felt a bit faint but shook myself awake.

"Don't get weird. We're just two California girls, yakking about home." She winked. "Have you considered selling your work? Or starting your own photography business? You should."

"I've never—"

Another muffled yell from Frank's office stopped me. He was yelling for me this time.

"I'm so sorry, excuse me." I opened his door, hoping to cut him off before he shouted again. "Frank, you have—"

"Is that Tris out there? What the hell have you been doing? Stop bothering the investors." He stepped around me and filled the doorframe with his awkward, unappealing body. "Tris! Come in! Let me get you a whiskey. Neat, right?"

Tris Jenson brushed past the two of us, saying, "Frank, darling, you sound like a beast, yelling at this poor girl. Don't you have an intercom?"

He glared at me. "She's fine with it."

Ignoring that, I said, "Can I get either of you anything?"

Frank opened his mouth but Ms. Jenson beat him to the punch. "No, thank you." She patted me on the shoulder. "Think about what I said."

I mumbled something and shut the door, leaving them to discuss how best to position her vast fortune.

How could I not think about what she said? Every word from her lips was a gem to be treasured, as far as I was concerned, even if none of it was realistic. It wasn't like I could control Frank. And start my own photography business? Being a person who liked to eat food and avoid rat-infested, moldy housing situations, I couldn't see the starving artist lifestyle working for me. *Maybe when I have an actual retirement account. Sixty years from now. But . . . damn.*

I straightened the frames on my desk, a grin hurting my cheeks. Michelle and Nicki slunk over, curious. The two research assistants hovered behind them, trying like hell to get in on the gossip.

"My God, did Tris Jenson just call you fabulous?" Nicki hissed, jealousy writhing across her face.

"What was she talking about, Paris?" Michelle seemed impressed, hands on hips. She smiled with encouragement, while Nicki simply looked hungry.

"Nothing. We were just discussing L.A." I shrugged. "She was very sweet." For some reason, I didn't want to spoil the dream by sharing it too soon.

"She's tough, that's what she is. She comes in here about every six months and it freaks out Frank," Michelle said. She turned to the huddled group of wide-eyed assistants. "You two," she said to the researchers. "You might as well update your trade reports in the biotech sector; he's going to ask for them in a minute. Tell each of the traders what you need. And you"—she turned to Nicki—"make a reservation at Tao for two people thirty minutes from now. Have oysters at the table waiting for them. Make sure they know it's Frank and Tris. Then go downstairs and make sure Frank's car is waiting, that there are two bottles of Dom Pérignon rosé on ice, and upload Nina Simone's albums for the driver."

"But—" Nicki sputtered.

"Go." Michelle's voice was low and menacing, like an Aryan German officer ready to beat down Nicki for the sake of the office. I couldn't help but be impressed by the mastery with which she controlled the situation and the people. She faced me, her blonde ponytail an exclamation point down her back.

"Stop looking so scared." She sniffed with disdain. "This is what we do. We figure out what Frank will want before he wants it. You'll figure it out, if you're here long enough."

Despite my better judgment, I asked her, "What should I be doing? Should I be doing something with her investment portfolio?"

"Call down to Tris's assistant; she's probably waiting at Tris's car; tell her what's going on. Then stand here. When they come out, follow quietly, ready to take notes or make calls, or run into traffic, whatever he wants."

"I'm glad you're here," I said earnestly.

Her face softened when she realized I didn't resent her for taking over; on the contrary, I was grateful. But then she gave me a quizzical look and asked, "And what *would* you do if I told you to go over Tris's portfolio? What would you be looking for?"

She wasn't projecting anything but curiosity, but bile rose my throat. After all this time, I'd let myself forget about the fact that I had zero experience actually managing or manipulating hedge fund portfolios. I had been lulled by my days of scheduling and buying tampons; I'd backed off from using my brain. Rarely was I asked to do anything directly related to finance, unless it was to run a report, which meant I had the time to sit at my computer and figure out what was needed. "Uh. I guess, first, I would assess the biotech—"

The office phone on my desk rang. I may or may not have literally hurdled over a desk to get to it—and away from Michelle. As I snagged up the receiver, I could see her become distracted by one of the researchers and wander away, but my shoulders refused to come down off my ears.

Nicki was calling from the lobby, her phone manner as unpleasant as her face-to-face manner. "I can't find any music by Nina Simpson. There's no such person as Nina Simpson."

"You're right, there is no Nina Simpson." *Your musical tastes run as deep as your thoughts on life.* "Michelle said Nina Simone. You know, 'I Put a Spell on You'?"

"Paris, you're an idiot. That was a guy." And she hung up.

I made myself look busy, moving papers from pile A to pile B to cabinet C, at the same time treating my frayed nerves with the sweet medicine of superiority, thinking of Nicki and shaking my head. When I heard voices approaching from the opposite side of Frank's door, I grabbed a notepad and my iPhone, ready for action.

Tris emerged without a glance in my direction, though she did set an empty whiskey glass on my desk. So much for bonding. And then out came our CEO. He was wearing Adidas tennis shoes with his suit.

"Frank . . ." I pointed at his feet, trying to catch his eye.

"Not now."

I started to follow but he stopped me. "Where do you think you're going? I need you to go through my appointments and phone calls for the day and reschedule everything."

Then he and Tris Jenson were gone. The crackle of energy left the room. Michelle was back at her computer, reabsorbed into whatever project I probably should have been doing, and the traders were gabbing, or flipping through Facebook and sliding through Tinder on their smartphones, their feet up on their desks.

For a minute, I considered talking to one of the traders about the biotech stocks Michelle mentioned. Hadn't the bubble burst in both bio and pharmaceutical? Was Frank sticking with this sector? I needed to keep on top of the financial papers, which would be easy enough since they were lying around here like abandoned children. I wished Frank would talk to me about his strategies, how he finessed the trends. That's why I'd taken the job, to learn about hedging from a master.

Instead, I gazed at the photos on my desk and broke into a grin. I could no longer bridle the giddiness. I needed to tell someone about Tris Jenson and my photos. Grabbing my phone and one of Lucia's cigarettes out of my bag, I waved it at Michelle and told her I was headed to the roof for a smoke break. The air was chilly but refreshing.

"Paris. What are you doing here?"

It was Nicki. She was leaning up against a pillar, smoke wafting out of her nose. Standing a foot away, her arms crossed against the cold, was Ericka.

I glanced at Frank's old EA in surprise but then shrugged and replied, "Smoking. What else would I be doing? Ericka, nice to see you again."

The woman smiled, though it was strained. "Paris, right? Nice to see you, too. Well, I'm off. Have a good afternoon."

"I'll go down with you," Nicki said, dropping her cigarette on the rooftop. She didn't look at me, or put out the burning butt, as they made their way back inside.

*That was so weird. Maybe they're girlfriends.*

# Chapter 11

A back-alley cat fight.

An opera singer, punched in the throat on the high note.

A soccer mom in a game rage.

I covered my ears, cringing, trying to block out the cats, singers, and angry moms screaming at me. Then, slowly, it hit me: I was dreaming. I cracked open my aching eyes.

*Where is that screeching coming from?* Could it be morning already? As far as I could tell, it was still dark and my alarm was silent. Then the sound stopped abruptly. *Thank you, Jesus.* I closed my eyes, slid further under the comforter.

The screech erupted again. I sat bolt upright. The noise was not coming from my alarm—it was the buzzer for my front door and it was as loud as a death harpy.

I scrambled into my living room and pressed the intercom button next to the front door.

"What!" I didn't bother with niceties. It was 12:32 a.m.

"Paris? Is this you? Did I wake you?"

"*Darien?*"

"Happy Norooz!"

I pinched my earlobe, really digging in with my nails. Nope, I wasn't dreaming.

"Can I come up?"

"I don't—" I stumbled in my sleepy state of alarm and my

fingers fumbled across the panel. I accidentally buzzed him in. "No!" I exclaimed, but it was too late.

I'd had just enough time to slip on a cardigan over my nightgown by the time he knocked on the door. My ex. What the hell was happening? Where was my bra?

"Why are you in bed so early?" Darien leaned against the doorframe, a bottle of champagne in his hand, tall, dark, and handsome in a cream-colored cashmere sweater. "It's New Year's!"

"I ha-have to work tomorrow," I stuttered, trying to gain control of my thoughts, and crossed my arms over my chest, trying to obscure my hardening nipples from the draft in the hallway.

The cold did help to sharpen my sleep-addled wits. I was so exhausted. I'd been up early and working late every day. Even on my requested day off for the holiday, Frank had called three times, demanding phone numbers and other information he easily could have found on his own—including wanting to know if the very young, attractive research assistant was single. Luckily, he wasn't interrupting anything, since I'd hung out at home in my yoga pants, celebrating the first day of spring by sharing a glass of doogh with my father over a short, light-hearted Skype chat, both of us munching on stuffed grape leaves and olives with our minty yogurt drink, keeping our talk focused on my photography classes and the weather.

"What are you doing here?" I asked. I'd made it through February without Darien, including Valentine's Day, and March had looked so promising, a fresh start for the Persian New Year.

"Hey, alright," Darien said, with a slight slur. "Sorry. I thought you might want to go for a drink, celebrate the hol-iday." He reached out a hand and ran it over my cheek, then lightly touched my ear. "I love that you're still wearing your mom's earrings."

I winced, and he dropped his hand. This was real. I was awake. My father had been right. "So you're in New York," I said, nonplussed.

"Yeah. I heard you were on the Upper West Side." He grinned. "I'm here, too."

"What do you mean?" Something in his tone, his giddiness, made me suspicious. "Are you saying you're living in my *neighborhood*?"

"Yes! How great is that?" His straight white teeth flashed in a beautiful smile. I hated him. Didn't I?

The tight-knit Iranian community back home was wonderful, but damn if they didn't gossip like old ladies at the water pump. Were they just handing out my address on business cards?

"Why? Why did you move *here*, of all places?" Part of me wanted to ask about his girlfriend. Was she here, too? A bigger part of me, however, wasn't prepared to be stabbed with that knife, not in the middle of the night, out of nowhere. The bottle of champagne in his hand didn't mean he was single. I'd learned that the hard way.

He paused a second and then continued, deflated. "I didn't move to Manhattan for you, if that's what you think. I've opened a shop here." His voice grew angry, his face tight. "I thought you'd like knowing someone from back home was close by. I thought we could be friends, Paris. I still care for you."

*I might be awake, but this is a nightmare.* I'd dreamt of this exact conversation twelve times a day. Each time it ended with him clutching me to his tall, hard body, admitting he loved me—but that was before I moved here. With time and distance, a demanding job, random barista flirtations, and flirting with Benji, the dream had melted away quietly, without me even really noticing. I missed being held at night, sure, but I didn't miss Darien. I felt free. Independent. Peaceful.

When I didn't respond, his edge softened. "Your dad will be relieved I can help look out for you now." He took a step toward me, waving the the Persian food he bought from the restaurant Ravagh. "Why don't I come in?"

There was so much to say to that. Flames filled my chest, burned hot. I stood my ground, filled the door so he couldn't enter my new world. "No. And I don't need to be taken care of by *anyone*, despite what you or my father thinks—especially not by a guy who cheated on me, or an old man who can't take care of himself." My stomach clenched. I had not realized until now that I wasn't only worried about Dad, I was also mad at him. Regardless of the logic, I felt let down by him. *I'm a self-centered asshole.*

Darien reared his head back. "Paris?"

"I know, I didn't mean that . . . about my Dad." I tried to rally my righteous indignation.

He ignored the dig. Frowning, he said, "Ehsan has had a rough time. A man with brown skin in his sixties? Word around the neighborhood is that no one will hire him. You know how it is, he writes down 'Tehrani' and these jackasses think he has a bomb tucked in his shoe." He shook his head in disgust. "I heard he tried getting a night job, cleaning up at a middle school; apparently, the principal told him they weren't set up for Muslims and that he'd be uncomfortable there. Ignorant sons of bitches."

"Damn it," I groaned, squeezing my eyes shut, trying to block out reality. "My poor father. I didn't realize."

"The Orange County gossip circles are saying he might lose his business." He sat the bottle on the floor and placed his hands on my shoulders. The weight was unsettling. "You should talk to him. Really talk to him. People from the community have offered help but he refuses, saying he won't take charity."

No. How could this be? My father had gone from running a successful business to a state of panic so quickly—unless he'd been hiding the depth of the problems with Tehrani Tax Services. Dad had not mentioned closing the business. He was about to lose it? And why would nobody hire him? It was shocking that in our modern times, in a civilized, multicultural city, racism was alive and well, dressed up in politically correct phrases.

Dad was a highly educated, peace-loving American, misaligned because of the lottery ticket his soul drew the day he was born, setting him down in the countryside outside of Tehran instead of Dallas or Kansas City. He grew up surrounded by men wearing skullcaps and head scarves, but fate just as easily could have surrounded him with cowboy hats and baseball caps—all the heads beneath being more similar than different.

I shivered in the cold and Darien's hands tightened on my shoulders. He drew me slowly to him and suddenly I didn't want to stop him. Leaning into his sinewy body, I felt protected and cared for. And wanted. His hard body fit against me perfectly, just as I remembered. His face hovered close for a brief second, and then his lips met mine. I immediately wanted more, my tongue and lips greedily moving against his mouth, my body moving against his. The tingle that roared through my veins woke me up, every sense on high alert. Unfortunately, that same alertness brought my brain to attention: *Danger! Danger!* it cried out.

With a self-control I didn't know I possessed, I slid away.

"I'm not doing this, Darien. We're done."

"Please, just let me in. I know you want to."

"Don't you have a girlfriend?"

"She's not you. Come on—"

"I knew it." I straightened my nightgown, furious at myself for allowing him back into my headspace, almost back into my bed. "I need to sleep. I've got a lot going on at work." The last person I needed back in my life was Darien. I did not want to start relying on him to be a confidant, a shoulder to lean on, or a lover. I knew where that path led.

"Can I call you tomorrow?" His face was hopeful.

Anger thrilled up my spine. With narrowed eyes, I said, "I don't think your girlfriend would appreciate it." Then I shut the door in his face.

I had to struggle with myself not to reopen the door, bashing down the jumping hormones begging for physical attention. *What's wrong with me?*

Wrapped in an old quilt, I sat on the fire escape and finally lit up one of the cigarettes I'd been carrying around for weeks. It was time to burn something down.

...................

The next morning, Michelle's blonde ponytail seemed less stern than usual, not as tightly slicked back. Even her face was duller when she caught up with me in the break room, her movements slow. She took down an extra mug and poured me a cup of coffee. "Some analysts and a trader are being let go today. Be prepared for high drama."

"Oh no! Why?" I put down the bag of groceries I had for Frank. Not exactly how I wanted to start out my "new year."

"I'm sure you've noticed we've been on the losing end of some big trades lately. Todd told me yesterday they have to cut back." She frowned. "It's not just us. A lot of hedge funds have had trouble restabilizing after the recession. We've done well, thanks to Frank, but that doesn't mean we don't take the same hits occasionally."

I took the coffee to my desk, hoping it would wake me up after a night tossing and turning and muttering to myself, but I eventually switched to chamomile tea and Alka-Seltzer in order to soothe my stomach. *Did I really smoke a cigarette last night? Did I really tell Darien he couldn't come in?*

The mood in the office was subdued, everyone trying to make themselves invisible. Thinking about it, I realized I should be doing the same thing. Panic blossomed in my chest when I saw one of the younger traders trying to hide his tears behind sunglasses as he packed up his desk.

*That could be me. Today.* I sat back. A realization struck me, the accompanying headache almost blinding. I needed this job. Really needed it. It was one thing if *I* was struggling financially, but my dad . . . I gritted my teeth. Whether I liked it or not, it was my turn to step up. For him. I struggled with my selfish anger with him for not being perfect, but if he needed me, I could help. My position at PRCM might not be my dream job, but it paid well. Extremely well.

I watched the trader trudging out with his small box of possessions. *I will be indispensable*, I decided.

I was absorbed in a report when my desk phone buzzed. "Yes?"

"Hi, this is Tony. Frank's trainer."

"I know who you are, Tony." I talked to the guy at least once a week, usually to let him know Frank was running late or out sick, but what the trainer lacked in brains showed up in his pecs. And he was the sweetest guy on steroids I'd ever met.

"Is Frank here? He asked me to come in, but I've been waiting in the gym for over an hour now. I'm way late for another client now. What should I do?"

I pinched the bridge of my nose. "Just go, Tony. I'm sorry. But make sure you bill him for your time."

I didn't want to get into it face-to-face with Frank, so I sent an instant message, telling him Tony had an emergency and had to leave. I knew that wouldn't stop him from bitching out the poor guy.

Then my cell phone rang. Weird. It was Frank, who was

in his office, as far as I knew. I hadn't seen him leave. And he usually just shouted for me.

"Yes?" I projected a kindness I did not feel.

"I'm out of toilet paper."

"Alllllright." I paused, waiting for him to go on. Finally, I said, "So, are you asking me to come into your bathroom and hand you a roll of toilet paper?"

*Why me?*

"What the fuck, Paris. Don't be a child. Bring me some goddamned toilet paper." He hung up.

I sighed. No need to worry about my job security.

If not for me, Frank wouldn't eat or have clothes to wear, nor would his family. I'm not sure what Sonya, his wife, did all day, but it had nothing to do with basic needs for any of them, including their nine-year-old son. I knew, because I set up her twice-weekly spa appointments, her daily luncheons and mani-pedis, and weekly visits to galleries where she bought "art," such as the hideous ball of metal hangers wrapped around each other recently installed in Frank's office. It sat on a marble pedestal. But I also coordinated with the house staff regarding Frank, Sonya, and their son's meals, their dry cleaning, and their separate car services. I wondered if any of them stopped for a second, did a three-sixty, and just appreciated their life.

Trying to blank my mind, I grabbed a roll from the staff bathroom, strolled across his office, and twisted the knob to his bathroom door. The door was locked.

"You're going to have to unlock it," he called out.

Grumbling, I set the roll on the floor and marched back to the break room. Nicki and Michelle were stocking shelves.

"What's got your Kotex in a twist?" Nicki said, her resting bitch face securely in place.

*Maybe I can get you fired along with everyone else.*

"Frank's locked in his bathroom. I need to unlock it. Any idea where the key is?"

"Ah. Sadly, this is not the first time," said Michelle, pushing Nicki to the side. "Here, this will do the trick." She handed me a butter knife.

She was right—a slight twist of the blade and I was in. *Lucky me.* I thrust the roll through the door, a hand over my eyes. If only I could have also covered my nose. The guy had no shame.

"Closer . . . closer . . . thanks."

The roll was snatched from my hand, and I bolted. I dropped the butter knife in a wastebasket on my way out of his office.

Hoping to wash my brain free of the last five minutes, I opened up Benji's website for his gallery. I wanted to make sure there was a class listed for that night. I needed to surround myself by beautiful art. A beautiful man wouldn't be hard to look at, either. *Okay, enough. Learn to make your own beautiful art and be satisfied with that. Benji is off limits, yo.*

I reopened the report on my desktop. The analysts and research assistants sent me information on ownership trends, showing me activity on our most sold and purchased stocks, so I could collapse and organize the information for the CEOs. I could see most of the trades originated from Frank, especially the shorts, though there were quite a few from Andrew.

Oddly, some of the transactions weren't attached to anyone. *Lazy bastards*, I thought. *How hard is it to write down who's telling you to make the trade?* I picked up the phone to call the lead trader but was stopped by a familiar shout.

"Paris!"

I pushed through his door hesitantly. First, I hoped he was dressed. Second, I hoped we weren't going to talk about the TP incident. Ever. Third, I was ready to take the bullet for Tony the trainer, if that's what this was about, but I hoped the wound would be small. And painless.

He squinted from under his floppy, dull hair. "I need you to go to a baseball game."

"I don't have to play, do I?" I smiled, relieved to have dodged a bullet, though I figured it was a fifty-fifty chance I'd be sliding into a base by the end of the day.

"My son's game starts at seven. You can ride with me." When I stood there dumbly, he ran a hand through his thin hair, squinting at me. "I need you to videotape the game for me. I can't stay."

......................

"I know, Gina, I know. I'll be there, I promise. I'm just going to be a little late. But how do I say no when he's firing people?" I trapped the phone against my shoulder, setting my bag and the company's video equipment on Kwan's desk in the lobby as I waited for Frank's car service. I'd run home to change and grab my camera, but now I plucked at my peacoat, hoping it was thick enough to block the March winds coming off the Hudson River. The Little League field was a few blocks from Ground Zero.

"Paris, we haven't seen you in almost two weeks. Frank Coyle doesn't own you. If you don't start saying no, you're setting yourself up to be treated this way forever."

"I don't want to be a pushover, but I don't have another job lined up. I can't just say no out of principle."

"Alright. I understand. But you have to promise me you're going to start sticking up for yourself. Besides, Lucia could really use some cheering up."

"What's wrong with Lucia?"

"She's been sick a lot lately, she even missed a gig yesterday."

"Give her a hug for me. And buy her some food. Remind her that cigarettes don't provide nutrition." She'd be thrilled to learn I'd finally given in and smoked.

Kwan, behind the desk, made eye contact with me and pointed at Frank, bouncing off the elevator. It was kind of nice to see him in such a good mood, on the way to his son's game.

"Gina, I'm sorry," I said. "I have to go."

"Okay—"

I hung up on her as Frank approached, wearing his favorite lime green dress shirt with expensive APO jeans. The shirt was unbuttoned too low, and again he was wearing the scruffy Adidas. He thought it made him counter-culture, matching trashy with high-end, when it just made him look like a *Saturday Night Live* character.

"Come on! Let's go!" He jiggled, waggling his eyebrows at me. It was disconcerting. And gross.

He went out to the car, leaving Kwan to help me carry my things. The heavyset guard reached the car first, breathing hard, and opened the door. I saw him glance in the back, pucker his lips, and then move to the front passenger door, loading the camera and video equipment onto the seat next to the driver. I looked at him curiously, but Kwan simply shrugged, a sad smile on his worn face. He waited for me to slide in so he could close the door.

Ducking my head into the back of the car, I saw what was happening. There was no room for the camera stuff.

In the back sat a small boy with brown mousy hair like Frank's, dressed in a white baseball uniform. He should have been happy or nervous on his way to a game, but instead, his bottom lip stuck out, his arms were crossed, and he stared sullenly at his father, who was bookended by two girls, both wearing tube tops for dresses. Bleached platinum twins with doll-like features painted on, no older than eighteen. If that. They brought to mind JonBenét Ramsey, which made me gulp down a sour ball in my throat. Frank had been excited to get in the car, not to get to his son's game.

"Paris, sit by Liam, he needs a pep talk. Almost time for the big game, right, slugger?" Frank fist-pumped the air. "I brought along a couple of friends to cheer him on, but he's being a little shy."

Liam rolled his eyes.

I slid in, trying not to touch anybody, but ended up crab-crawling over Girl Number One to reach the seat next to Liam. *Wow, her legs are so smooth and firm*, I thought. My brain was too stunned to come up with anything better.

"Hi, Liam, nice to meet you. I'm Paris, I work with your dad." I offered my hand and he did shake, finally, once, softly. Then he looked out the window.

"Dad," Liam asked in a neutral tone as we pulled away from the curb, "isn't Mom meeting us at the game?" He looked pointedly at each girl.

*Brave kid.*

"Yes," Frank said, blowing into Girl Number Two's ear while handing Girl Number One what was clearly not her first martini of the day. That was the end of the conversation.

*I'd love one of those martinis.*

"So, Liam, how long have you been playing? I loved to play baseball when I was your age." It was a lie. I'd spent the majority of my time in the library or in the computer lab, though I did love to swim in the Pacific and float on a surfboard in my bikini. Anything that brought me into close proximity to the surfers.

The boy warmed up to me as we drove, eventually nestling into my side, a baby bird seeking warmth, as he went on speed-talking jags about famous players, the benefits of stealing bases, and his home run stats from last year.

". . . is just a preseason game, but the coach is tryin' to decide 'tween me and Johnny for this season's pitcher position. I'm way better than Johnny . . ."

I smiled and nodded, no idea what he was talking about most of the time. I hated kids, or at least I'd thought I hated kids. The nine-year-old, with his adorable freckles, purposefully kept his gaze directed at me, his face animated with the love of his sport. Neither of us wanted to look directly at the freak show happening across from us.

"Driver!" Frank leaned forward, breaking a three-way clinch.

I cringed, pushing the button for the intercom. The driver couldn't hear him through the glass.

"Did you need something, sir?" The driver's voice crackled out of the speaker, emotionless.

"We're going to be making a stop on the corner here, at Smitty's."

Liam vibrated with angst. "Dad! We're going to be late!"

Frank waved in front of his face. "Come on, champ, we have plenty of time. I'm just dropping these two off."

Liam relaxed against me, both of us unable to hide the relief we felt at the departure of the twins. "Oh, okay."

Frank squinted over his martini at his only child. "Yep." He tossed back the rest of his drink, his hair flopping to the side. "Alright, out, out, out." The interior filled with shrieks and giggles as he grabbed asses and boobs while they tried to squish through the narrow opening. Without a glance back, he followed them out the door and into the bar.

I turned to face Liam, sure he would be in tears.

"I hate him," he said quietly, dry-eyed. I believed him. His features were laced with rage. "Coach wanted us there early to warm up. The game starts in a half hour."

Better that the boy was furious rather than hurt, just so he could get through the next few hours. The driver and I exchanged a glance through the glass. Behind the boy's back, the grandfatherly man roughly pushed back his driver's cap and mouthed the words, *What a motherfucker.* I nodded. Liam might not have been crying but I was about to.

Ten minutes passed. I went in after Frank.

He was sitting at a table next to a stage with three guys in suits. "Paris! Let's have a drink." The girl working the pole had admirable skill. The blonde twins were nowhere in sight. The muscled bartender probably had asked for their IDs.

"Liam's going to be late for his game."

He put his elbows on the stage. "Go ahead, take him over. I'll call another car, meet you guys there. Don't forget to video-tape. I want to see how he does."

I pursed my lips. *Father of the year.* "Are you sure, Frank? He really wants you there." I cringed. This wasn't any of my business.

"His mom will be . . ." His voice drifted off when the dancer, covered only in a string of beads, moved in front of us. She turned and bent over, offering a spaced-out smile over her shoulder. Within a second, she was in an improbable pose, one which would have ripped ligaments and muscles if I'd tried it. She opened every orifice up for inspection.

I left, not bothering to wait for a reply. As soon as Liam's game was over, I was picking up the wanted ads. If nothing else, apparently anus bleachers were in high demand. *It can't be worse than this.*

# Chapter 12

"You guys are leaving?" I put my tote bag down on a stool at The Rooftop's bar along with my camera and the video equipment, while Gina tugged on her coat. She shot me a baleful glance, reminding me once again of a French bulldog. Now was not the time to be amused, however. Lucia swayed beside her, more pale than usual, ignoring me.

I touched her sleeve. "Are you okay, Lucia?"

"I just need sleep." The model shrugged, her blue eyes foggy, her voice raspy. She didn't have a death stick in her mouth, but maybe her body was trying to tell her something.

Gina stepped under Lucia's armpit, sliding the much taller woman's arm around her shoulder. "I've got this, Paris. Don't worry about us." Lucia leaned on her gratefully.

"Don't play the martyr, Gina. I got here as soon as I could. And I'm here now. Let me help."

"It sounds like Frank needs you more."

"It wasn't Frank, it was his son, Liam. I couldn't just leave him—"

"Yep, okay. You were doing something important. Got it. We'll talk later."

"You don't understand . . ."

But they were out the door, two drinks half-finished on the bar. I slugged back one, avoiding lipstick imprints, hoping the alcohol killed whatever disease Lucia may have left behind. The next drink turned out to be club soda. Who the hell was drinking club soda?

I put my head in my hands. I was cold and tired and frazzled, having come directly from the game to meet them. I could really have used a friend. True, I had been late or unable to show up a number of times in the past three or four weeks, but Gina and Lucia both had jobs and had to put up with crap they couldn't control, too. They should understand. Storming out seemed to be blowing things way out of proportion.

A martini magically appeared on the bar in front of me. The bartender, the one with a handlebar mustache, caught my eye and tossed his chin down the bar. There was Benji, sandy hair tousled as usual, in a pair of corduroys that clung to his quads. The photographer lifted his glass and offered a salute, then got up.

The stress ball in my stomach grew. I'd seen him a few days ago as he conducted a class. We hadn't been able to talk personally, but I could swear he focused his smile on me more than anyone else. *Sigh.* I so badly wanted to hang out with him, but his girlfriend had to be on her way or already in the bar somewhere. *It's alright, this is purely innocent. He's talking to me because I'm his student.*

"Hey, you okay?" He reached out a hand toward me, and I wildly imagined him pulling me to him when instead he wiped at something on my coat. "You got a little something there."

I glanced down. "Dang it." I scratched at the yellow splotch. "It's mustard. I had a hot dog at the game tonight."

"You were at a game?" His brows rose.

"What, I don't look like I appreciate sports?"

He shook his head, and I laughed.

"Yeah, well, you might be right, but I was at a Little League game. I videotaped my boss's son." I pointed to the camera equipment next to me and felt sadness roll back over me. "Tonight was his first night pitching in a game."

"Why so glum? Did he crash and burn?"

"No, he actually did great. But neither of his parents were there. His dad ditched him to hang out with strippers." I'd finished off my martini in five or six gulps. It was a slow night and the bartender had another one ready immediately. *I should stop now*, I thought, and tossed back my third drink in fifteen minutes. I normally stuck to a two-drink maximum, but the hounds were loose.

"And his mother never showed at all, though she was supposed to be there to take him home." I slurped at an errant drop in the bottom of the glass.

Every time Liam had stepped up to bat or ran out to the pitcher's mound to take his place, he would scan the crowd. I'd wave to him, as did the driver, but the boy's shoulders would still drop. The driver could have waited in the car but the old guy felt obliged to support Liam, knowing how his own grandkids felt about their games. But he was cursing a blue streak at Frank under his breath the entire game. If cursing actually cursed people, Frank and Sonya had a hellfire barbecue to look forward to, and they would not enjoy it.

So, two strangers rooted on a nine-year-old, a sad little boy who threw his heart out. We stopped for ice cream on the way back, and I rode with him to his house to make sure he wasn't going to be there alone.

His mother was inside, entertaining her friends.

I tipped the driver heavily when he dropped me off at The Rooftop, but I had every intention of getting reimbursed. My drinks bill was going to be added to the tab.

Benji listened quietly to my story, nodding and exclaiming in the right places. "That poor kid. No wonder rich kids grow up to be assholes." He leaned into me and clinked my glass. My fourth martini. "I can see why you're upset. It's hard to stand back and watch someone do that to their own kid."

I nodded slowly, tears in my eyes. The liquor was not helping to keep my emotions in check.

He took a drink and eyed me seriously, sitting close enough that our arms brushed against each other with each rise and fall of my chest.

"So what are you going to do?" he asked.

"Sit here and feel sorry for him. And myself."

He took another slug of beer, put down his glass, wiped his mouth, and jumped up from his stool. "I know what'll cheer you up."

"What?"

"Let's go develop your film from the game. I just restocked my darkroom."

"I don't know . . ."

"Come on, this will be a good student-to-teacher bonding moment. Let me guide you, my *padawan*."

"So, I'm the Karate Kid to your Mr. Miyagi?"

"Seriously, you didn't catch the Star Wars reference?"

"Uh, no. Nor am I ashamed of that."

"Funny. I can easily picture you dressed as Ahsoka Tano. She's a badass."

*He pictures me? Who the hell is Ahsoka Tano? Should I be offended he's not picturing me in Leia's metal bikini? I smiled. No way should I spend time in a darkroom with this guy.*

"Are we going to walk to your studio?" I asked, ignoring my inner voice while trying to keep my outer voice from slurring. I was tired and a little tipsy. I eyed the number of empty glasses in front of me. *It's funny, I don't feel drunk. And yet, here I go.* I agreed only because his studio was so close to my apartment.

He slung my video equipment over his shoulder. "Is that okay?"

On so many levels, it was okay.

"What about your girlfriend?" But he didn't answer, as he was five feet ahead of me, cutting a trail through the rowdy Rooftop crowd. To be fair, I'd whispered it. He'd said this was a teaching thing. Tired of being lonely and depressed, I shut my brain off.

As we walked through an electric New York City night, we held a pleasant quietness between us. I shot photos of the crowds and colored lights and street vendors shimmering in the chilly, early spring air. I was drawn again to doors, some open, some shut, some locked, some worn, some refurbished, some broken . . . The imagery and symbolism appealed to me, though I didn't dare apply any of it to myself in this scenario. I just wanted to enjoy the moment.

We shed our coats once inside the red door of his gallery. "Hold on, I'm going to run up to my apartment and grab a bottle of wine. You can get started if you want. You know where everything is." He grinned, running a hand through his dark blond thatch of hair. "I'll bring some food, too. I don't want you drunk, not when we're using processing chemicals. I wouldn't put that beautiful face in jeopardy."

With that, he was gone, bounding up the stairs like he was on a parkour course. I hadn't realized he lived above his gallery. Or that corduroy pants could stretch that way.

Despite what he thought, I wasn't exactly drunk, though not sober, either. I felt awake and alert, energy tingling through me. But was I making the decisions of a drunk? He'd just called me beautiful and went to get more wine so we could spend time in a small, dark space together. I felt the tingle settle in my heart. And between my legs.

I wanted to be in that darkroom. I could keep my cool.

Besides, I was ready to show my "teacher" I really had been paying attention to what he'd been saying in class. Mixing the three different chemical baths kept my mind occupied, working out ratios and measurements while the hottest photographer in New York stomped around upstairs and then back down. By the time he'd set a laden tray on a counter in the corner, I was ready to turn out the lights.

Waiting for our eyes to adjust to the dim yellow glow of the special light, Benji gathered supplies and pried the lids off the film canisters, his fingers strong and graceful.

"It was my dad who taught me to do this," he said, his freckled face serious as he slowly pulled the coil of film free.

"What?" I was startled by his comment, so absorbed was I in watching him move.

"My dad. He loved photography. I'm lucky. Not everybody has a parent who'll share their passion and their time with them." He bent over his workbench, bringing the scissor blades together on the film with a brisk clang. Angrily, he said, "I really feel for that kid, Liam."

My heart ached all over again. "I know. How can a father do that?" I bit my tongue, hard, to keep from tearing up. "My dad would die for me. He did risk his life to bring me to America. Sometimes I can forget that, since I don't remember anything from my childhood except things like my dad taking me and my friends to the boardwalk and buying us sugar cones and watching *Buffy the Vampire Slayer* with us, or him sitting through ballet recitals and math competitions." I brought a stack of photo paper to Benji. "Is your father gone?"

"Yep." He thwacked a canister to jar the lid loose. "Heart attack. Right after I graduated high school. But my mom kept it together. She made sure I got through college and she wouldn't let me give up on my dream of being a professional photographer. She's my biggest supporter." He looked at me. "You'd like her. She'd like you, that's for sure."

Confused by why he might possibly say those things, I said, "My dad is my biggest supporter in all ways except this." I spun in a slow circle, gesturing to the pictures hanging around the room. "He wants to make sure I can take care of myself and be totally independent, which he thinks means having a steady job in a secure industry. Art is not secure."

"What does your mom think?"

"She died when I was a toddler. I don't remember her. But I know she was a strong woman in a time when that was dangerous in Iran. My father fulfilled her last wish by getting me out, so I could be free to be whoever I wanted." I grimaced. "Except for a photographer."

Benji handed me a glass of wine, his face soft and sweet. "Here's to the good mothers and fathers." He raised the crystal goblet and stepped next to me.

I raised my glass and we clinked. "Yes. And here's to Liam."

We drank silently.

After an hour of drinking and processing, Benji finally rubbed his eyes and said, "Whelp, let's call it a night."

"Oh." I put down a sheet of contact paper. I'd been having so much fun, caught up in our comfortable spurts of conversation and then silence as we worked side by side, that I'd forgotten how late it really was. I took a step back, fatigue suddenly washing over me, and managed to stumble over air. Benji caught me before I face-planted into a tray of chemicals.

"Hey! Remember what I said about protecting that beautiful face." He had grasped my shoulders to steady me, his breath on my cheek.

He cocked his head to the side, uncertainty swimming through his hazel eyes, only inches from mine. "So, what do you want to do now?"

. . . . . . . . . . . . . . . . . . . .

I came partially awake, cold air creating goose bumps on my

skin. Without opening my eyes, I tugged the sheets up over my chest.

Why was I naked?

My eyelids flicked open. The ceiling above the bed was a clean white and devoid of cobwebs. Where was I?

Flashbacks of a wild night tumbled out of the darkness, waking up my body just as much as my mind.

Smooth, strong hands. Fingers. A tongue. *Oh my God, that tongue.*

Benji, a blissful smile on his sleeping face, was beside me, bundled into the bedding. His bedding.

*Oh my God, again, that tongue.* Our tan and cream skin sliding, pushing, pulling against each other. I almost groaned aloud when I remembered his hand gliding down, his fingers lightly brushing against the outside of my panties.

That was mere minutes after he'd told me I could sleep over, but "not to worry," he'd "leave me alone." In response, I'd taken off my pants and shirt, standing before him proudly in my underwear, with my hands on my hips. That image of myself, strong and in control, was amusing, especially considering I was currently scouring the same room, trying to decide my best exit strategy so as not to wake Benji.

But, oh . . . there was another snippet of a memory, him on his knees, the tip of his tongue moving over my inner thigh, pushing aside my panties with his nose . . . I shivered. "You smell like honey," he'd murmured, and teased me until finally he'd slid his tongue in, deep, making me cry out.

"We should stop," he'd said then, standing up to tuck my head against his shoulder, hugging me. "You should sleep. I don't know if you're sober enough to make this decision."

I'd wrapped my arms around his midriff and squeezed. "I promise, I know what I'm doing." And then I'd tugged down his pants and pushed him up against the wall.

With dawn now creeping into the room, I held my breath, wide-eyed, admiring him. I wanted him again. The things he'd done. We'd done. I started to reach out to him, my body reacting to the heat between my legs.

*Oh hell no*, my sober brain yelled out. *I think you've forgotten one very important thing.*

His girlfriend. I bit my lip. The bartender girlfriend who'd never shown up. I pinched my eyes shut with a sudden, excruciating wave of guilt.

*How did I let it get this far? How could I have forgotten about her? At what point last night did my moral compass twist so far south?*

I moved with the stealth of an embarrassed ninja, inching off the bed and gathering up the clothes I could find easily and tiptoeing—quick, quick—into the hall, where I dressed at the speed of light. My bra and T-shirt were missing but I'd rather swing free under my coat than risk confronting Benji. I had yet to decide if I was more disgusted with him or myself.

. . . . . . . . . . . . . . . . . . . . .

The walk of shame. It'd been a while.

Luckily, I'd gone to the bar last night dressed in my warm clothes from the baseball game. I didn't look out of place on a Saturday morning, bundled up on the street outside Benji's gallery. I had my coat buttoned to the top of my neck to hide my nude torso, so it wasn't my clothes drawing attention—but I felt like my tangled hair and the mascara under my eyes made every dude under forty do a double take. The women were too busy avoiding eye contact, lest their own sexed-up selves be revealed.

What the hell had I been thinking? When did I start letting my vagina make the decisions? I was too old to play this game with my heart. I didn't need half a boyfriend. I didn't want to spend dates hidden away at tables tucked into a corner by the bathroom. Nor did I want to carry the guilt that comes with snagging a sister's man. Guilt . . . *too late.*

I hailed a cab. I wasn't in the mood to deal with the idiosyncrasies of subway riders and I needed to get to SoHo. I'd make my friends talk to me.

Gina answered the door, blinking hard, wrapped in a kimono bathrobe. "What are you doing, Paris?"

"I need reassurance that I'm a good person. So . . . I'm sorry?" I held out my arms, offering a hug.

She grumbled good-naturedly and gave me a bear hug. Or a bulldog hug. "Alright, tell me what's going on." Then she tugged me inside, stumbling into the kitchen to make coffee with her eyes half closed. "Let's be quiet, not wake Lucia," she whispered with a morning rasp.

There was a loud retching noise from the bathroom.

"Or," she said at a normal volume, "be as loud as you want." At the alarm on my face, Gina said uncertainly, "She'll be okay," but looked toward the bathroom with a frown.

Another long retch, followed by a groaned Italian curse.

"Does she have the flu?"

We heard the toilet flush and Lucia running water. A minute later, she stumbled into the kitchen, haggard, her short blonde hair askew. Gina jumped up and pulled out a chair for her.

The model dropped into the seat, loose, like a rag doll. Then, Lucia cleared her throat and moaned dramatically, a palm held flat to her chest. "*Sono Incinta. Sono Incinta!*"

Gina gasped and turned white. "No, Lucia. *Non sei così stupida!*"

"What? What is it? Did you just call her stupid?" I said. The drama seemed straight out of an Italian soap opera. Then it dawned on me.

The nausea. The club soda. No cigarettes.

"You're pregnant?"

The thin, gorgeous model nodded miserably, while Gina stared off into a corner. Time in the kitchen froze.

Finally, to break the silence, I repeated, "You're pregnant?"

Gina was the first to snap out of it. She leaned into Lucia, flipping a hand toward the model's still flat stomach. "Seriously, how did this happen? This is the twentieth century—"

"The twenty-*first* century," I whispered, trying to stop myself.

Lucia slowly bent forward over the table and rested her head on her arms. From the crook of her elbow came her lilting Italian accent, heavy with exhaustion. "The pill was making me fat. But I'd only been off for a couple of weeks . . ."

"What! No condom?" Gina slapped her palm on the table. "I don't understand." Confusion rolled off her short frame. "I'm trying not to judge, but, I mean . . . when? And how come you didn't tell me?"

"Don't be mean, Gina." I laid a hand on her arm.

She shook me off, glaring. "I'm not being mean, I'm just trying to figure out what in the fuck is happening here." She gripped the edge of the table. "What you don't get, Paris, is that our families are Catholic. Lucia's family practically *bleeds* Bible verses. We have to break out the wall cross and the statue of Mary every time they come over and drop to our knees and swear we are looking for husbands. An unwed pregnant Italian girl? Please. This might be the twenty-*first* century, but the people in our neighborhood live in the fifties. Their heads will explode."

Lucia started quietly crying, her shoulders shaking. My heart cracked. She'd always been the stoic, unemotional one. A jagged voice came from under her arms. "It was at the sports show. At the Javits."

Gina and I both leapt to the same conclusion, but Gina pushed back from the table sharply and shrieked, "*You were raped?!* Oh my God, I'm going to fucking kill—"

"No! *Torto!* You are wrong!" Lucia lifted her head, swiped at her eyes, squared her shoulders. "It was my choice." She was composed now, her voice stern. "I told the show manager if he switched me to the lead stage and featured my name, I would sleep with him. He wasn't *cretino*. I had to talk him into it. He was grateful!" She waved off our looks of surprise. "*Dai!* Stop with those faces. It means nothing to me."

Gina hunched over, bewildered. "You've done this before? I don't believe you. I know you. I know how proud you are."

I had to listen close to hear Lucia's response. "You know I have a hard time connecting with people, Gina. I decided, better this way, where it means nothing and yet could finally break my career out of the trenches. No one gets hurt."

Gina shouted, "No one got hurt? You're pregnant!" She paused, breathing heavily, standing in the middle of the kitchen now.

Lucia lashed out bitterly. "It *is* my career that is hurt! My mamma will survive the shame, but my modeling days will be over. I am so close! What do I save, a baby or my chance at being a Victoria's Secret Angel?" She was crying again, snot marring her perfect face.

Gina's voice dropped. Calmly, she said, "You did this to yourself. I mean, for fuck's sake, you didn't even use a condom. Smart. Real smart."

"This is what you have to say to me?"

I scooted my chair back so quickly there was a screech. I knew I wasn't yet someone who should have any say in this discussion. "Okay, I'm gonna go. You guys have a lot to talk about." I wrapped my arms first around Gina, who was unresponsive, and then Lucia, seated at the table. She actually hugged me back. I kissed the top of her head, aching for both of my friends.

"But I'm here if you need me, Lucia. If you need to talk or . . . whatever."

I don't know if either of them heard me. I snuck out the front door and latched it quietly behind me. A wave of sadness, and then loneliness, swept through my body, almost bowling me over.

Adjusting my coat, making sure no one could see bare flesh through the buttons, I thought, *May we live in interesting times . . . Whoever said that was one cold bastard.*

# Chapter 13

It was the last week of March. I'd been there for two months, but the past weekend had dragged by for so long, it felt like I'd been in New York for a lifetime. Worrying about Lucia and avoiding Benji's texts, I sat in my apartment and berated myself.

Finally, it was time for the Monday morning pep talk with the PRCM crew.

I dragged myself into conference room three, where the light tumbled in from the window overlooking the city and landed on Frank. He was lit from behind in what would normally be described as a halo, but for some reason the light seemed to darken around his head. Even in the sun, he had horns.

"Every one of you is out on your ass by the end of this week if you don't get your shit together. This slide continues, and I swear to God I'm going to make sure even the post office won't hire you."

Frank's squint didn't hide the red sparks shooting out of his pupils as he yelled and hammered the table.

"You," he shouted at our newest analyst, a twenty-three-year-old straight out of school. "Why the fuck are you crying? There's no crying in here!"

Fresh tears spurted from her eyes. "My-my dog die-died this morning," the girl said, her breath hitching.

Our boss opened his pursed lips to say something but I cut

him off. "So, Frank, the staff's been talking, and we're trying to decide what kind of cake to bring in for your birthday. I'm thinking we get a lemon poppy seed and a chocolate, really live it up. Are you good with that?"

He leaned back, his hands behind his head. "Huh, well, that's nice of you guys," he said, his features blank.

The young analyst shot me a grateful look, trying to gather herself, but I ignored her. I had to keep Frank focused on himself or he was going to freak out again.

"You know what?" Frank muttered. "I hear that Cirque du Soleil has started doing private parties. We should totally do that." He grinned, gaining steam. "Yeah. Women on a swing. Climbing ropes."

Everyone in the room was suddenly taking notes or buffing their fingernails, making no eye contact with Frank. "Let me see what Todd says but . . . that . . . would be fun." Soothe and accommodate, that was my job. Todd got paid the big bucks, he could be the one to say no.

We'd just laid off a host of employees and our portfolio continued to tank, but Frank wanted to make a show of throwing around money. *Business Weekly* and *Forbes* would have a field day if they caught wind of his bacchanalia birthday plans.

After the meeting, I took the elevator down to Todd's office.

"I know, Paris, I already heard." The gray-haired COO rose from his desk, surrounded by intimidating, wall-to-wall shelves overstuffed with books that looked like they'd actually been read. As usual, he wore an impeccable pinstripe suit. He pointed to one of his armchairs. "Have a seat. And don't worry, I'll talk to him."

Todd had the gravitas and sophistication befitting the leader of a large hedge fund. He was the face of our operation, and, really, the heart and spine. Andrew was vital to the company in some way, I assumed, though I barely knew what the CEO's face looked like. And Frank might have been the reason the company stayed in the gold, but no one wanted to see *his* face.

Todd settled back into his desk chair, a high-backed, tufted leather executive throne with lumbar support out the yin-yang. It was a chair I planned to purloin if he walked out on this gig before I did.

"It's probably a good idea for you to create a short list of alternative birthday celebrations that I can present to Frank. Something . . . low-key." He rested his hands on the desk, his fingernails manicured and buffed. "It appears you've settled in. Any other fires I should know about upstairs?"

"Nothing I can't handle." I wriggled around. "You know, I was wondering, though, if maybe I should sit down with Frank and work out some kind of schedule. See if he's ready to bring me in on some of his portfolio deals. I really thought I'd be doing more with the funds by now."

The older man rubbed his fingertips over his chin, quiet for a minute. "Well. I'm not sure that's technically part of your job description. I suppose it can't hurt to ask Frank. Just don't get your hopes up."

On the short ride back up the elevator, I tried not to let depression drag me down. But it was too late.

I averted my gaze from the mirrors, tugging on one of my hoops until it hurt. I was comfortable with my looks, usually believing myself to be attractive enough. I'd always had boyfriends in school. Sometimes, when I happened to catch a glimpse of myself in a joyful moment, I'd even see what my dad saw when he'd tell me I was beautiful. He'd twirl me around and tell me I looked like Princess Jasmine from *Aladdin*, just like my mother.

I knew Frank wouldn't have hired me if he thought I was ugly. Safe to say, PRCM was an ad for attractive, smart people. But on bad days, the mirror told me the truth, highlighted what I was afraid was the real me. My features large and absurd. Or plain. Boring. Or downright ugly, my insides exposed on the outside.

On these dark days, I thought my special power must be that I could project whatever it was someone else needed me to be, what they needed to see, my true self aptly hidden. Accommodating their wants and desires. My calm threw a spell over people I interacted with, so they saw me as capable and witty and attractive. But on days like this, the mirrors reflected the truth of it, the peasant rather than the kick-ass princess. The selfish, cowardly boyfriend stealer.

And every time my phone lit up with a call or text from Benji, my insides felt that much uglier. I was going to have to get it over with soon, tell him I'd made a mistake, that I couldn't hurt someone else or be a second choice, waiting in the wings. My insides were going to turn to coal if I didn't make this right.

*Wow. Time to pick up that Wellbutrin prescription. Why don't we have a therapist on staff? God knows, these people could use it.*

Heavy with self-loathing, my head hung low, I stepped off the elevator on my floor and almost ran into a man wearing size twelve loafers. I recognized the designer. I lifted my head slowly. Darien.

"I've been looking for you!"

"What are you doing here? At my office?" Why couldn't *he* look like the ugly devil that resided in his soul? But no, unbearably handsome. The devil in a blue suit.

He handed me a paper cup. "A chai. Persian blend. A peace offering."

I took it tentatively, unsure of the content or the intent. The smell of ginger and thick cream and chai spices made my mouth water, but no way was I going to let him see me inhale.

"I know I came on strong the other night. You're ignoring my calls . . ." He paused, but I didn't say anything so he kept going. "That's okay, I understand. I shouldn't have ambushed you like that."

At my raised eyebrow and glance at the unexpected drink, he half-laughed. "Yeah, okay, maybe I'm doing it again." He rushed on. "But I really, really want you to know I'm here if you want a friend. I'm not asking for anything more, Paris."

"So. That kiss at my apartment. I should have known you were passing that out to all your *friends*—"

He winced. "A little grace. That's what I'm asking for here. We're new to the city. If you don't want to be intimate, that's understandable. But we can help each other." He tipped his head down the hallway, down to the open pit where my desk was. "It can't hurt to share networks."

"Are you serious—"

He adopted a wounded mien, a kicked dog. "No, no, not just that. I really do care for you. You know that." He reached out a hand and brushed my hip.

"No, I don't know that. I don't think your girl knows that, either." I tried to hand him back the chai, but he shoved his hands in his pockets. I shrugged, took a sip. It was too sweet. "You—"

"Paris! Who's this?"

*Oh sweet mother of God.* It was Frank. In a dress shirt, slacks, and beat-up Birkenstocks. Nicki, clipboard in hand like a Hollywood extra, was close on his heels, glee emanating off her like old lady perfume. I couldn't think of two entities I would want to be part of this interaction *less* than Frank or Nicki. Maybe Death incarnate. No, scratch that. *I'd fucking love it if Death showed up right now and whisked me away.*

"Um, hi. Darien, this is Frank Coyle. The CEO."

Darien stuck out his hand, smooth, a car salesman. "Hello there, I'm Darien Basir." Beat. "Paris's boyfriend."

I grimaced. *The audacity.*

Nicki shifted from hip to hip in the background. I could feel her giddiness but ignored her.

Frank, at least a foot shorter than my ex-boyfriend, squinted at Darien's hand for a second, then pumped it loosely, once. His hand was tiny and pasty in Darien's big man hand. He flinched when Darien squeezed.

Staring at Darien, I threw daggers from my eyes. He seemed to catch one in the frontal lobe, finally, and let Frank's hand go.

"Heyya," the CEO said, craning his neck upward, spreading his stance, and crossing his arms across his chest. "What brings you to the office? Here for Paris? Or are you an investor?"

I almost laughed out loud at my boss's dropped pitch, going from a tenor to a baritone, but I simultaneously wanted to scream in frustration. *Men.* Quickly, I said, "Oh, he's not an investor. He was here to bring me a tea. He's leaving."

Darien tried to wrap an arm around my shoulder. I awkwardly shrugged away from him and he laughed. "Ha ha, you. So shy, this one."

Frank frowned at me. "You need to get back to your desk."

"Yes, of course. Like I said, Darien is leaving." What a fucking coward I was. Always had to keep the peace, though both these men had no problem acting douchey.

Thankfully, the elevator popped open.

"Paris!" Liam jumped into the hall and sprinted up to me, wrapping his short arms around my midriff, smiling up at me as if I were his long-lost best friend.

I felt immediate gratitude to the kid, and then a surprise burst of emotion. The sweet little boy was unconditionally showing me affection, simply because I'd been nice to him once. I squeezed him back, grateful to see he seemed to be doing okay despite his awful parents.

"Hey, slugger! Long time no see. What are you doing here?"

"We have a conference with my teacher."

"I told you I'd meet you at the car, Liam." Frank stepped around the group in the hallway, swaggered into the elevator. "Come on."

I tousled Liam's hair. "Good luck." *The teacher must be hot if Frank is going to a school function.*

Frank yelled from the elevator, "You! Redhead, whatever your name is, let's go. What's the holdup?"

Nicki swept past me, her remodeled nose in the air. "Just so you know," she stage-whispered, "Frank was looking for you earlier. He said you're irresponsible."

Damn it, I'd been gone for less than fifteen minutes. Then again, did I want to go on another field trip with Frank? The last one had been so not enjoyable, but now Frank's son was stuck with those two.

Liam gave me one more squeeze. "Bye, Paris!" He hustled into the elevator behind Frank and Nicki, correctly guessing they'd leave him behind if the doors shut before he got in.

The CEO's hand emerged from the elevator at the last second, grabbed the closing door, and pushed it back. He bent forward and shouted, as if I weren't three feet in front of him, "I'm going to be back in an hour!" He released the door and offered a look as if I should know why that was so important. I simply nodded, trying to give the impression I was on the same page.

Then the doors slid shut. I whirled back to Darien.

"My boyfriend! Why would you even say that? Why are you even here? You left *me*, remember? And I've made it pretty clear I have no interest in you now."

"Sorry, sorry. It just seemed the easiest way to explain us."

"There's no us!"

"Why do you care?" His eyes became slits. "What, are you interested in this guy? He's your boss. Is that how you roll now?"

"Are you insane? You did not act like this when we were together, why in God's name would you act like this now? Are you trying to get me fired? Is that what you want?"

He backpedaled. "No, I swear, I don't know what came over me. I just wanted to see where you worked, meet some of the people you spent your days with. And I wasn't kidding, networking would be great."

"Seriously?"

"I can see this didn't go down the way I meant it to—"

"And what about your real girlfriend? You've sidestepped her every time."

"I'm not sure where that's going. We're really more like friends." He leaned against the wall, visibly shedding the jealous act, morphing into his sensitive-guy persona. Always the actor. "No one gets me like you do, Paris." He grinned. "And it looks like you've overcome your fear of children."

I had the chance for intimacy right in front of me, a strong pair of arms to hold me at night. My apartment was drafty and lonely. I didn't even have a cat. I wanted love. But I did not want to wake up to lies and arguments and disdain. I did not want conflict.

Suddenly, I realized if I *was* willing to face conflict, I'd pick Benji. *The other guy with a girlfriend*, I reminded myself sternly.

I put on my game face.

"Eh, I don't know, Darien. You're a child and I don't like *you*." I winked as if I were teasing, punching him on the chest, pretending it was a playful blow but hoping the sting lasted.

"Damn, Paris." He grabbed his chest. "That kind of hurt. You must be working out."

"Yeah, good one." I smoothed down my shirt, moved back a pace. "I've got to get to work. Thanks for the chai, but call next time." I turned and strode down the hall before he could draw me back in.

"What, no hug?" he called down the corridor. But when I glanced over my shoulder a minute later, he was gone.

Back to work. Thank God.

The irritants were gone.

I loped over to my desk and grabbed up the office phone. "Hey, Kwan, can you try to catch Nicki before she gets in the car with Frank? Tell her she needs to get him some real shoes before he goes into the school. And make sure there's water and snacks for Liam in the car. Thanks."

It was a long day, but quiet. I worked through a number of projects with no interruption.

Later, I heard Frank before I saw him. As I looked up, I saw Nicki settle into her desk chair slowly, as if she'd just run a marathon. Liam was nowhere in sight. I hoped he was spending time with a friend, another nine-year-old with parents who would cook him a well-balanced meal and ask him questions about his favorite color and consider adopting him.

Frank, disheveled and revealing far too much chest hair, stood in the pit, in front of the analyst he'd made cry that morning.

"Hey there," said our middle-aged boss, waving his hands under his sweat-stained armpits. "Why don't I take you out for a drink? Take your mind off your dead dog?"

"Me?" The girl put her hand to her chest, a deer in the headlights.

"Yeah, you look sad."

"It has been hard . . ." She petered off weakly.

"Damn, is it hot in here or is it just me?" He ran a hand across his forehead, creating streaks in the perspiration. "You know, my kid keeps saying he wants a dog, but my family shoots them back in Texas. I don't really see the attraction." He patted her on the shoulder, leaving a damp handprint. "A couple of tequilas will make this better."

By the time I reached them, the office was silent, waiting to see how she responded. Beyond a gasp, she seemed stymied.

I broke the spell. "Uh, Frank, Andrew wants to see you in his office. He said it's important," I said loudly.

The CEO frowned and tromped toward his partner's office. I widened my eyes at Michelle and she nodded; Frank brought out the mental telepathy in us. The savvy assistant picked up her phone and said something quietly. Andrew's door popped open a second later, just as Frank got there. The two disappeared inside.

The hum of monitors and trading and gossip turned back on. The young analyst sat back down. "Michelle, he asked me out for a drink. What should I say?"

"No," we said together.

"But I just started. I want to keep my job."

Michelle leaned in, her ponytail swinging forward with definitive purpose, and said quietly, "Then say no in a way that lets him off the hook, like, 'Oh, I can't, my fiancé's parents are in town, but thank you. It was nice of you to want to cheer me up.' Pretend you don't know what he really meant." Michelle sighed, straightening her ponytail out of habit. "Yeah, I know, sexual harassment is illegal. You shouldn't have to tiptoe around your boss's ego, and it's definitely against company policy to date your superior. Unfortunately, Frank doesn't pay attention to any of that." Her voice became serious. "If he becomes pushy or he tries to touch you, you tell Todd or me. Stick up for yourself, tell him to stop. It might create conflict, but you can't let it slide. A job is never worth more than your integrity. Right, Paris?"

"Right."

*Hypocrite*, I thought.

## Chapter 14

I spent the week avoiding Benji's calls, working on an acceptable birthday "surprise" for Frank, and trying to get a hold of my dad. I was starting to think he was ignoring me like I was ignoring Benji. Thankfully, Darien seemed to have backed off.

Until the ass hat sent me a text.

*I'm glad I ran into you. Tell Frank I said hey. Maybe one of these days when the office is slow, he'd be interested in chatting? I'd love to pick that guy's brain.*

I erased his message. I wanted to erase his narcissistic, delusional face from this planet. Did he think I couldn't see through his desperate attempt to use me to get to Frank? I wished with all my heart he was in front of me right then. The pain I would deliver . . .

Then Frank called me in to go over his agenda for the weekend.

"Frank, I totally forgot to give you the recording of Liam's game." I thrust a labeled flash drive at him. "Sorry about that, didn't mean to keep it so long."

Actually, I had not forgotten. Instead, I'd spent multiple nights going back into the recording and erasing some of the audio, thanks to YouTube tutorials. Though the limo driver and I had bonded over our shared dislike of Frank's fathering methods, I hadn't always remembered to mute the mic. I'd learned a lot about video production in the last few days.

Frank grabbed the flash drive and tossed it to the side of his desk, amidst a stack of magazines and newspapers he'd already read.

"I've been meaning to talk to you about that."

*No, please!* I did not want to rehash the experience. I'd have to swab out my brain again.

He tugged his wallet from his suit jacket. "Here." He withdrew a number of hundred dollar bills. "This is a bonus. Good work with Liam. He liked you." His nasally voice sharpened. "And I liked that you kept your mouth shut."

"Thank you. I liked him, too." I took the money and stood there like an idiot, unsure of what else to say. I didn't want to deconstruct his afternoon with the Funsy Twins and their sister, the cleanest stripper in the world, but I also was not going to turn down a bonus I had definitely earned.

Luckily, his attention span was that of a gnat.

He brought up a host of spreadsheets on his desktop, fiddling with codes, numbers, and formulas. He immediately became absorbed, forgetting I was there.

"Sorry to bother you, Frank . . ." He didn't look up. "But when you're done with that, if you have a second, could you look over that report on the trends I sent you last week? I need to talk to you about which traders were making some of the unlabeled trades." I needed to get the finalized report to Todd and Andrew.

Dismissing me with a flick of his fingers as if I hadn't just spoken, he said, "My wife called, she wants some caviar for our weekend guests, from that place on Seventh Avenue. Petrossian. Get a lot."

*A lot. Sure.* I knew his chef was on vacation, and the maid was at a funeral, so I didn't bother calling the main house staff.

Still, I wished there was someone who could tell me how much "a lot" was. There was no way I wanted to go to 7th Avenue and back for caviar. But as I was dialing, I realized I *could* use the company car to stop at the bank and deposit my fresh wad of cash along the way. Frank had given me over two thousand dollars; I doubted he knew he'd given me that much, but I wasn't going to say anything.

I could even pick up a few things for Lucia, like ginger cookies, or pickles, or whatever crazy food she could keep down that day. She was almost six weeks pregnant and she was terrified and anxious and confused about what she wanted. It didn't help that she and Gina were in an odd place. I'd stopped by twice that week, but Gina was distant with both of us. She said she was wrapping her head around "things."

"She is so angry," Lucia told me one afternoon, when Gina came into the kitchen, grabbed a bag of chips, and went back into her room without saying a word. "Not because I am *con il bambino*, but because she thinks I let a man use me. I have explained I was using *him*, but that doesn't seem to make it better. I'm not a bad person, am I, Paris?"

"No. You're just human. A complex human." I sighed. "She's still your best friend. You just surprised her."

Lucia was lonely, bothered by Gina's rejection while she dealt with the question mark growing inside her. God, I did not envy her on that score. She was a hot mess. A baby would make her runway career impossible for now, possibly forever, and, worse, she was sure it would destroy the relationship with her family. Even so, it would be worse if her family found out she'd had an abortion. I also knew, deep in her gut, she feared she was going to hell regardless of her decision, having been threatened with brimstone and flames every time she'd sinned as a child. *Ugh. It's all so complicated and horrible. If she wants this baby, she's going to have to fight for it.*

Ginger cookies and pickles would be little comfort in the face of such turmoil, but it was the best I had to offer.

Once I was relaxing in the back seat of the town car, I suddenly remembered I'd forgotten to give Frank his updated agenda for Saturday and Sunday, which also had contact information he needed. I could email it to him, but he rarely looked at his emails or texts unless they were from investors—or women named Bunny. I called Michelle, but a nasally voice answered.

"Nicki, hi," I said. "I need you to print off Frank's updated schedule from my desktop. Knowing Frank, he might leave before I get back with his caviar."

"Why did you get to leave?"

Biting my tongue at her snotty retort, I said, "I'm doing what I'm supposed to be doing. I'd like you to do the same. Please give him the schedule." I hung up on her before she could argue with me, but I texted Michelle and asked her to check in with Nicki, to make sure it had been done.

Responsibilities delegated, I leaned back and appreciated the city streets, trying not to think too deeply on any one thing, taking the moment to just breathe. To be.

This time last year, I was working with securities from a bank desk, spending my free time helping my dad and taking Torah interpretation classes online, while watching Darien continue to drift away. My dad's business had seemed to be going strong, despite some dips, but that might not have been the truth. The two men in my life at the time had lied to me, one to protect me, the other to test out the greener grass on the other side of the fence.

Now, I worked for a madman but made a good salary at a successful hedge fund company, lived in New York, was in love with photography all over again, and I'd met . . . Benji. I hated to accept he was a cheater like Darien, but I would meet other men, right? I'd be fine. Lucia and Gina would be fine. My father would be fine. Frank would be . . . blown up in a terrible toilet tragedy. I smiled, pressed my nose against the car window, and breathed; fog blurred the harsh outlines of reality sliding by.

My phone buzzed. A text from Benji.

*Please don't be mad at me anymore. Come to the class tonight, we'll talk. But even if you won't talk to me, I have something you need to see . . . No, not that, sicko ;)*

My heart palpitated. Logically, I knew I had to stay away. Heartwise, I just couldn't believe the sweet soul I'd bonded with emotionally and physically was playing me. He wasn't smooth, not like Darien.

Then the phone buzzed again.

*Dear Parisa, will you call me tonight? This is your father. I have to tell you about the new zoo I went to today. It only had one animal. A dog. It was a shitzu. Love, Dad.*

My dad had finally figured out the text function. I chuckled when I heard him say "shit zoo" in my head, his accent thickened by laughter. He cracked himself up. But what had taken him so long to get back to me? Why did he need me to call? The bad feeling came back to life in the pit of my stomach.

A third buzz. A text from Frank. I was a popular girl, all of a sudden.

*Where are you?*

I'd been gone for maybe twenty minutes.

*Maybe I should have finished those conversion classes. Maybe God would like me more.*

. . . . . . . . . . . . . . . . . . . . .

"Dad, you said to call you. Call me back when you get this message."

The intercom next to the front door buzzed as I turned off my cell phone. My heart surged, just for a second, wildly thinking my dad had surprised me and flown here, to give me a hug and tell me stupid jokes and make baklava while we discussed what I should do with my life. Then reality sank back in.

"Who is this?"

"It's me. Benji."

"How do you know where I live?"

"You put your address on the form for the photography class. I'm sorry, Paris, I'm not trying to stalk you. You didn't come to class tonight. You've made it clear you don't want anything to do with me, but this is something else. It's important. Can I come up and talk to you for a minute? I won't make a move, I promise."

He sounded so sweet, downtrodden even. I had to stay resolved. *Is he really that sweet if he's willing to sleep around?*

"Fine. Just for a minute." My voice could freeze vodka.

When I heard footsteps approaching my door, I swung it open before he could knock. I lost my cool immediately. "Does your girlfriend know you're here?" I demanded, my voice on the edge of a shriek. I'd already asked that question once this week, to Darien. How had this happened?

Benji, sexy as hell in a tight blue T-shirt and jean jacket, shifted a large package to his right hand, his eyebrows raised in bewilderment.

"What? What girlfriend?"

"Don't screw with me. I know you have a girlfriend. The bartender at The Rooftop." I layered on the spite with a trowel.

"Are you talking about Cassie?"

"I don't know her name. The one who looks like she runs boot camps." I crossed my arms, my feet in a basketball stance. I was staying strong.

He blew out his breath and ran his hand roughly over his

chin. His freckles darkened with the flush that crept up his neck to his hairline. The gold in the center of his hazel eyes flashed. "Cassie. She and I went out on a date exactly twice. That was it. I never slept with her, and she was definitely never my girlfriend. She's nice, but dumb as a box of rocks."

"Why should I believe you? One of the servers told me about you two. Why would she make that up?"

"I don't know. You'd have to ask her. But seriously, twice. She's moved on, believe me." He put his hand over his left pectoral. "Or don't. But I promise, cross my heart, I am not in a relationship with Cassie."

I fidgeted, shifting back and forth, suddenly off-balance. I wanted to believe his words, but was I being a sap?

It was the unvarnished shock, with a touch of hurt, on his face that sold me. "Paris, I'm sorry you ever thought that. I would never cheat on someone. Not ever."

My chest clenched when I realized Benji was a good guy, totally innocent . . . but I wasn't. I was the bad guy here. I was the one who, believing Benji had a girlfriend, went with him to his gallery that night, knowing full well what would happen. I'd justified it to myself by saying the martinis clouded my judgment or that it had happened too fast, but neither of those things was true. I was an asshole.

I was Darien.

A total asshole.

And the beautiful man in front of me knew it.

"Can I come in now?" He held up the package, his emotions masked. Except for a slight downturned mouth, revealing a sadness. "I really do have something to talk to you about."

My shoulders hunched, my tail between my legs, I stepped back and allowed him room to step into my apartment.

He stopped in the middle of the living room and spun, slowly. "This is nice." He walked over to my red wall and studied my photo collection. His face relaxed into a partial grin. He gestured to the wall and said, "This! This is why I'm here."

"What do you mean?"

He tore the brown wrapping off the package and withdrew an eleven-by-fourteen framed photo with a blue ribbon stuck to the glass cover plate.

It was one of the photo samples I'd left with him during the first class. The red-and-orange door in front of the Newport bookstore.

"What's this?" I'd been keeping my distance, either out of shame or fear of a tongue-lashing, but my intrigue freed my self-consciousness. "How come you have my photo?"

"*New York* magazine is publishing it in the next issue, as the grand prize winner in the Up and Coming Artist Contest. No joke." He pulled off the blue ribbon and handed it to me. On it was printed *#1 Mom*.

"Ignore that," he said when he saw me read the label. "I bought the ribbon down the street. I wanted to hand you something."

I laughed, confounded. "I don't know what to say."

"You should be proud of yourself, Paris. This is an accomplishment. A big honor."

"I can't believe you did this for me."

"I wouldn't have if you didn't deserve it." He turned his face away from me. "And, yes, I entered the image into the contest long before we slept together."

"Oh."

"Do you mind telling me what's going on? I'd thought we'd become friends. I figured you woke up and realized my nose hair was out of control or my housekeeping skills sucked, or that I was just too boring. Was it really because you thought I had a girlfriend?"

"Yes." I coughed out the word, ashamed.

He sighed. "Then we've lost time over nothing." He paused. "On the bright side, that gives us a lot to talk about at dinner. We're celebrating at Calle Ocho. Best Cuban food in New York."

"I—"

"Shhh. Grab your jacket. We can finish this conversation on the walk over." He put his fingers on my lips, briefly, but then stepped away with a twinkle in his eye. He wasn't going to immediately fall into my arms, but that was fair.

*It's not much of a conversation if I don't actually say anything*, I thought, but my heart felt light as I lifted my coat off the hallway hook. It was lighter than it had been in a long time. I had a chance to be a better human.

My phone rang as I was locking the door. My dad. "Do you mind if I take this? I can talk as we walk, but I need to make sure my dad is okay."

"Of course." He pressed the elevator button.

"Dad? Hi, I've been trying to reach you. What's going on?"

"I am sorry, little one. I was practicing my texting. Everything is fine."

"You keep saying that. But you didn't answer your phone." I tried to keep my tone nonchalant. "Darien said he heard you might be selling the business. You have to talk to me, Dad."

"I . . . I have been busy. It is true, I am going to sell the business. But that is a good thing. I can get another job, one with less responsibility. Do not fixate on me, I have told you everything is fine here. You worry about yourself. Are you alright? Happy?"

"Listen, I'm going to send you some money."

"No, little one, you save that money. It is time to downsize my life, now that you are gone, taking care of yourself. I might even sell the house, rent something small. I will be fine. This will work out. You need not worry yourself. It is time for you to shine."

Going down the elevator with the handsome photographer beside me, who was pretending not to listen, I realized my love life was coming into view on the horizon but the life I knew at home was disappearing. *Maybe selling the house? That's crazy. He loves that house.* My dad had said nothing about his problems getting someone to hire an aging Middle Eastern man. He obviously did not want to talk about it—but how was he going to find full-time employment when he couldn't even get a part-time janitorial job? I didn't want to shame him, but I couldn't just pretend this wasn't serious.

"Dad, please, wait one more month before you make any decisions. I'll send you enough to cover your bills for now. Let's see what happens."

"Ah, well, perhaps one of us will win the lottery. You never know, the Powerball is at two million. That is a 'lotto' money." He proffered a weak chuckle that made me want to cry.

"I love you, Dad." I hung up.

In the lobby, Benji politely gave me another minute, pretending to scan Instagram, standing close enough his leg brushed mine. He didn't ask any questions about my dad, or Darien, as I downloaded the Venmo app on my phone and wired the bonus money and most of my savings to my dad, regardless of his protests. What else was I going to do? I couldn't let him lose his business or sell the only home he'd known since moving to America. He'd spent his life caring for me. I really, really hated knowing I no longer had him to support me, but I couldn't selfishly worry about myself, not when he was trying his hardest to keep his life together and being treated poorly for his efforts. I was young and I had skills and opportunities and choices he didn't have.

Swiveling to face Benji, who'd been quiet throughout the interlude, I said, "How much does it cost to run an ad? And what's a good name for a photography service?"

# Chapter 15

*If you have to have two jobs, make the second one pleasant.*

I was lucky to have a skill I could parlay into extra cash, while a good chunk of Middle America was forced into working two or three crappy jobs in order to feed their families. I had an opportunity for two income streams. One paid my rent and the other was not . . . really paying, not yet, but it was enjoyable, and I could see the potential, if I worked hard.

During the first week of April, I wandered the city. I stumbled across artistic inspiration and possible backdrops while hanging fliers and talking to businesses who dealt with weddings and big events. I occasionally suffered a twinge of guilt or fear, praying no one from PRCM saw my advertising. I was breaking a firm company policy by moonlighting, but I had weighed the benefits and harms and decided the risk was low while the need to help my father was high. But it would suck to lose my well-paying job, especially before I was making any real money taking photos.

I felt a surge of pride the day I did a shoot for a mom in my building. She wanted a headshot of her toddler, for her budding acting career. The mother was pleased with the plethora of smiles I was able to get out of the kid—I'd followed Adam Sandler's lead and smacked my head on an open cupboard and my pain made the kid howl with laughter. The mother referred me to a number of her stage-mom friends, after offering me a box of Band-Aids. I went away with cuts and bruises and a wide smile.

By the second week in April, I started getting calls from models, thanks to Lucia. A handful of her friends needed to update their comp cards and iPad portfolios. I had to up my game. I couldn't just run into a wall to get the right shot. These people knew what they wanted and had high expectations.

"I brought you a prezi," Lucia said, dropping a leather duffle bag onto my couch. She'd come over with no warning. I was in my after-work, not-for-viewing-pleasure pj's, while she was wearing a yoga outfit and yet looked like she'd just stepped from the pages of a glamour magazine. At almost nine weeks, she was an advertisement for beautiful mothers-to-be.

I swiped at the hummus on my pajama top and then pointed to the duffel. "Is there a head in there? I don't have the strength to deal with that."

Instead of answering, she reached down, unzipped the bag, and upended the contents onto the floor: lotions and wipes and insect repellent and nylons and a lint brush and panty liners and dress jewelry and scissors and sunglasses and hair ties and false eyelashes and flesh-colored thongs and pasties . . .

I blinked, slowly. "What the hell?"

With a proud, graceful swish of her arm, she said, "*La mia collezione*—my kit. If you are going to set up shoots, you will need this. You will not have to stop if someone starts their period or forgets a bra, or if you need a different *aspetto*." She prodded a floppy hat with her toe. "A different appearance. A cute hat can changed the tone of a shoot."

"You are so right!" I threw my arms around her but the tall model backpedaled and touched her short, spiked hair.

"Yes, yes, I am *favaloso*."

"It's true, you are fabulous, Lucia. *To behtarin dooste mani*—you're a good friend." I plucked a child's plastic teapot out of the heap and handed it to her. "Do all the professionals have this in their quiver?"

"If they're *intelligente.*" She balanced it on her palm, held it at chin-level, and batted her eyelashes at me from behind the child's toy.

I laughed. "The blue really brings out your eyes." A few random, whimsical props couldn't hurt. "Aren't you going to need this stuff?"

She kept her eyes trained on the floor and muttered, "Not for a while," as she knelt next to the small mountain of items. I helped her put the objects back in the bag, including a hardcover book with the pages torn out and a bag of fake mustaches, waiting for her to go on, to bring up the pregnancy. The baby bump was showing. A few more weeks and she'd be at the end of the first trimester. I thought the baby must have a heartbeat already, but Lucia wouldn't talk about it. I couldn't imagine having an abortion after you've heard a heartbeat. The baby would start moving at three months. I didn't want to think about that. If Lucia went through with the pregnancy, it would affect her body, sure, and it would cause havoc in her religious family, but it seemed like her emotional baggage, as a Catholic herself, would be more bearable. She had to decide soon, however, before the decision was taken away from her. What was she going to do?

I kept my mouth shut. If Lucia wasn't in the mood to confront the hard stuff that morning, who was I to push her?

"Have you thought of a name yet?" she interrupted my reverie.

It took me a second to realize she wasn't asking me for my opinion on baby names. "For now," I said, "I'm keeping it simple: Photography by Paris. I can use interlocking Ps as my emblem."

Lucia nodded. "Sounds cosmopolitan."

After I forced her to hug me for real, she sashayed to my door, opened it, and turned, half in and half out. "I almost forgot." She dug around in her bag and drew out a carton of Benson & Hedges. Tossing them to me, she said, "I don't need these anymore."

We held eyes for a minute before I said, gently, "So, you're keeping the baby then?"

Her gaze became fierce and hot. She stood tall with a hand on her belly, her response firm. "Yes." Then she nodded, stepped out the door, and said, "*Ciao, bella.*"

With that, she was gone.

*New life. New beginnings.*

Invigorated, I threw the cigarettes into a drawer with the other packs she'd given me—I could sell them on Craigslist, if I ever needed some quick cash—and curled up with a pad of paper, a pen, and a glass of pinot. Time to create an actual business plan. I finally felt like I was doing something worthy of my time, helpful to others, and fulfilling.

As long as Frank didn't find out. I'd signed at least three different forms stating I would be loyal to PRCM, agreeing I would not take on a second job. Was it worth it if I got caught? *I don't know. I hope so. I don't know what else to do. I guess I'm not as loyal as I thought I was.*

That thought reminded me of Benji. I'd believed him to be disloyal but had since discovered he'd told me the truth; he had only dated hot bartender a couple of times. Was he ever going to be able to trust *me*, knowing I'd been willing to sleep with him while thinking he was spoken for? I disgusted myself. For the last few weeks, since the night he gave me the award and took me to Cuban, we'd gone to dinner and movies, but nothing more. He'd told me he wanted to go slow and I had no choice but to go along.

I climbed into my cold bed.

As I drifted into sleep, alone, I regretted agreeing to Benji's plan: hand holding and cold showers. I didn't blame him for not wanting to dive into anything with me right away. I'd shown a very unsavory side of myself. Benji had no way of really knowing I was bothered by that, too, that I'd always prided myself on being loyal and ethical. *Yet, given a chance, I had acted just like Darien. Ugh.* I rolled over and hugged my pillow. I deserved to be sleeping in a lonely bed.

When my cell rang a few hours later, at two in the morning, I popped out of a deep sleep and scrambled for the phone, praying he'd decided to renege on the deal. Maybe he was standing outside my apartment with a toothbrush and a lust-filled smile.

But no, it was a number I didn't recognize. Ready to unleash on the bastard who was calling me in the middle of the night in order to find out who I was voting for or if I wanted a spa vacation, I yelled, "Who is this?"

"Good Lord." A shrieking roll of laughter. "Paris, bring it down a notch."

"Frank? What are you doing? Whose phone is this?"

"Easy, easy." He was using his slimy voice, the low drawl he thought made him sound sexy. "I left my phone and wallet at Aquavit. I need you to go get it and bring it out to my house in Oyster Bay." He had no shame; he knew that I knew his wife and son were upstate. He belched. "You can stay out here."

My brain came fully alert, trying to come up with something, anything that would derail the request without pissing him off.

"Oh, gosh, Frank. I totally would, but it's after two. I can't get there before they close."

"The hostess is waiting for you. I've already spoken with her."

"How about—"

"Ask them if they've got any of the Swedish meatballs left." His slurred muttering over the top of me made me want to tear out my hair.

"Or, how about if I go get it and bring it to you first thing tomorrow morning? It will take me over an hour to get it and drive out there."

"Are you arguing with me? I have four thousand dollars in that wallet. You're the only one I trust to bring it out here. Don't fuck with me. I need it tonight. And I want those meatballs. And some of those sugar beignets."

*Are you for real? Can't you just write your hooker a check and buy her some pizza?* "I'd have to take a taxi—"

"Fine." He hung up.

I grabbed up a pillow and screamed into it, long and loud. My neighbor probably thought I was dying or having fantastic sex or both. *Why me?*

I called the PRCM car service but no one answered. I hated taking Ubers or taxis this late at night. I could get kidnapped and no one would realize what had happened for days—Frank would be furious if I didn't show up, but he wouldn't think to report me missing.

I decided to text Benji. He wouldn't see the message until morning but at least the police would know where to begin their search for my body.

*Hey,* I texted. *I have to deliver something to my crazy boss, way out in Oyster Bay. I'm taking an Uber, but I wanted someone to know if I go missing. Ha ha. I'll text when I get back home, so you'll know I'm alive.*

My phone rang again as I hurriedly put on clothes. "Dammit, Frank," I muttered to myself, but it was Benji.

"Oh my God," I said into the phone, embarrassed, "I did not mean to wake you up! Go back to sleep!"

He laughed. "I've been working on a new exhibit; I haven't

been to bed yet. And I'm thinking I'm in the mood for a road trip . . ."

He had a car. But was it right to rope him into this? I peered through the blinds and appraised the landscape. Dark alleys, sirens, drunken shouting.

*I might be embarrassed I bothered him so late at night, but I'm not stupid. A car ride with a hunk, or with an unwashed old man?* "Thank you."

# Chapter 16

My mind, sodden, worked overtime to process the numbers on the computer screen in front of me.

Benji had dropped me off at my apartment at five that morning, after spending the night driving around on behalf of the esteemed Franklin Coyle, who had not bothered to say thank you. He couldn't, because he was passed out, snoring in a deck chair by the pool. Someone had thrown a towel over him, presumably the hooker with a heart of gold. *Hope she helped herself to something nice before she left.*

I put his wallet and phone on the kitchen island next to his keys, offered Benji a meatball from Aquavit's foil-covered plate, and then balanced the dish on my boss's chest. If I was lucky, a raccoon would smell the Swedish snack and attack the sleeping man-beast. We left him and his food next to the pool.

Back at my apartment, I spent a good five minutes trying to beguile Benji to come inside, but he was right, I needed to sleep. My drooping pajama bottoms, disheveled hair, and mucky breath probably didn't help my cause. Outside my door, he'd gently held my face in his hands and kissed the tip of my nose.

"You are so beautiful, Paris. Inside and out."

I'd fluttered. Throughout the day, his words stuck with me, like a glowing light I kept coming back to as I got coffee, or sat in a meeting, or read at my desk. Oh, how I wanted to live up to that compliment, to please him. To keep him close, to keep his deep, hazel eyes focused on me with that same caring intensity he'd revealed in that moment.

In that minute, I'd grabbed him, holding on. "Thank you so much, Benjamin Stark, for tonight. I owe you a million times over."

"I'll take that payment right now." He'd bent down and pressed his lips to mine, molded his body to mine, pulling me up so our groins were mashed together. He was perfect. One hand had threaded into the hair at my scalp and held me to him, the other cupping a buttock, his tongue slow and measured in my mouth, demanding attention. He was not sloppy or awkward or aggressive; he was an artist. After a breathless moment, he broke away with a small laugh. "Oh, Paris. If only you knew how much that was worth."

As I unlocked my door with a shaking hand, he'd said, "Hey, look at me."

I had turned and he'd snapped my picture with his phone camera. "Something to look at while I fall asleep." He'd grinned and then loped down the hallway.

A text drew me out of my dreamy state. I blinked back into real time, at my desk in the middle of a long afternoon.

*To my new favorite person . . .*

Benji included a link to an old YouTube video of Van Morrison singing "Brown Eyed Girl." I'd never really paid attention to classic rock, but it was a lot different when you could picture a hot photographer singing it to you in the bathtub. I listened to the song thirty-two times in a row. He was singing directly to me. I was Benji's brown-eyed girl. I was Benji's.

*Whoa. Okay. Moving pretty fast here. Take a breath.*

Frank had called in sick, not surprisingly. I hoped he was suffering from raccoon rabies along with his hangover. I stayed because he told me I needed to sign for a package and put it in his safe, but no one in the office needed me for anything.

Most of the traders were having a Candy Crush tournament, as far as I could tell. I'd already put in more than enough hours, starting at 2:00 a.m. I could have spent my time researching current trading trends. Instead, I Googled "dating tips" and "when is he your boyfriend" and "how do you know he's cheating" because you know, once bitten, twice shy, and all that.

An hour later, I was weighted down by the wide world of cynical women and their capitulation to nights alone with Netflix and dildos, and the searing abhorrence or feverish passion for *The Bachelorette*. I did glean a few helpful ideas, like I should try to be as real as possible around him, so six months down the road "he's not irate when you have to admit you can't actually ski and you wished he hadn't bought that expensive black diamond package in the Alps." Another good tip was to find something you have in common other than drinking. I felt smug in that arena. And, most importantly, have your girlfriends vet him before you're serious. *That's a damn good idea*, I thought. *If I'd listened to my girlfriends back in California, I would never have suffered the dick that was Darien.*

Finally, the FedEx delivery woman trudged up to my desk, glassy-eyed and reeking of weed. "Do you speak English?"

I sighed. I didn't get that nearly as much as my dad, but still. Annoying. "Maybe."

"The anorexic chick at the front desk said Frank is back here. Are you Frank?"

I started to laugh but then realized she wasn't joking. "Um, yes, I speak English, and no, I'm definitely not Frank. But I will sign for him."

She thrust a small box at me, moving away before I had a firm hold. The heavy package dropped to the floor between us. There was a jingling counterpoint to the thud. I froze, but the delivery person meandered away without the smallest glimpse backward.

I stared at it. *Shit.*

I picked it up and casually, oh, so casually, eyeballed the room. The office was half-full of people being held hostage by their computer screens. Nicki and Michelle were off in a corner, gossiping with a new analyst. No one had seen the big drop.

I removed the Book of Frank from my locked desk drawer and strolled into Frank's office, slow and calm, binder and package in hand. *Nothing to see here.* I nudged the door shut behind me with my foot and flipped the binder open to the combination page. Mumbling the numbers under my breath, I left the binder on a chair and opened the safe. I set the package into the iron box, trying not to shift the broken glass, and re-spun the dial.

For all Frank knew, the item had arrived broken.

I slunk back out, guilt finding an easy, well-worn foothold.

I was supposed to meet Gina and Lucia for appetizers and drinks—virgin drinks for the pregnant girl. The two were back to talking, somewhat, but Gina was unsure of how to help her friend when it came to her family or, more importantly, now that she'd decided against an abortion, if Lucia should give up the baby for adoption or keep it. But Gina also continued to pass judgment on Lucia's reason for sleeping with the guy. Apparently, it was okay to bring home strangers from a bar, but not to use sex to get ahead in your career. On the other hand, Gina had told me privately she was kind of happy at the thought of a little Lucia running around the world. Once again, my friends proved to be complex but caring women.

I could offer an open mind and a kind ear. I thought about inviting Benji but decided he didn't need to be part of the baby saga, not until Lucia had made a decision.

I yawned a huge, gaping yawn, ending with slitted eyes that were hard to reopen. *Okay, I'm tired. Maybe a little nap first.*

I shut off my computer, went home, and fell asleep in my clothes.

The angry calls from Gina and Lucia, waiting for me at the restaurant, did not wake me up.

......................

The next morning, I fired off a string of apology texts, and then ordered a chocolate-dipped fruit bouquet delivered to their apartment.

At the office, I still felt like I was moving underwater.

"Paris! Par-iiiiiisssss!"

I jerked, sloshing coffee onto the desk and my hand. Sucking my skin, I cringed. Had Frank opened the broken package? I was hoping he'd forgotten about it, or that he really couldn't open his own safe. I put my head up and walked into his office confidently. Whether or not I decided to take the heat depended entirely on the next few minutes. I didn't mind owning up to something I did wrong—as a matter of fact, I preferred to purge my sins—but if the package was inconsequential, or he was a total douche, then I would rather burden my non-Catholic soul with a lie than be fired from the only job that was keeping my father, and myself, from the poorhouse.

"Do you know why I called you in here?" His doughy face was inscrutable.

"Um . . ." I felt like I was in a sitcom from the eighties, the scared student facing down her insipid principal in a bad suit. What was the right answer?

Glancing at the wall safe out of the corner of my eye, I realized the door was shut. Suppressing a sigh of relief, I thought, *He doesn't know the combination . . . oh hell. The Book of Frank. Did I leave it in here yesterday?* I flicked my eyes around but saw it nowhere.

"You are supposed to be in charge of my medication. I've been out of it for two days. Two days!"

He did look more crazed than usual, with greasy hair and bugging eyes. He had three screens set up and linked to his computer, and his desk was six inches deep in trade sheets and financial printouts. I edged further into the middle of the room, to be closer to the door.

"You're right, I'm sorry, I don't know how I missed that." I maintained a gentle tone. Then he threw an empty prescription bottle at my head, the wind moving my hair as it flew past. "Hey!"

He pounded his fist on his desk. "Look around here, Paris! I am the one holding this place together! Me! If I wasn't telling those moronic ballbags out there where to take a piss, they'd be sitting in their own piddle." He twirled one of the computer screens toward me. "See this? I'm currently tracking nine hundred and sixty-two trades. If I'm not paying close attention, some other fucking gunslinger is going to steal the horses."

"I'll go right now—"

"The head of NBC isn't going to settle for a fucking pony, Paris!" He pounded his desk again. "My concentration is shit! Maybe *you* can tell me which of these is a goddamn Arabian!"

I scooped up the bottle from the floor. "Okay, Frank. I got it. I'll help you corral the horses—"

"What in the *holy fuck* are you talking about? Get me my goddamn medicine!"

Michelle burst through Frank's door just as I was reaching for the doorknob. "Frank! I can hear you clear across the office. What's going on?" Her blonde ponytail bobbing, she tried to ascertain the damage.

I grabbed Michelle as I marched past and pulled her out with me. She shut the door and gently pried my fingers off her forearm. Seeing my face, she patted me on the shoulder. "Are you okay?"

I nodded. I held up his medication bottle and shrugged, afraid if I said anything I'd start crying. I hated being screamed at, I definitely hated having things thrown at my head, but I really, really hated it when I failed to do something I was expected to do. It certainly didn't help matters that the Book of Frank was missing and the CEO would probably find it, read the snarky comments about himself, and then fire me, even though I hadn't written them. Well, not many of them.

Then, something on the bottle caught my eye. The date. The prescription wasn't set to be refilled until the following week. Frank had been double dosing himself.

Alright then. Onto the next problem. Frank's binder . . . where had it gone? He didn't have it or he'd have thrown that at my head, too.

I told Michelle I was fine and then frantically rechecked every drawer, already knowing it wasn't in my desk. It had to be in his office, maybe under a chair. As if my blood pressure wasn't high enough. Frank was going to assume I was its creator, reducing his life to a three-ring binder. So much of it could be construed as condescending. Because it was.

# Chapter 17

Returning from the pharmacist, I found Nicki in Frank's office, on a stepladder, screwing L-brackets into the wall. He was gone.

"What are you doing?" I didn't really care. I put his medicine on the desk and then scanned the floor under the desk and side chairs.

"Well, since you decided to take a long lunch, Frank picked me to be the one to put up a shelf." She held out a hand. "I already broke a nail. Thanks a lot."

She had no idea what a cliché she was. "Why does he need a shelf?"

"He wants to display his wife's newest piece of art." She snorted and stepped down. "So stupid."

There, on his desk, was the ripped-open envelope and a pile of blue shards of glass, some chunks bigger than others. Whatever it used to be would remain a mystery.

Nicki slid a glass shelf over the brackets, climbed down, walked over to the desk, and then scooped the crystal shards back in the large, padded manila envelope. Then she marched back to the wall and dumped the shards into a pile on the shelf. She stood back and looked at it, smirking.

"He told me it was abstract, representing the fragility of the human psyche. I'm pretty sure he just made that up."

"He saw this?"

"Oh yeah. He made everyone come in and admire it. And then told me to hang a shelf, that he wanted to see it from his desk."

She stepped back to the wall and adjusted some of the pieces, trying to give the mound some semblance of an aesthetic shape.

The brackets tore loose and the shelf fell off the wall. We stared at the mess on the floor.

"Did you find the studs first?"

"You think you're so smart, you do it!" She huffed, and then marched out.

I called in one of the handymen from building services to hang the shelf, which Nicki should have done in the first place. While he measured and pounded nails, I got on my hands and knees and looked for the binder under the sofas, then under the cushions, with no luck. It took the guy three minutes to get it done, most likely because he wanted to be gone before Frank came in.

As the handyman left, I "artistically" arranged the blue shards and stepped back to assess my handiwork. *Nope, looks just as stupid from a distance as it does close up.*

I went into Frank's bathroom to wash glass slivers from my hands, and to find white toothpaste to fill the first set of drill holes. There, on the back of his ridiculous toilet, was the Book of Frank. I groaned. So, he had found it. And he was using it as reading material while he pooped. I should have known.

Gagging, I wiped down the binder cover with a Lysol cleaning cloth and took it back out to my desk. I refused to picture the bacteria clinging to the pages inside as I tucked the binder into the drawer and locked it.

He hadn't returned by the time I left for the evening. I figured there was a fifty-fifty chance Frank would forget about the binder by the time he returned, especially since he hadn't come in to get his meds. I'd had them messengered to his house, with a note for the cook to make sure he took them, but who knew if he'd listen to her. *He should be good and crazy by now*, I thought, relieved to make it out the building without a showdown.

.....................

That night, just as I was sinking into my couch with a bowl of chocolate peanut-butter ice cream and an episode of *Gilmore Girls* teed up, Frank called.

Berating myself as a coward, I answered. "Hi, Frank."

"Hey! Where's the binder?" I could hear water hitting water in the background. He was peeing while talking to me. I shuddered.

"Oh, uh," I said, thinking fast, "I took it. I locked it back up, since it has your banking information and passwords in there."

I heard droplets, and then the sound of his zipper.

"Yeah, that's probably a good idea," he growled, "but I want to finish reading it." The toilet flushed. "I could totally help you add more to it. We could use your content when I hire a biographer to write my memoir."

*Oh my God*. He liked it.

The whole notebook revolved around managing his moods and idiot choices. There was a section on the crazy, disgusting protocols he had implemented for maintaining his hygiene. There were lists of words and phrases not to use because they made him "throw a screaming fit like a deranged toddler." There was a page on how to walk and hold yourself, offering the least amount of possibilities for him to ogle your ass or breasts. Michelle had recently added in what to do if he continued to "accidentally" brush against you or rub his privates in public, who to contact in HR. I'd been praying I wouldn't have to use that information.

He thought I was responsible for its creation. Instead of getting fired, the narcissist thought I was brilliant. I was about to tell him Michelle deserved the credit, when he changed topics.

"By the way, you need to hire a new research assistant. You know what I like." He wasn't referring to smarts. "I want you to fire the skinny one tomorrow."

"Why?"

"She came into my office and I gagged. She stinks. I don't like how she always smells like burnt cookies. Or how she says 'thank you.' I've told her, but she keeps doing it. That's disrespectful. And I'm really tired of repeating myself to her. I've told her to go get the wax cleaned out of her ears, but she hasn't done that, either. I don't need her bullshit."

"What am I supposed to tell her? I'm pretty sure you can't fire someone for smelling like cookies or being polite."

He hung up without saying goodbye.

*Frank, the great mumbler, next in line for Humanitarian of the Year.*

I was suddenly too depressed to watch *Gilmore Girls*. I walked into the kitchen, placed my melted bowl of ice cream in the sink. I felt bad for the young assistant, but there was nothing I could do. We had no union. She could probably try bringing suit against Frank, but I doubted she could afford a good lawyer, much less the horde of attorneys that PRCM would throw at her. It was so unfair. *This man has a few switches locked in the off position. His brain does not function properly.*

I went out on the fire escape, a cigarette in hand.

I was struck by the night's cityscape, the jumble of bright colors lighting up the sky. I put down the death stick and retrieved my camera instead. Clicking away, practicing with different filters and lenses, I thought, *I wish Dad could see how happy this makes me. I'm doing what he wants, appreciating beauty in the simple things. And I'm good at it. I can make a go of photography, be successful. I know I can.* My father had brought me up in the world of business and hard work—I knew what it took to make a small business function. I fantasized about hanging each shot I took on a wall in my own gallery.

Half an hour later, I was soothed and had a new roll of pictures to develop. Which reminded me of a certain photographer.

Thinking of Benji and his developing room lightened my mood further. The tune to "Brown Eyed Girl" played as the soundtrack to a new, fairly intense fantasy.

# Chapter 18

As I got ready for work, digging through piles of clothes and hastily applying makeup, I had the TV on in the background. A dancing circle of prepubescent white girls in old-fashioned dresses and with wilting bluebells in their hair were wrapping ribbons around a May Day pole in Central Park, celebrating the budding leaves and flowers and the baby squirrels of spring.

A gaggle of my aunts, uncles, and cousins were partying Persian style in Iran, at their mid-spring festival. I knew this because my dad, who'd sold the business without consulting me and refused to talk to me about where or if he was working, forwarded a photo the family had sent him: a large, happy group of people crammed into a small backyard festooned with lights and streamers. That was immediately followed by another text from my dad, which was a photo of a cow giving birth. A very clear, detailed picture. *Happy Maidyozarem!* he said.

It was gross, and it was annoying—*that cow got some action, how come I can't get any?* Not that I wanted to be pregnant, but it would be nice if Benji made his way past third base sometime soon.

Benji and I were having a good time, though. He was a good listener and easy to look at. When I could get away from work early enough, or wasn't called away at the last minute, we hung out in hole-in-the-wall places. At the colorful and loud Mediterranean

Festival Restaurant, we worked our way through the menu, or we scarfed up tabouli and cheese and spinach-stuffed pastry in Gazalas, and we laughed and drank and talked about art and building our photography businesses and family.

I closed out my dad's texts. I was tired of worrying about him, especially when he wouldn't tell me what was going on. Here I was, trying to figure out how to help him out financially, and he was the one acting like an irresponsible child. Didn't he care that he was going to lose our family business? Benji had tried talking me into flying back to Newport, but there was no way I had time for that. I was thrilled I had even one night for Benji, which wasn't always true, thanks to Frank. We'd agreed to meet at a new place to test out their happy hour. The thought of it would help me get through the day.

Work was even busier than usual. The two CEOs were leaving the next day for Galveston, on a rare dual outing, to meet with the heads of a rumored "vast corporation." I was faced with coordinating a number of things. Yet, despite this, Todd had come in to the office and said he was taking Nicki for the next few days.

"Right now? Can I send her up after we get through this list of phone calls?"

"No. I have a backlog of paperwork that needs to be taken care of immediately. You'll be fine."

The junior assistant smirked at me and followed Todd to the elevator. *Good riddance.*

Since I was in charge of everything, including meshing emergency contact numbers with my executive assistant counterpart in Galveston, I knew Andrew and Frank were meeting with a conglomerate of oil tycoons. It was going to be a bunch of middle-aged men addicted to Viagra, competing to see who had the biggest conquest story. Part of what I had to accomplish before tomorrow was to find two high-profile models willing to accompany Frank and Andrew to a business dinner as their dates. *How much money does it take for a Victoria's Secret model to hide her disdain?*

I also knew the details from Michelle. She'd been stomping around the office, her long hair twitching like a horse's tail across her black blazer, steam rising off her angry hide.

"I'm the one who told Frank about the takeover and I told him who I thought was making the money over there. He promised he'd take me with him," she fumed, slamming papers down on my desk. "And now Todd has Nicki working on some secret project? This is bullshit."

Poor Michelle. She believed Frank would ignore his sexist, classicist nature and reward her hard work, dedication, and smarts. *Sigh.* She had a master's from the University of Michigan and parents in the auto industry. Without an Ivy League degree, he wasn't going to take Michelle seriously. He thought state schools were filled with hillbillies and English majors.

*So . . . wait. I'm from a state school. Why am I sticking around?* "He'd told you he was going to let you be part of their meetings?"

"Not in so many words." Despite how she was acting, Michelle knew the reality: Frank was never going to allow someone else to take credit for the deal and certainly not an assistant. We brought him toilet paper. We weren't thinking, functioning human beings. I could see she'd let herself get caught up in a fantasy, only to be crushed.

Michelle and I had watched Frank and Andrew moving around on the other side of their frosted office doors, in a world that seemed inaccessible. Michelle then harrumphed and stormed off to the break room. She'd been helping with Frank's departure issues, but that appeared to be over now. Luckily, I'd become adept at anticipating his needs.

Michelle might have been distraught, but I was far from it.

With Nicki's snideness gone for a few days and Frank's Frankness on the way out of the office, I was ready to celebrate even before Frank left. I decided that, after drinks with Benji, a late dinner with Gina and Lucia would perfectly round out the night. It was rare I had this much energy.

"Hey, Gina," I whispered into my phone. I didn't want to capture the attention of any of the traders, or God forbid Frank, who might then set me on some freakishly time-consuming task. "I'm free tonight. You guys want to grab dinner?"

"Yah, right, Paris. You're going to make it to a dinner?"

"Frank's leaving tomorrow, gone for the next few nights. My workload is going to be deliciously light."

"And the new boyfriend?"

"I'm trying to make time for you guys, I swear. It's not Benji who forces me to break plans at the last minute."

"How would I know? I never see you anymore. Benji could be an imaginary boyfriend."

I'd been trying to get him and the girls together for a while, but work, or exhaustion, or Lucia's twenty-four-hour morning sickness, got in the way. And, yes, I'd passed up opportunities because I'd wanted to be alone with him. "Why don't I bring Benji along tonight? Unless you and Lucia are fighting again."

"We aren't fighting. We were never fighting." She huffed, then sighed. "She's adamant she's going to have this baby. I love her like a sister, Paris. On one hand, I think she should have an abortion, just start over with a clean slate, get back to her career. It's not too late. Her family never needs to know. But another, bigger part of me understands. I mean, there's a little life in there."

"I love you both. I'm here, too. I'll help however I can."

"Well, anyway, let's start with you committing to a dinner. Time to rake your guy over the coals. First test will be to see if he's a good human. For example, does he eat diner food?"

"Not everyone thinks a diner is high cuisine."

"It's not high cuisine. It's the *best* cuisine!"

"I'm not sure what diner you've been going to."

"Oh my God. It is so obvious you weren't born in Jersey. You know nothing, Paris Tehrani."

I spent the rest of the afternoon making sure the staff at Hotel Galvez in Galveston, a five-star luxury hotel, had the penthouse rooms adequately stacked with booze and sugar-free candies and knew to expect an "eccentric" guest. I was also coordinating meeting times, restaurant reservations, party RSVPs, drivers, helicopter hops, and the private jet for both Andrew and Frank. Frank, as usual, created an extra challenge—he was unable to tell me where he wanted the driver to pick up his luggage when it was time to depart. I found it bizarre that he had multiple houses within a two-hour radius of one another. He believed in options, like picking out a shirt for the day. Sonya and Liam Coyle stayed in the Lenox Hill brownstone most of the time, since it was the closest to Liam's school, but that didn't seem to be a tether for Frank.

Happy hour was quickly approaching. I decided to wrap up the final details the following morning, like finding models willing to go on a date with a rich goon. I packed, quietly, so I could slip out without anyone noticing. As I was about to make my escape, however, two extremely tall men in flashy suits appeared at my desk.

Baring his white teeth in a striking smile, one of them asked, "Yo, is the big guy in?"

The other guy, with sharp brown eyes and a broken nose, said, "Damn, girl, he always make you work this hard?" He raised an eyebrow at the papers and files spread across my desk. There were stacks on the floor next to me. Frank took a lot of paper to manage.

"Oh, hello. Yes, he's in. Let me tell him you're here." I ignored their flirtation and their questions. They were investors, both of them in the headlines: NBA players famous for their affairs and multiple baby mamas, though neither seemed to care about their reputations. Every woman in the PRCM office had been the victim of an ass grab from one, or both, of the professional athletes.

They didn't have an appointment but Frank threw open his office door and acted like his fraternity had come to town.

"What up, dudes?" he hollered, bouncing on his heels.

*I can't believe these guys are willing to be seen in public with him.* But, of course, it came down to money. Frank was the money guy. It was why he could act like a piggish buffoon and dress like a hobo and still get into the best restaurants with a drop of his name. He'd made a lot of people a lot of money.

I called PRCM's car service and then Bar Pitti to make a reservation and preorder appetizers with a round of martinis for them. Frank had been going there weekly, ever since he'd cornered Gwyneth Paltrow at the bar one night and she'd had a drink with him.

I texted the CEO the details, reminding him he'd be flying out tomorrow afternoon, and that I had everything ready to go. I hoped he'd take that as an invitation to stay home until it was time for him to board. Stepping onto the elevator, I tried to think of any other reason Frank might call me, so I could resolve it before it came to that. But as I descended into the lobby, I let it go and smoothed my long hair. Benji was waiting.

. . . . . . . . . . . . . . . . . . . .

We watched the May Day events on the TV over the bar in The Mermaid Inn, slurping down cheap oysters and Bloody Marys. The small, trendy restaurant had their rolling doors open to the sidewalk, which was refreshing until the air chilled as the sun descended. Benji noticed me shiver, even with my coat on, and he wrapped his jacket around my shoulders, rubbing my arms briskly.

"If we want to make dinner with your friends, we'll have to leave soon. Good thing, or I'm going to freeze while you're all cozy in two coats." He ran a hand through his dark blond curls, which always made me melt. Then he took a swig of his beer, set it down, and said, "Hey, I have something important to talk to you about."

I stopped chewing, tried to swallow without choking. *Is this it? Are we finally going to spend the night at my apartment? Or maybe he's breaking up with me* . . . I didn't want to be chewing like a cow with a cud while he regarded me so intently from his barstool.

"I set up a job for you."

I wasn't tracking. "Huh?"

"One of my bigger clients owns a string of boutiques downtown; they want a whole new advertising spread. They are willing to take you on as the photographer, as a favor to me. I showed them your portfolio and they like your work."

"You are kidding me."

"Nope. One hundred percent for real. It's time you got serious."

My face felt numb, my stomach hot. My hands started to shake; I tucked them between my legs. "Serious. Seriously. You're serious?" He nodded. "But, I . . . okay, so . . ."

Benji's hazel eyes crinkled with laughter. "It's okay, I'll talk you through it. It's an important gig, but you can totally do it."

"When do they want to get started?"

"That's my girl. This weekend. Late Saturday afternoon."

My brain whirled with excitement. Normally, I was on call weekends, since Frank couldn't go a day without needing me to find his wallet or to solve a ridiculous personal problem, like what cologne he should wear. But he was going to be far away that weekend, with Andrew watching over him.

........................

"On a scale of one to ten, would you agree that Paris's snoring is at an eight?"

Gina peered expectantly at Benji over several empty wine bottles and dirty plates, the white linen tablecloth spattered with marinara sauce and Chianti. Galli, in SoHo, served huge portions of pasta at normal prices, and Gina and Lucia had deemed it fit for consumption.

"I do not snore!" I said, indignant.

"Well, you'd had a few glasses of wine that night, baby . . ." Benji dramatically swept his gaze over the table and the empty glass in front of me, grinning wickedly. "I find it charming. Maybe tonight I can record you."

My heart skipped a beat. He wanted to spend the night with me. I grinned back.

"There is nothing charming about it," said Lucia, lifting her glass of sparkling water in a toast to my septum. "Unless you enjoy the sound of a wide-open engine." She sniffed pretentiously. "Please tell me you're not a NASCAR fan."

It made me happy to see her and Gina amicable. Lucia had told me they didn't talk about the pregnancy. When she'd mentioned maybe keeping the baby, Gina had walked out, but first hotly reminded Lucia she hadn't even told her parents about the pregnancy—how did she plan to hide a baby?

It was hard not to notice Lucia's cute little baby bump on her thin frame. But if they could find a way to eat peaceably together, I was happy. Even when they were mocking me.

"What's NASCAR?" asked my handsome photographer, with a crooked, far-too-innocent smile that led me to believe a Saturday at the track was likely in my future.

While my friends joked together, I smiled warmly. Not just because my people were getting along smashingly, or even because Benji had finally thawed on his no-sex policy, but because it hit me that he'd used a term of endearment. "Baby." *So natural, so sweet. How I love this man.*

I sat up straight. I loved him? I plucked that thought out of my head, laid it gently in a metal tin, sealed it up, and tucked it into a dim corner of my mind to be explored when I was alone. I was intent on having mind-blowing sex and cuddle time. True, neither of us was interested in being with anyone else right then, but deep, permanent feelings—which could leave deep, permanent scars—needed to be dealt with carefully.

Lucia, her hand on her rounded stomach, more sexy as a pregnant woman than I would ever be on a normal day, put her drink down and studied me. "*Bella*, I need to ask you a favor." She opened up the calendar on her phone and showed me an appointment note. "I have a sonogram scheduled for Saturday morning. Would it be possible for you take me?" She tilted her head at me, avoiding Gina's gaze. "Gina is working. If you can't, Paris, it's okay. I can get there myself."

"No, I would totally love that! Will we see the baby? Are we finding out if it's a girl or a boy?" I knew I was her second choice, but I was happy to fill in until Gina chilled the hell out.

She laughed. "The *bambino* is as big as a lime, but it's too small to see the gender." She rubbed her tummy. "We will hear the heartbeat."

"That is so cool," Benji said, with such earnestness, and so loudly, we turned to him in amazement. "What?" he said. "I like babies."

We were laughing and teasing him when the waiter approached the table. He frowned at our boisterous group. "Would the ladies or gentleman care for dessert? The menu is limited," he said stiffly, implying we should get the hell out of there.

Benji offered him a slow smile and tried to slide the dessert menu out of the waiter's pinched fingers. There was a slight

struggle, but Benji won, holding up the laminated sheet triumphantly. "Ladies, I'm thinking chocolate. You?"

"Ahh. One more reason to adore you, Benji," said Gina,
wrapping an arm around him. "You're a keeper."

I opened my mouth to agree when my phone went off.

Lucia, Gina, and Benji went dead silent. Their heads swiveled to me in sync.

"Don't answer it, Paris," Gina said, low and intense.

I stared at the screen. It was Frank. Of course it was Frank.

Gina saw me hesitate. She scoffed, "What, the office out of
Coffee-mate?"

Lucia put a hand up in the air like a referee. "Gina—"
Pregnancy had turned the Italian model into a nurturing ball
of empathy.

Benji's hazel eyes rested on me, unreadable. He said nothing.

On the fourth ring, I said, "I am so sorry, guys. I have to at
least see what he wants. He's my boss."

I knew how lame that sounded when I said it. *Whose
boss calls after hours? Well,* I argued with myself, *the boss
of someone who gets paid a decent wage.* Someone with no
safety net and a dad with money problems to think about. I
answered it.

"Paris? Are you there? Jesus."

"Hi, Frank. I'm here. What's up?"

He laughed. "My friends. They're up. So am I. We need to
take care of some wood."

"What?" I was confused. Wood? Was he building a fire?

"Go to the office, get all the cash out of the safe, and take
it to Madame Elena's on Park Avenue. Send three women over
to the Hyatt, have them ask for MacGyver."

"I . . ." *What?*

"Jordy prefers Asians. Chris will be happy if she has a
vagina. Me, I prefer a Bubbles over a Jasmine. And when I say

'Bubbles,' I mean a natural blonde with big tits." He was loud and chipper, the hard beat of a club behind him.

"I'm not—"

"Listen"—he dropped his voice, a rough whisper—"you either do this for these clients or we lose not just them, but *all* our investors from the league. Get over yourself. You've got an hour or you're fired."

My cheeks tingled, the skin tight around my eyes. My flesh was so hot, I felt like I could sear a steak on my face. Hopefully, it was dark enough Benji couldn't see my flush or my shaking hands.

I was in a lose-lose situation. No way could I accommodate everyone's needs. I had to triage, like a nurse at an accident site with no time to think; it was my career that looked like it was going to bleed out the quickest. I had to believe my other relationships were strong enough to survive.

Benji's mouth dropped open when I stood up, but Gina and Lucia did not share his surprise. Both women glared and turned away.

"I know, I know! Please don't be mad," I pleaded with them, tapping an Uber request into my phone at the same time. Then I struggled into my coat. "I'll be back in an hour, and the next round will be on me, I promise."

"I am not waiting around for an hour. You will not be back by then, anyway." Lucia shifted her gaze to Benji and then me. She was trying to tell me this was not going to make my boyfriend feel very appreciated, but . . . *yeah.*

Gina leaned back in her chair and took a sip of wine, running a critical eye over me. "From the looks of you, you're gonna be MIA for a while." She drained her glass.

I didn't want to look Benji in the eye but he was staring me down. "I'm sorry," I said, lamely.

Abruptly, he jumped up and buttoned the top button on my

coat. "It's windy out there." He looked at his watch. "And it's so late . . . I'm coming with you."

"No, no!" I said, frantic. There was no way I was ever going to let any of them know what I was about to do. I knew I was crossing some line, I just couldn't see a way around it in such a short time frame. "Seriously, I'll be back in an hour. I need to stop at PRCM and get something from Frank's office and then take it downtown. Easy peasy."

Benji shrugged, but I could see the hurt in his eyes. And suspicion. "Okay, but I think I'm done here, if they are. I don't want dessert anymore. How about you girls?" They shook their heads. They'd already been gathering up their things. The only one who was happy was the waiter, who dropped off the bill with a smirk.

"I can meet you guys some place for drinks . . ."

"Nah, I have to work tomorrow," said Gina. "And Lucia doesn't drink, remember?"

I blushed all over again. "Oh. Right. Sorry." I turned and put my hand on Benji's arm. I hated that he was suspicious of me now. "Do you want to meet up later?"

"You know, I think I'm gonna call it a night." He kissed the top of my head, kind but dismissive. "You text me when you get home, let me know you made it there safe."

My Uber app flashed—the driver was waiting. Benji had rescinded his offer to sleep with me. The last time, I'd snuck away believing he had a girlfriend, and I was about to screw it up again. I was being punished. But I didn't have time to argue with him.

I ran out the door, my body heavy. *Ugh. What am I doing?*

# Chapter 19

"I quit," I whispered into the mirror.

My threat fell dead in the empty morning air of the PRCM restroom. My ashen face, peering back at me, did not respond.

Terror quickened my heart and drew the blood from my brain. I was about to give up not only my security, but also my father's.

But Frank had crossed the line. Well, really, I was the one who'd chosen to cross the line, to appease Frank. *But who in the name of God forces someone to find hookers for them?* The devil. Frank Coyle. That's who.

I could not sell myself like this any longer. I was losing my identity—and Dad would be irrevocably disappointed in me if he knew I'd gone into a house of prostitution last night and rented women for investors. My mother was rolling over in her grave. I would die before I let my father or Benji know about my sojourn to Park Avenue. How could I have been so weak? So easily manipulated?

How was I any different from Madame Elena or any of the lovely high-class whores lounging around on her velvet couches, waiting for a man to come in and tell them what to do? At least they were being honest with themselves and were well compensated in return. I was busy pretending, just like Michelle, that my boss would one day come to respect my talents and further my career in finance, and I had to simply put up with his "quirkiness." But "quirky" did not really fit Frank; he'd made me break the law, in the most embarrassing, shameful act I hoped to ever live through, and I'd watched him abandon his son and cheat on his wife and belittle or harass employees, including me, time and time again.

What was my payoff for supporting Frank in his bullish demagoguery? My friends weren't talking to me, my boyfriend thought I was selfish and possibly hooking up with my boss, my dad needed me and I didn't have time for him, and the owner of a whorehouse had offered me a job. Frank had become my world, whether I'd wanted it or not. How had I let this happen?

Nicki pushed through the bathroom door and came to rest beside me at the mirror. She fussed with her long red hair, then said, "Frank's looking for you."

"What are you doing up here, Nicki? Aren't you supposed to be downstairs, working with Todd?" I'd hoped I'd at least be free of *her* that morning.

She angled her pale hatchet face so her eyes met mine in the mirror. "You are unbelievable, you know that?"

"I'm not in the mood for whatever this is, Nicki. What are you talking about?"

"No need to be coy," Nicki scoffed. "Michelle already knows."

*Oh my God, how does she know about last night?*

"Knows what?" My desire to scream at her mounted by the second.

"That you're going to Galveston with Frank to help him with the deal. Michelle's deal. Nice job, Paris. You just pissed off the one person here who liked you."

It was my turn to scoff. "Hey, gossip girl, you don't know what in the hell you're talking about. I set up the trip—I'm not going." *I'm quitting, you back-stabby little bitch.*

Nicki flipped her hair around, diva style. "Uh huh," she said, and flounced out the door.

I followed her out. Michelle glared at me from her desk as I trotted past. I wanted to tell her whatever she'd heard was only a rumor but I sent a look of apology instead. I needed to get this over with. I needed to quit. My steps grew more determined as I threw open Frank's frosted door and advanced into the office, ready to set myself free, no matter the cost.

Frank leapt up from his desk, saying, "Don't say a word, Paris."

"But—"

"I'm serious." He came around the desk, wearing sweatpants and sandals with his lime green dress shirt. Despite jumping up, his demeanor was calm. Frank pointed to the set of armchairs. "Sit down with me for just a minute. Let me do the talking."

He'd never asked me to sit before. Even when he brought me in to work on projects, he seemed to resent it when I sat in his presence.

I stayed standing. "I have something important to say, Frank."

"I know. I'm not stupid, despite what you think." He sat in one of the chairs, crossed his legs, folded his hands in his lap. Like an adult. Well, if he'd been wearing real pants.

"I can tell from your face that you're angry with me, that you're going to quit. But I'm asking you to reconsider. I should never have asked you to go to Elena's last night. That was wrong of me. I'm sorry."

I stepped back involuntarily. Not just because he'd apologized, which was unheard of, but also because he sounded so normal. His tone, pitch, and words were those of a normal middle-aged man, apologizing to a peer.

I squinted my eyes at him, crossing my arms. "I don't

believe you," I said, just to make sure he received the message loud and clear.

"I don't blame you. I was kind of a dick . . ." I made a disgusted noise and he stopped for a second. "Okay. Yes. I've treated you terribly." He bent forward with his elbows on his knees, propping up his face. "What can I do to make this right? I need you to stay."

My suspicions shot up to alert level ten. He was so obviously performing—acting in the way a contrite human being would, using the vocabulary of a professional in an office setting. His posture was like that of a kid listening raptly to a story, and his eyes were wide and innocent . . .

*I think he may be a sociopath.* He knew *how* he was supposed to act, but he only let societal norms dictate his actions if it benefited him.

"Why do you care if I quit? Any monkey can do this job, Frank. Why did you bother hiring someone who wants a career in finance? Because this is a career killer, right here."

For the first time, I was speaking to Frank honestly. I remained calm. I knew I was on my way out and I felt nothing but relief. "With every menial or unsavory chore you've had me do, my brain has eroded. I thought I'd be walking away from here smarter and more capable, but I swear to God I've lost brain cells. You've taught me nothing." *Except how to deal with insane people.*

"So . . . if I taught you how to work with the hedge funds, you'd stay?"

I paused for a minute. Wasn't that what I wanted? To learn and grow into a competent financier?

I sat down, trying to see all the angles. "Seriously, why do you care if I quit or not?"

His face contorted until he finally hit on what he thought conveyed sheepishness. It was like watching a *Doctor Who* episode, the one with shape-shifting aliens. "Andrew's tired of dealing with untrained people." I could see the darkness sliding around just below his remorseful gaze. "He said he's leaving the company and taking his funds if another assistant quits because of me."

*So, Andrew is finally stepping up.*

"Don't get me wrong, Paris," Frank added quickly, squirming his lips into a too-wide smile. "This is really about you. I can't lose you. You're the best assistant I've ever had. I can't function without you." He scanned my face as if to see if I was buying his bullshit. I managed to avoid gagging, barely. He hurried on. "But I can also be a mentor. I can do that. I promise. We can start when we get back."

"I told you, I—Wait. Get back from where?"

"Andrew broke his leg at the gym this morning. He can't go to Galveston. He said I have to take you or he's calling off the deal. So did Todd."

He was muttering, but I was pretty sure he'd just said I was going to Galveston. *Too much. Brain overload.*

"Paris, you put together my schedule, you know I have to make it to meetings, and dinners, and parties, and keep everything straight. You can sit beside me—you'll make me look good. I'll buy you a new dress."

*This is really why he wants me to go. He needs me to wipe his ass while creating the facade that women are attracted to him.* I let my face show my scorn. Todd and Andrew wanted me to go because they expected me to keep Frank in check. Left to his own devices, he'd be a headline on the nightly news.

"I don't even know if I want to stay at PRCM. Why don't you take Michelle? You should be taking her anyway. She brought you the information about these guys in the first place."

He sighed theatrically. "Michelle isn't very pleasant. She's bossy. The men I'm working with do not want to deal with a female who will insert herself into the conversation." He held up his hands in protest. "Don't look at me! It's not my fault they're sexist."

I was surprised he knew how to use that word correctly, considering his face was in the dictionary under the term. *Don't trust this guy*, I reminded myself, *he's become rich from manipulating people as much as he manipulates the markets. He knows exactly what to say to get what he wants from me.*

But what if I really was going to be mentored? I already knew he was the devil, and how to work with him, so what could it hurt to stay a little longer? *I mean, besides losing my personal life and relationships.*

Was there a way to stay at PRCM and keep my friends? If I could make them understand how important it was that I made this work, that I established my career in a real way and made real money so I could support myself and my dad . . . But they already knew that. They thought I was letting Frank walk all over me, and them by extension, while he offered me nothing.

"If I'm going to stay, and that's a big *if*, you have to stick to your word and teach me things. And we'd need to set up boundaries. Like calling me in the middle of the night. That's out. Or referring to me as your 'Persian princess.' Or having me tell your wife you're playing golf when I know full well you're not. I'm not going to lie for you."

His eyes flashed.

I knew I was pushing it, but I'd already quit, essentially. I leaned into it. "No throwing things, and no more hookers. Ever."

Propelling himself out of his chair, he hovered over me. I shrank back in the seat. He didn't notice, just plucked at a loose thread on his sweatpants, nervously shifting from foot to foot, far too close to me.

"So, then, you're going to Galveston?" he asked.

When I didn't answer right away, he sat back down, slowly, gripping the arms of his chair. He opened his mouth and his voice came out an octave higher. "I'll give you a raise! A significant raise!"

That made me sit up straight. "Can I take a second to process this?"

"The plane leaves in three hours."

*Michelle will kill me. It's not fair to her.* I stood up. *But she'd do the same thing. Who turns away a decent raise?* I stepped away from Frank. *Besides, I'm her boss.* Striding out of his office, I said over my shoulder, "Give me ten minutes to make my decision."

He didn't answer. My head spun as I shut the door, the floor seeming to move under me.

Todd, always the gentleman in a beautiful pinstriped suit, leaned against a corner of my desk, waiting for me. He exuded patience and control. He should have been the CEO.

I dropped into the desk chair and put my head in my hands, partly so I didn't have to see Michelle, still glaring from across the room. "I don't want to do this, Todd. Even with a raise."

He lifted a gray, bushy eyebrow. "He offered you a raise?" His long fingers patted my shoulder. "Good." His fingers clamped down briefly. "Paris, we need these investors. The company needs a shot in the arm—or we're going to get sick and die. If you don't go, Frank will fuck this up."

I blinked at the sophisticated COO using a curse word.

"You know I'm right," he said. His body tensed. "Maybe you don't have any reason to be loyal to the company, but I need you to do this." He smiled sardonically but then became serious again, standing up. "Every employee here needs you to do this. I can't leave; he doesn't listen to me anyway. He has to stay on his meds, keep the drinking under control, and not create a national incident. You've handled him better than anyone has before. You're calm and you make good decisions."

"I'd be his babysitter."

"Yes."

"To tell the truth, Todd, I don't feel safe around him."

My cell rang. Glancing at it, I didn't register who it was at first. Sonya. Frank's wife. I slid it to voicemail. I'd deal with her later. But the cell immediately rang again. Sonya again. *Great, what does she want?*

With a sigh, I said, "I'm sorry, Todd, I better get this." I showed him the screen and he nodded, folded his arms, and settled in for an obvious eavesdropping session.

"Hello?"

"Paris? Is that you?" The voice was scratchy blue steel.

"Yes, hi, Mrs. Coyle. What can I do to help you?"

"As you know, Liam's birthday party is on Sunday at six."

"Okay." This was news to me. She must have just planned it or her cook would have let me know.

She clicked her tongue. Loudly. "Paris, it is your job to make sure Frank's there. On time, with a present."

"I haven't agreed to go to Galveston yet, Mrs. Coyle. I can't guarantee I'll be there to get him home on time. You'll have to talk to Frank."

Todd shook his head and waved a hand in front of me, while the air on the phone went dead. Then Sonya said, "What's this about Galveston?"

"Oh, uh . . ." I widened my eyes at Todd, who shrugged helplessly. "I'm sorry, Mrs. Coyle. Frank has a meeting with investors this weekend—"

"And you're going to stay in Galveston with him. Interesting." She hung up before I could say anything further.

I glared at Todd. "Maybe you could have warned me before I answered."

"Frank never tells her when he's going somewhere 'fun,' and she is definitely opposed to him taking along attractive young women." He tucked his hands in his pockets. "Anyway. It's not like you're going to be best friends. I'm surprised she remembered your name. You are a peon to her. We all are."

Todd was trying to change my mood. I couldn't care less what Sonya thought about me. Liam, on the other hand . . . I did care about the little boy. His dad was never going to make it back in time for his birthday party. Unless I made that happen.

So many reasons to go. So many reasons to stay.

What was I going to do?

# Chapter 20

I left the PRCM building, making my way back to my apartment in a fog. *My life is like a Choose Your Own Adventure book, and I have to choose which storyline I want to continue. Romance? Family? Career?* I felt like whatever option I chose, I was slipping into a nightmare scenario.

Collecting my mail on the way through the lobby, I automatically sifted through the envelopes on the elevator. One address caught my attention. The fog boiled off.

A letter from Capital First, the bank that owned the mortgage on my father's house. As a matter of courtesy, since my name was listed somewhere in the deed, they were writing to regretfully inform me that, after many attempts to contact Ehsan Tehrani, they were taking possession of the home listed at 174 Kings Road, Newport, California. The foreclosure would be final in fourteen days.

I swooned. No one was there to catch me.

The decision to stay at PRCM was made for me. I threw open my closet, dragged out my suitcase, and tugged clothes from the hangers, tossing dresses and blouses in a pile on my bed as I made phone calls.

"Dad? Dad, would you answer your phone? You've been telling me you're fine and now you're losing the house? What is going on! Dad, I want to help, but you have to call me."

Frustrated, I called Gina next.

"Hi, Gina—"

"Yes?"

"It's Paris—"

"I know who this is. This is Paris. My old friend who's MIA."

"Alright, I get it. You're mad. But I have to leave for the weekend, and something big—"

"Why are you leaving?"

I hesitated. "Frank needs an assistant with him for this trip to Galveston, to woo new investors. But, listen, seriously, I need to talk to you about—"

She cut me off again, her New Jersey accent thick and angry. "I guess you've forgotten Lucia's ultrasound this weekend. You said you'd go with her."

I groaned, slapped my forehead. I'd forgotten to add it to my calendar. "Oh, jeez, tell her I'm sorry—"

Gina hung up. She'd done that to me a number of times lately. *I'm not sure I always deserve it.* Of course, I was feeling a little defensive. She hadn't given me a chance to tell her what was going on with my dad's house.

I stood next to the bed, my stomach rolling. Finally, I dialed Benji's number. I wouldn't be able to handle it if he hung up on me, too.

"Paris? I'm so glad you called. I am sorry if I was a jerk last night."

Last night seemed like a lifetime ago. "Hi, Benji. Please don't apologize. You weren't a jerk." *Well, maybe a little, but so was I.* "I think I've worked it out with my boss so that won't happen again."

"Thank God! That guy treats you like a dog. I mean, seriously, he couldn't get what he needed from the office himself? Is your time less valuable?" He breathed loudly. "Anyway, glad you're doing something about it."

*Gah.* So much was wrong. I'd ditched him on a date, I was hiding the fact I'd gone to a brothel, and he was about to find out I was leaving with the same boss I'd just said was no longer going to steal my time.

"So, yeah," I said. "I told him I wouldn't take that kind of stuff from him anymore or I was going to quit. He actually promised to start teaching me how he works with funds. But . . ."

"But what?" His melodious voice turned suspicious.

I dropped the shirt I'd been folding and sat down on the edge of the bed, clothes and shoes scattered around me.

"Well, I sort of have to go on this trip. To Galveston, to meet with new investors. But we'll be back by Sunday! I have to go—"

"Sunday?"

"Yeah, I know . . . oh, no."

"You're going to blow off my boutique clients? For Frank?"

I had trouble catching my breath. After him shutting me down last night, having to visit a whorehouse, and then attempting to quit my job this morning, I'd completely forgotten about the professional photography shoot he'd set up for me. "Do you think they'll let me reschedule? This is really important."

"Um, you're serious right now? You don't have to do anything you don't want to do, Paris. You don't *have* to take this photo shoot, though that is a huge mistake. You also do not *have* to go to Galveston. Didn't you just say you weren't going to let Frank do this anymore?"

"The company really needs me—"

"They can't send another assistant? You're going to make me look stupid if you don't show up, plus you're throwing away a huge opportunity you probably won't get again. What's important to you, Paris?"

Just then, my phone beeped. My father was calling in. *Worse timing ever.*

"Listen, I have to get this. It's my dad. He's the reason I'm going on this trip. I'll explain everything, but let me talk to him. I'll call you back in a minute."

"Really, don't bother." Indignation dripped from his words. "You seem to like getting pushed around, but I don't." He hung up.

*No! This is so unfair!*

I tried to switch over to my father, but he hung up, too. I threw my phone, hard. But on my bed, because I couldn't afford to buy a new one.

I was angrily jamming hair products into a Ziploc bag when the phone rang again. I looked at it like it was a snake, about to bite me. It was my dad.

"Dad! What is going on with you!"

He didn't say anything.

"Dad?"

Nothing.

"Dad? Are you there?"

Then I heard his voice, faintly, in the background, and the rustle of what sounded like cloth over the speaker. I couldn't make out what he was saying, but I did hear him laugh, followed by a loud female cackle. Then the woman said something in a foreign language, maybe Russian.

"Dad! Daaa-aaad!" I yelled. *He ignores my calls and then he butt-dials me! Goddammit.*

"You're ruining my life!" I screamed into the phone but immediately regretted it. I held my breath, listening, praying he hadn't heard me.

Instead, I heard him say, "I have been looking for my pants for days now. But they are camouflage."

A pause, then an unfamiliar woman's voice said, "Oy, Ehsan, you are so funny!"

*Seriously? He's letting our family house go into foreclosure because what, he's too busy hooking up with someone?*

A surge of rage swept through me. Was I the only one who cared that the earth was crashing down?

.....................

Running in high heels and a skirt, my rolling suitcase flipping around behind me, I regretted my decision for the eight hundredth time in a row. Across the runway at the Teterboro Airport, I could see the crew detaching the boarding stairs. I tried yelling but could only wheeze.

Finally, with a deep intake of breath, I burst out, "Hey! Wait for me!" My voice cracked, thanks to an hour of crying, but they must have heard something.

Two mustachioed guys in blue jumpsuits cranked their heads around and stopped. They moved the stairs back into position, smirking and blatantly eyeing the skirt sliding up around my thighs.

The inside of the Wheels Up jet was exactly as I'd seen on dozens of movies, the opulence overwhelming. Cream-colored leather and teak everywhere, with a full bar, a huge media center, gorgeous couches and reclining armchairs. A young female flight attendant, who looked at my blotchy cheeks and swollen eyes with sympathy, stowed my luggage and went off to help the pilot, promising to return with a food and drink menu.

Frank lay limp in one of the loveseats, already asleep, his phone, wallet, pants, and an empty whiskey glass on the floor beside him. The prostitutes must have kept him and his friends up late. Now I had the pleasure of seeing him in tight white underwear and a dress shirt, drooling on the leather. I found a blanket and threw it over him, for my sake, not his.

I studied his face through narrowed eyes. Even as he slept, he was unattractive.

But when I saw his iPhone, I had an idea. I quietly retrieved it and found a seat farther forward in the cabin, a cozy armchair with a lap desk. I turned away from him and set to work.

After a two-minute search on Google, I had the directions for how to turn his phone into a homing device. I wasn't too worried he was going to wake up and catch me—but I was taking my health into my own hands, literally, by holding his bacteria-laden phone. *I can't get syphilis from touching something, right?* I dug a bottle of hand sanitizer from my purse, doused my hands, and then his phone.

I activated his global positioning system. Then I downloaded the Find My Friends app and gave authorization for Frank's phone to allow my phone to track him, providing me with a map of his location within a five-foot radius. I should have felt bothered by the huge, probably illegal, intrusion into his privacy, but I felt only relief that I'd thought of it, tinged with concern that someone else could just as easily be tracking me. *But that would mean someone out there cares where I am and took the time to go through my phone.*

I didn't want to think about my friends right now. Or Benji. They'd turned their backs. It hurt they wouldn't let me explain my reasons for staying with Frank. And then there was my dad, who would die if he knew what was going on with my job and my boss. Yet he was going to lose the house, after already losing the business, if I didn't do at least one more dance with this devil.

*Do the ends justify the means? I have no fucking idea.*

......................

"We'll be landing in about ten minutes. Can I get you another drink before I buckle in?"

The attendant was so fresh-faced and happy, I wanted to punch her. But not nearly as much as I wanted to punch Frank, who'd woken up about an hour before, put on a pair of sweat-pants, and turned on the TV, ratcheting up the volume on a basketball game. I thought the speakers were going to blow, but no such luck. I'd put in my earbuds and listened to soothing music, staring at the white clouds below us, picturing myself as a bird, floating, at peace, free . . .

"No, thank you, I'm fine." I'd limited my drink intake to one glass of chardonnay, since I had no idea what kind of energy the next few days were going to take. Frank, on the other hand, had no such compunction. After his third drink, I'd quietly asked the attendant to mix the whiskey with water and bitters. He didn't seem to notice. His palate was expensive but not developed.

When we arrived at Hotel Galvez, he stepped out of the limo and stretched loudly. I followed suit, minus the soundtrack, try-ing to loosen the muscles in my calves and between my shoul-der blades, taught with stress and travel. And grief.

"Hey, Paris, catch!" I turned and gasped as his wallet thwacked me in the chest and fell to the driveway.

"Oh, sorry. I thought you were looking," said Frank, dis-tracted. "Use the American Express to check us in. I'll be by the pool." With that, he kicked off his sandals and pushed down his sweatpants, leaving them in a puddle on the cement. *Oh my lord*, I thought, covering my eyes. I took a second to steel my resolve, and then I slowly removed my hand. He strode into the lobby, shoeless but not in his tighty-whities. I gushed a sigh of relief. Thankfully, at some point, he'd put on swim trunks. I wasn't about to ask him about it; who knew where that con-versation would lead.

Nor did I want to have another conversation about him throwing things at me, but it appeared he was already nudging at the line I'd drawn in the sand earlier that same day.

The driver was unloading luggage from the trunk.

"This one is mine," I said to the porters swarming the car, "but these two will go to the penthouse."

Frank was in the biggest, most expensive suite, overlooking the Gulf of Mexico. I was in what was supposed to be Andrew's suite across the hall. I gratefully realized this meant I could hear his door open when he tried to escape, but we didn't share a wall. I did not want to hear any noises he might make, for any reason.

My rooms faced inward, with French doors and a long, wide balcony looking over the pools. Below, Frank was easy to pick out in his lime green dress shirt and swim trunks, sitting on the edge of a lounge chair next to a gaggle of sorority girls in bikinis. I couldn't hear them, but the girls had their backs to him, and one wrapped a towel around herself and scooted her chair further away, clearly not excited to have a middle-aged weirdo crashing their conversation.

I sighed and went back inside.

After a shower, I unpacked slowly, enjoying the large, beautiful suite, with the sound of the ocean and the smell of clean salt air making me feel like I was back home in California. Then there was a knock on my door.

"Hey, why are you over here?" Frank's doughy face was pink. Sunburnt. *I didn't know the devil could burn.*

"What do you mean? Am I supposed to be somewhere?" I looked at my watch. "Your first meeting is at the French restaurant. It's not for another hour."

"No, I mean why are you sleeping over here? My suite has three bedrooms."

"Oh. Well. We already had this room for Andrew. Besides, it's company policy employees can't share hotel rooms." That was a total lie. There was no such policy, but he'd never know that.

"That's a stupid rule. I'm sure Todd came up with it. God, he's so paranoid." He crossed back to his door. "I hate staying by myself," he muttered, childlike, fumbling with his room key.

I let my door close. There was no way in hell I was going to sleep anywhere close to that guy.

*As a matter of fact* . . . I dialed the front desk manager. "I need to ask a favor, and please, *please* keep this to yourself, but please don't give anyone else a key to my room. Especially Frank Coyle."

"Of course, Ms. Tehrani. Our policy precludes us from giving out room keys anyway, but I will make a note." His voice was smooth, pleasant. If he thought it odd I'd make a specific request to keep my boss out of my room, he did not react noticeably. "May I assist you with anything else?"

"Nope, that's great. Thanks."

It was going to be a long weekend. I didn't want the hotel staff to burn out early.

# Chapter 21

An hour later, I was ready, but Frank wasn't responding to my texts.

*Driver will be here in twenty minutes. You'll find a navy striped shirt and turquoise tie packed for tonight. It will contrast nicely with the restaurant's decor. I know you like to stand out:)*

Power dressing had been Michelle's idea, but she wasn't in Galveston so I figured it wouldn't hurt to let him think I had something to do with it. My assistant had researched every location of every meeting and, before she found out I was going, purchased clothes in power colors suitable for the different aesthetics. Psychological warfare at the smallest level. It was genius, the kind of thing Frank would love.

I'd explain the origin to him someday. And that Michelle had created the Book of Frank, not me. Just not this weekend. I needed to seem like I was in control.

*Great, he's going to be late. On the first night.*

I knocked on his door. Twice. Three times. *Goddammit.* I went back to my room and retrieved the extra key for his room I'd gotten from the front desk at check-in—hypocritical, sure, but obviously necessary.

"Frank?" I said from the door.

Heavy moaning.

*Sweet Jesus. Please, Lord, let him be dying.*

Walking through the entryway, past the coat closet, I held my breath and peeked around the corner. I could see the back of his head as he sat on the couch, intent on the TV. The moaning came from the TV, but maybe not all of it. A circle of naked white dudes, holding their man-parts, knelt around a frizzy-haired woman writhing around on the floor in ecstasy—or possibly having an epileptic seizure. It was hard to tell.

*Is he watching that on purpose?*

I backed up slowly, quietly, wishing I could return to my room, lie down on the table, and perform a lobotomy on myself. Instead, I wrenched Frank's hotel door open, slammed it shut, and shouted from the entryway, *"Frank?* Are you here? Should I come in?"

He groaned in a way I hoped signaled frustration. "Yeah, hold on, I'm coming."

The double entendre made me gag.

"I'll be outside, at the car!" I cried around the corner and scurried out. I didn't want to see if he was zipping up his pants.

I would not be using his room key again.

When he crawled into the back of the car with me a few minutes later, I was relieved to see he wore slacks, dress shoes, and the blue shirt and tie. He had to know, in his heart, that he had to do everything right with these oil guys or he'd be putting his company in jeopardy. Hopefully he was smoother at manipulating them than he had been with me. I'd stayed because I needed the raise, not because I believed any of his words. And for damn sure not because I respected him.

. . . . . . . . . . . . . . . . . . . . .

The preliminary meet-and-great went smoothly. Frank and two of the oil magnates sat around a table going over the next day's agenda and eating lavish French dishes, thick pools of butter on each plate.

After a round of introductions and the tipping of large cowboy hats, Frank had tried to get me to sit next to him at the table, his soggy hand on my waist as if I were his date. But it was not meant to be. On many levels.

"Little lady, this is just going to bore you," one of the men said, adjusting his belt buckle over his gut and openly running his eyes up and down my dress, finally settling on my face with a puzzled expression. Probably he was assessing my brown skin in order to place me on his social strata totem pole. "Why don't we meet you in the bar when we're done here?"

I froze, my ass hovering over the chair. Awkwardly standing, I peered over my shoulder to be sure the guy from *What Would You Do?* wasn't behind me with a camera, filming a segment on sexist pigs. Nope. I cemented my features into a small smile, restraining the inner female warrior who wanted to come out and smash this Neanderthal in the face with a crowbar. It was a look I had perfected in my time with Frank, patient zero of the caveman epidemic.

"Uh, sure." Bellying up to the exquisite marble bar lined with expensive cowboy hats, I avoided eye contact. The majority of bar stools were occupied by the upper echelon of Texas, men riding high on the North American gas and oil boom—but a sixty-year-old man in a Lamborghini is still a sixty-year-old man, and I did not want anyone to think I was on the prowl for a sugar daddy or a hot night with a sweaty old guy.

I told myself not to be hurt by the probably racist, definitely sexist experience with the businessmen, but it was a matter of willpower to not succumb to depression. And if I was going to be barred from meetings, what did Frank think I was here for?

I ordered a drink and then tried to reach my dad, and then Gina, but the only people willing to talk to me were the drunken letches who thought I was for hire. I wanted to also try Benji, but I knew he wouldn't pick up and that would just crush me. I liked him so much, with his sweet humor, and artistic genius, and loving hands . . . picturing him lying next to me that night so long ago, wrapped in a sheet and laughing. I fought back tears. *I put my relationship in jeopardy. And my new business.*

*And for what, for this?* I thought, leaning away from a bar customer who scooted closer and closer to me, and farther away from his wife. It was hard to hide my extreme annoyance by the time Frank lumbered into the room to get me.

On the car ride back to the hotel, Frank muttered into his phone, recording notes to himself, stopping occasionally to scratch his head and research something on his iPad. He was preparing for the real meeting tomorrow. I breathed shallowly and avoided swift movement, lest I startle the beast in his natural habitat and draw attention to the Iranian American girl frozen in the corner.

I busied myself by sending another round of text messages to my dad and Gina, who were pretending their phones had died. One or both of them may have been wishing I was dead. I started a message to Benji about twenty times, but deleted it before ever hitting send. It wasn't just that he was mad, it was that I'd disappointed him so badly when he put himself out there for me. I simply didn't know what I could say to make it better, to erase the disgust from his voice. I hadn't done it on purpose, but I had done it.

We arrived back at the hotel without incident. Against the odds, Frank bumbled his way straight back to his room, not bothering to say goodnight as he went in, still making verbal notes in his phone.

I checked his iPhone GPS every five minutes until I could no longer keep my eyes open. He did not leave the hotel that night, at least not as far as I could tell. I fell asleep quickly, falling into the heavy slumber that comes from sobbing for too long.

Frank was alive the next morning. He was even dressed in his preordained suit and tie choice, ready to go when I called to tell him the car was available.

We met in the hall. He straightened his tie, glancing at me as we walked. "You look nice, Paris. Are you ready? Today is going to be interesting, you should learn a lot. Let me know if you have any questions."

Shocked, I could only nod. *Who is this man, and what has he done with my boss? Maybe this weekend won't be as bad as I thought.*

As I followed Frank Coyle through the lobby to the outside world, I searched for wood to knock on.

# Chapter 22

The boardroom was beautiful, a bank of tall windows offering a vista of the white-beached shoreline and clear-blue water seamlessly blending with the sky at the horizon. The long table was burled maple, the chandeliers composed of tasteful crystal drops. My chair, tucked into the corner, was a bit of architectural magic that supported and comforted my body as I took notes.

The council members perched around the long table; happily, three of the seven were women. However, the blowhard who had banished me last night was in charge, wielding his power like a bludgeon. He treated the men and women equally to large servings of condescension and aggression. Frank looked like he wanted to hump him, or be him, or both.

"Mr. Coyle, I believe we're ready to hear what you have to say."

My whole body cringed as Frank leapt from his chair like a clown from a jack-in-the-box. But when the hedge fund manager took over, he transformed into a different man. His hunched shoulders straightened, his paunchy stomach disappeared, his normal squint opened up to reveal intelligence in his green eyes, and his stringy hair . . . was still stringy, but he projected charisma and confidence, abandoning the aura of a beat-up middle school teacher.

"You men and women have been at the top of your game for a while now. But now you want to take your earnings to the next level. That's what I do. I'm the best there is in this already elite club." He smiled, revealing surprisingly white teeth, then cocked a hip and pointed a finger gun at Blowhard. "I'm a bankster."

*Oh my God, we're done here*, I thought. *What a dork*. But no. The Texans ate it up. Laughter bounced around the room. I rubbed my neck, amazed. Then Frank astounded me further by letting the humor float for only a few seconds before bringing the conversation back on track—instead of beating the joke to death, which is what he did back home, even though the jokes were never funny in the first place.

"It's true, the markets are volatile right now, and not apt to be resolved soon, not worldwide. The riotous habits of the industry will make it difficult to provide solid returns month after month. That is the nature of the beast." He shrugged one shoulder, sighed dramatically, and crossed the room. "Sometimes we will have a bad month. We will lose money, and diversification will not always adjust for this. Not right away. You should be prepared.

"But notice that I said we may not balance our earnings *right away*. Because this is the long game, folks. You are oil people. You know the long game. You've lived the long game. But you don't know *this* particular game. Not like I do." He jammed his finger in the air. "No one knows it like I do. And I make money. Lots of money."

My mouth was agape. *This man is so competent. In charge of the room. Selling like a motherfucker.*

Over the next hour, he explained trends and prospects, forecasting a rosy future for these wealthy folks, with plenty of evidence that he could make that future happen, answering questions with aplomb and not a hint of intellectual snobbery. It was a thing of beauty.

*Why can't he be like this every day? Imagine the loyalty*

*he would inspire.* PRCM would be a much healthier creature if the man before me came to the table more often.

When he finished, there were handshakes and back slaps all around.

Then they broke for a light lunch, catered in the private dining room. A martini lunch.

Frank, of course, reverted to his normal, socially awkward self as soon as the first martini was down, but he didn't become obviously drunk over his fresh fish salad, thank God, nor did he say anything outrageous or unprofessional. Sure, it was a tad weird when he interrupted a woman who was talking about fracking in the heartland of America in order to make a comment about llama farms, apropos of nothing, explaining how he loved them as a child and so purchased his own llama farm, and offered to fly everyone there that afternoon and pet his big, fluffy animals. I didn't know why, but the Texans once again thought he was hilarious.

As the laughter wound down, he opened his mouth to keep going but I kicked his ankle under the table. It was the only time since meeting Frank I was glad I was sitting next to him. And he actually understood the kick, squinting his eyes but shutting his piehole, especially when I gave the faint but distinctive finger-across-the-throat sign for "shut the hell up." My guess was he'd been kicked under a table before.

"Mr. Coyle," I interrupted politely, "that conference call you asked me to schedule is in twenty minutes. I have the notes set up in your hotel room."

"Wha—"

I kicked him again. He winced.

"The call with Andrew and Todd. They would like to be looped in."

He rolled his eyes, exasperated, but the head Texan pushed back from the table and stood up.

"Ah, well," said Blowhard, "we're done for now anyway. Why don't we meet for dinner at eight? We can work out the finalities then." He snapped his chubby fingers and an assistant leapt out of the background. "Make reservations for a banquet room at The Railhead." He slapped his hands on the basketball stomach under his silk shirt and winked at Frank. "Best barbecue in Texas."

Walking into the southern heat, out of the office building, Frank unleashed his irritation. "What was with the kicking? And why am I talking to Andrew? He knows what I'm doing."

"There's no conference call. I just figured I'd save you from a lunch meeting that seemed to be dragging on forever." In reality, I was saving him from himself. We had a few hours before dinner and I needed to make sure he was able to close the deal. Otherwise, my life had been derailed for nothing.

"Very clever, my little Persian princ—sorry, I mean, good thinking, Paris. Those suits *were* pretty boring." He reached over and flicked my ear, as if I were a child. "Let's go find some fun."

I flinched away. *Who does that?* "Uh, I think we should go back to the hotel before we do anything. It's only a couple of hours before dinner and I'd like to freshen up, take a shower. It's so muggy here."

He leered, the liquor adding a shine to his ugly pig eyes. I'd purposefully referenced myself naked in order to distract him. But in hindsight, it not only made me feel dirty, it also made me feel unsafe.

"Sure, fine then." As the driver opened the limo door for him, he said, "Driver, just take us down the main street and then back along the beach road. You can see the sunbathers from the road, right?"

Once we were inside, the limo powered away from the curb abruptly, making me sway. Frank watched my chest, more blatantly than Blowhard the day before. Crossing my arms, a learned response since I was fourteen, I tried to limit the jiggle. *I will totally rip off a hunk of his face with my teeth, à la* Silence of the Lambs, *if he touches me.*

I tried to delay in the lobby so he'd walk up without me, but he stuck close, at one point putting a hand on my hip to guide me around a corner. I pretended to scratch my arm and moved away. I kept my face poised, careful not to sway my hips or say anything that could even remotely be considered suggestive. I minimized myself, becoming a robot, a nonsexual being. At his penthouse door, I was acutely aware that Frank, who was my height and actively worked on acquiring liver disease and diabetes, could physically overcome me and drag me into his room. Worse, I was sure he wanted to.

He started to speak. "Hey, why don't—"

"I'm gonna return a call to Todd," I said, talking over him. "Let's meet back here in three hours and head over to the restaurant?"

He frowned at me and grumbled as I slid into my room and closed the door behind me. It took willpower not to whip it shut. I locked the bolt, carefully, quietly, so as not to insult Frank.

*So as not to insult the man who has pawed at me and said awful, suggestive things! What the fuck is wrong with me?* I should have told him off, many times, and pushed his hand away whenever he touched me, but instead I minimized his actions so that by the time I was alone in an isolated place with him, he felt entitled to say and do whatever the hell he wanted to. *Frank has been allowed to treat women like dirt. I'm allowing Frank to treat me like dirt. I have set feminism back fifty years.*

My desire to appease everyone was truly doing me no favors.

I threw on a sundress, not taking the time to shower. Instead, I grabbed my camera and snuck back out. Leaving the lobby, I checked Frank's GPS. He was in his room.

I meandered down the beach, taking photos. The peaceful lull of the waves and the wind settled my angst. Digging my toes into warm sand, forcing moist air deep into my lungs and blowing out with gusto, I found myself missing Dad and our home.

I took pictures of beach grass, and shrieking kids running into the white frothy gulf, and cormorants, and leatherback turtles. Caressed by the warm sun and ocean breezes, I enjoyed the glorious afternoon. I was grateful I didn't see any snakes or alligators. I'd be too busy screaming and peeing myself to take pictures.

Too soon, I had to turn back. I checked my phone for the hundredth time. No one I loved had tried to contact me, and the one I abhorred was still in his room.

Carrying my sandals, I made my way back up the beach, toward our hotel, preoccupied. Why had I let Frank, and other men, cow me so many times? I hated that I crossed the street instead of flipping off catcalling construction workers because I was afraid of conflict. Of them, really.

But eventually my focus shifted from general sociological ills to the specifics. Why had Benji given up on me so easily? That hurt. And why were Gina and Lucia refusing to talk to me? It wasn't fair. Finally, why had my dad waited until it was too late to get my help? Anger and sorrow swirled through my brain and my heart.

My feet left sandy prints as I crossed the pool area into the lobby. A familiar hoot of nasal laughter came from behind me. I twirled and faced the opening to the Hotel Galvez's upscale bar.

I looked at the Friends app on my phone. The blue dot that was Frank sat in the exact location as when I'd left the hotel.

Yet, as I entered the dim lounge, I immediately spotted his slouched figure on a barstool, at least five hundred feet from his room, flirting with a woman who couldn't have been younger than seventy-five, held up by an exoskeleton of diamonds and Botox. A margarita the size of a bucket was in his hand.

Damn it. He must have left his phone in the room. I should have thought about that before.

As I was trying to figure out how to get Frank out of the bar, the scrawny older woman next to him wandered off in the direction of the restroom, hip-checking each table she passed. From beside Frank, I motioned the bartender over.

"Hey there, this guy needs to go. Can you settle up his tab and put it on his room? Penthouse A. And please bring a cup of coffee, to go."

"Pssht. I don't need coffee." But Frank didn't argue further, just got up and wandered out. I got the coffee and followed. He was already in his room but answered the knock at his door. He had his phone, talking loudly into it while trying to wave me into the room with him. My feet remained firmly planted in the hallway.

"Dude, right on. See you in ten minutes." He hung up. "Wanna come in?"

"Who was that?" I asked, handing him his coffee from the hallway.

He did not slur his words, which I hoped meant he was sober. "One of the oil guys is sending his car around to get me. He wants to show me the golf course he just bought, and then we'll meet at the barbecue place."

*This is not going to end well.*

Frank had a supernatural tolerance for alcohol, but this was not the day to test it. Could I somehow finagle a ride along? Probably, if I showed some cleavage and an interest in partying. But no, I had to draw the line somewhere. And, really, dinner was not too far out and he'd be with one of the investors . . . How bad could it be?

"Don't forget your phone," I said.

# Chapter 23

When I arrived at dinner, there were no other women at the table, except for one of the Texan's assistants, a terrified college girl whose face spasmed with relief when I came in. Where were the female CEOs from that morning?

Frank was there, thank God. I'd followed his jaunt around town on my iPhone as I paced the length of my hotel room, suffering through bouts of the nervous shakes, praying the technology demons weren't lying to me when they reported his blue dot went directly to the golf course and then to The Railhead. I was grateful to see his bloated face and squinty eyes in the banquet room, seated at the center of a table meant to fit at least sixteen, an empty seat on either side of him. Oddly, the six well-dressed male occupants were spread out, empty chairs between them all.

"She's here! Let the party begin!" gurgled Frank, choking on a drunken giggle. The oilmen chortled along with him, fiddling with their ties and twirling their mustaches. Frank raised a glass of red wine and toasted me. "The other girls will be here soon, I'm sure."

I lifted an eyebrow at the female assistant, seated at the end of the table. She looked down at her hands, misery radiating off her in waves. I drew out the chair next to Frank but he said, "No, Paris, sit down there, next to her."

*I guess I'm not the life of the party after all.*

I sniffed and straightened my new black organza dress, smoothing a hand over the peacock on the side, embroidered in such a way that it looked like an elegant tattoo. The dress and I deserved way more respect.

I moved down the table. I'd seen the girl earlier, but we hadn't spoken, as I'd been busy taking unnecessary notes and watering down Frank's lunch drinks while she'd been sent on multiple latte runs.

"Hi, I'm Dee," she murmured, nervously adjusting a bra strap under her tight red cocktail dress. "I am so glad ya'll are here, you just don't know!" She peered around, but no one was listening to us. "This is so weird. I'm only a junior assistant. Why'm I here?"

I would probably have to help her figure out which was a fork and which was a spoon when dinner was served, but she seemed nice. "Dee, I'm Paris. You're here so these boys have a lovely young woman to stare at while they suck on their barbecued ribs."

She bit at a fingernail nervously. "I don't know . . . Your boss said you were bringing along some friends who were models . . ." She pointed to an empty seat and dropped her voice even lower. "My bosses are pretty dang excited about it."

The bottom fell out of my stomach. *Oh. My. God.*

I had stupidly assumed when Andrew broke his leg and I was forced to come along that Frank no longer needed a paid "date" for the evening. I'd already canceled their contract. And, anyway, I'd only been asked to book two women—their agent referred to the dinner as a "modeling" gig—but the empty seats at the table made it look like the men were expecting a herd of beautiful ladies to show up.

"Dee," I said around a slow, thick tongue, "this is an emergency. Do you have any friends free to have dinner with us?"

"Sure," she said uncertainly. "John and Trent are waiting for me at the bar down the street—"

"Girls!" I hissed at her. "We need girls!" I wanted to bash the stupid off her sweet face. "There are no models coming!"

The light came on in her eyes and brightened slowly. "Oooohh." She put a finger to her temple. "So you want some of my girlfriends to come here? Now?"

"I'll pay them five hundred bucks, each, if they can get here in the next twenty minutes. Just to sit, eat, and look like they're interested in whatever these idiots want to talk about."

She slit her eyes. "I don't know any . . . bad girls."

"I am not asking you to pimp out your friends!" My face flushed. Wasn't I? How was it I was acquiring women for Frank for a second time that week? Gina would tell me I was going to hell if she knew about my new life in the world of harlotry.

Logically, I told myself the college kids were going to get a nice-sized check for listening to boring stories about the glory days of high school football but, emotionally, I felt as slimy as I had two nights ago, when I handed ten thousand dollars to Madame Elena. At least I knew Frank was fine with me spending money from his safe on women, because there was no way I was going to jeopardize my soul *and* do it on my own dime. "The only thing they're required to do is eat and talk," I whispered to Dee. "I'll be here to make sure no one messes with them, I promise."

. . . . . . . . . . . . . . . . . . . . .

It was a long twenty minutes.

When I'd announced "my friends" would be there soon, Blowhard and the other Texans smiled and nodded, while Frank yelled "Huzzah!" and guzzled another glass of wine.

The mustachioed CEO closest to me leaned across an

empty chair and said, "I swan, Yankee, you're quicker than a hiccup, ainchya?"

"I . . . guess?" I couldn't tell if the good ol' boy, who was wearing what I was pretty sure was Louis Vuitton, really spoke that way or if he was in character. His cowboy boots looked to be worth a house in Ventura and definitely had never been close to a cow patty.

He winked. "I was just wondering why a smart gal like you is stickin' with this rowdy fella."

"That is an excellent question," I said.

Blowhard, resplendent in a Gucci suit from the big and tall section, his silver hair whipped into a frenzy—*Is that helicopter hair?*—pointed to the server hovering in the doorway. "Buddy, bring in a round of Cuervo. The 1800 Colección. Leave the bottle."

"Ah, could we get more bread, too, please?" I asked quickly.

I slid the wicker basket next to Frank's plate when it arrived, but a few slices of warm sourdough bread were no match for the copious amounts of liquor Frank was downing. Or for the e-cigarette he suddenly had dangling from his pale lips as he vaped the hell out of some extremely fragrant weed. I whipped my head around, trying to assess the impact on the Texans— the Texans from tobacco Texas, where a bud gets you thrown in jail for two years and an e-cigarette earns you a beating. Luckily, our new investors were fixated on a perfumed trickle of femininity.

Five beautiful girls in trendy designer clothes and the highest high heels I'd ever seen filed into the banquet room, waving to Dee and throwing smiles via shiny red bee-stung lips around the table as if they owned the place. If they weren't models, they should have been. I breathed a sigh of relief and gave a thumbs-up to the young assistant next to me, who smiled nervously. *I wonder if any of them need head shots*, I thought, deciding to give them my business card on the way out. I was way past caring what my boss thought about me moonlighting.

Frank floundered out of his chair. It was the first time I'd gotten a good look at him since I'd arrived. He was wearing the pale lavender shirt and tie I had set out for him earlier—provided by Michelle, in order to stand out against the burnt-red walls of the boardroom—but he was not wearing the same slacks.

Bright orange pajama pants. He was wearing bright orange pajama pants. With Birkenstocks. I had to blink twice to make sure I wasn't hallucinating. *He is unbelievable.*

"Ladies, ladies! So nice of you to join us! Let me help you find seats!" he slurred, bumbling around the table to the small group. The women herded together to avoid the crazy guy bearing down on them. The oilmen stood, quickly, politely, drawing out chairs for the various girls fleeing Frank's reach.

The two seats on either side of Frank remained empty. At first he sat quietly, eating and smoking and drinking, surveying his kingdom with an air of satisfaction. Then he became increasingly agitated, shifting around, sighing, trying to interrupt conversations, shooting four or five shots in a row, slamming down each glass.

Finally, he got up to make rounds. I grabbed his arm as he crept behind me, forcing him to stop. "Frank! Where are your pants?"

He looked down at the pajama pants, irritated. "Paris, I'm wearing pants. Are you drunk?"

"Your suit. What happened to your suit pants?"

"I spilled coffee on them. These are way more comfortable, anyway." He started to rock back and forth, an ugly metronome.

I knew I should have escorted him from his hotel room to the car. *This is what I get for taking my eyes off him for five minutes.*

"It's so hot. I'm not wearing underwear." He waggled his hips, which were level with my face.

I blanched.

Then he whooped and yelled out in a terrible southern accent, "Ya'all should try it! Take off yer undies!" He threw up his arms and performed the Macarena at high speed. "Let 'er all hang free!"

Below the thin material, his penis swung around like a tetherball in a hurricane.

A few of the younger CEOs laughed, but the girls made mewing noises and averted their eyes, lips pursed in disgust. Old Blowhard, mildly amused but tuned into the vibe of the women around him, said, "Boy, sit down before you break somethin'." Then he patted the supple flesh of the young thing next to him. "Y'all got nothin' to worry about, he's just feelin' his oats."

As Frank leaned over the other corner of the table, discussing boxers versus briefs with a couple of the guys, I slouched down in my chair.

"I'm sorry," Dee said. "And I thought *my* boss could be an asshole. What is it you do for him exactly?"

"Everything."

"Everything?"

"Close to. I've sold my soul to this guy."

"You're his everything girl."

I winced. "Don't tell him that. He'd make me a name tag."

"I hope he pays you a lot of money."

Frank came up behind us just then and squatted down. At least his commando crotch wasn't in my face. "Hey, Paris. Who's your friend?"

"Frank, this is Dee. You met her earlier."

"Yep, right. Local girl. Listen, Dee, I need some blow."

She paled. "What?"

"Find us some coke, will ya?"

He wandered away before she'd gathered her wits enough to answer. She started to push away from the table.

"Where are you going?" I snapped at her.

Her face drooped, resigned. "My bosses said we need to keep him happy." She stood up, inching the red dress down to mid-thigh.

"You cannot get him coke!"

"Why not? One of these waiters will know someone—"

"No! He's a billionaire! If you get him coke and he ODs . . . who do you think that's going to come back on? You. You'd be the drug dealer who killed the CEO of a major hedge fund!"

She stared at me with big doe eyes. "What do I tell him?"

"Nothing. Look at him." Frank was banging a spoon against the table to the tune of "Jingle Bells," replacing the lyrics with "Jiggle boobs, jiggle boobs, jiggle all the way . . ." A couple of the debutantes must have figured out how rich he was, because they were singing along and slinging back shots with him.

"He has the memory of a two-year-old right now. He's not going to remember anything."

She nodded, crinkling her nose. "You really do have to do everything for him. Like, keeping him out of jail, I mean."

"You have no idea."

The dinner went on forever.

And then at some point the party shifted to the nightclub next door.

We lost about half of the oil CEOs and two or three of Dee's girlfriends, but Blowhard and Louis Vuitton were still with us. Everyone was blottoed, including Dee. I just wanted to snap my fingers and be at home, back in my own bed, with my own comforter. With my own boyfriend . . . who I was afraid was no longer my boyfriend.

"Frank, you should slow down," I said to him as we weaved our way through the crowd to reach a set of couches. "Actually, we should just go. Right now, they're happy with us. Let's keep it that way."

He pushed his greasy bangs out of his eyes and squinted at me. "Don't be pissy. Loosen up."

I considered smashing a plate over his head to knock him out and then dragging him back to the hotel but knew one of us had to maintain an air of sanity for the sake of the investors.

Dee was sent to the bar with a drink order for the crowd.

One of the coeds squeezed in next to Frank, moistening her puffy lips and pressing her breast into his arm. "You are soooo lucky. I really want to move to New York." She batted her freakishly long fake eyelashes. "We should sit down and talk about some possibilities for me at your firm."

The CEO on the other side of the gamine tapped her on the shoulder, trying to get her attention, but she stayed focused on the drunk, ugly one. God only knew why she chose that billionaire over the other, more sedate billionaire. Sitting across from them, I pinched the black organza of my dress between the pads of my fingers, concentrating on the ridged netting, training my mind on something inanimate. I'd sunk pretty low over the past few weeks, but I wasn't willing to sit on his lap and beg for a job. I had scruples.

Frank lifted his arm and dropped the dead weight across her shoulders, crushing the oil CEO's fingers, and curled her in to his side. "I have a firm position for you right here." He patted his crotch. "I'm ready to talk now." He leaned over and licked her cheek.

I don't think she was expecting such an exuberant response.

"Gahh . . . good . . ." Her self-control was impressive, the way she transformed her breathy cry of revulsion into a word and made it look like she needed to tuck her hair behind her ear while surreptitiously rubbing slobber off her face. Instead of jerking away, the polite southern girl slowly sat back and said, lightly, "I need to use the restroom. Jenny, come with me?" And with that, Frank was once again sitting with empty space on either side of him.

*A magician, that one.*

Dee materialized, juggling four drinks. "The waiter is bringin' the rest in a minute," she yelled.

Frank, who'd appeared on the edge of comatose for the last hour, suddenly sprang to his feet.

"Hey! Look at this!" He started dancing in front of her, kung fu style, with chops and high karate kicks. Like a seven-year-old cracked out on cotton candy, seeking attention. Before she could back away, Frank turned sideways and let fly a high kick. He caught Dee in the ribs.

It was like watching an eighties movie in slow-mo. The sweaty glasses slipped from her fingers, propelled through the air, a waterfall of liquor spraying the crowd before the crystal hit the floor and exploded. Dee landed on her back in the midst of it all, red dress cranked up to reveal scanty Hello Kitty panties. The hapless errand girl screamed as glass burst into shards and rained down on her.

Shrapnel. The great party foul.

"Cute underwear," said Frank.

. . . . . . . . . . . . . . . . . . . . .

The Doogie Howser of EMTs strapped Dee to a stretcher. Her girlfriends had followed the gurney out to the curb, fluttering around uselessly, creating a plethora of deep cleavage as they bent over her and the tongue-tied baby-faced health-care provider. Dee resembled a human pincushion, with slivers of glass sticking out of her bare skin. And there was a lot of bare skin.

"Is she going to be okay?" The deep, nervous voice came from the Louis Vuitton suit. I was impressed one of Dee's bosses had torn himself away from the heaving dance party inside. Until his follow up question: "Do you think she'll be okay by tomorrow?"

It was the way he said it. Even the man-child EMT seemed put out. "Sir, she's fucked up. What did you do?"

The rich dude backed right off.

Dee, bleeding from a dozen gashes, raised a pitiful finger and then let it drop. "Am I gonna die?"

"Ma'am, we're takin' ya in right now, but I think these are all superficial wounds."

One of the coeds broke in. "Oh my gawd, Dee, my daddy says his plastic surgeon's on the way. I will not let these hillbillies touch your pretty little face!"

Dee groaned and gripped EMT Doogie's sleeve. "Drugs first. Ya'll got some painkillers?"

The ambulance door slammed shut a minute later and I came out of my daze. Frank. *Where is he?* The hairs raised at the back of my neck.

Inside, pushing past the drunk, over-excited dancers, I reached our corner. The table was surrounded by a happy group of drag queens. Frank was nowhere in sight.

"Sweetie, can I help you?" The short Puerto Rican with Hollywood-perfect makeup was overtly friendly. I envied her long black hair, suffused with a fluff and shine I wanted for my own long black hair. The only thing that marred her feminine allure was the Adam's apple. Even so, she was far more beautiful than most of the women in the room.

"Did you see the guy in orange pajama pants who was sitting here earlier? Do you know which way he went?"

"Oh, honey, no. We've been dancin' up a storm. I'd definitely remember someone wearing pajamas." She wrinkled her nose.

Then she bent forward and lifted the hem of my skirt to appraise the material. "But you are fabulous! Girls, look at this dress!"

*Finally!* It was about time someone noticed my dress.

"And those gold hoops are perfect, stunning against your skin."

Their bubbly focus on my attire distracted me for a second.

"Have a nice night!" I wanted to slide onto the couch with them, hang out with the laughing, amicable crowd. But no, I had to track down my drunken boss before he burned our company to the ground.

I crisscrossed the room. I didn't see him anywhere or any of the oil guys. And Dee's friends had disappeared. I was suddenly back in middle school, eating a lamb sandwich and studying for a chemistry test at a table by myself because my friends had skipped school without me to go watch the newest Harry Potter.

I'd been ditched.

Tugging my phone out of my purse, I noticed missed messages and calls. Of course, none of them were from Frank. Gina was finally reaching out, and once again, I didn't have time for her. There was also a message from Benji. Trying not to think about it, I switched away from the unread texts and tried Frank's phone.

Nothing. After calling him three times in a row, I finally left a nasty message.

His GPS. *I am brilliant!* I trilled triumphantly in my head. The blue dot showed Frank was at the club, in the south corner, not moving. I prayed he was passed out.

I pushed through waves of sweaty, drink-spilling people. The blue dot was at the far end of the bar, where I could see a cluster of guys in their thirties and forties discussing the 49ers in loud voices. One of them was in a chauffeur uniform. As I got closer, I recognized our driver, a beer in his hand.

He looked back at me in surprise. "Ma'am? I thought y'all had left. Your boss said he didn't need me."

"Oh hell! Who did he leave with? Which way did they go? Were they walking?" My voice shook.

"Ma'am, I'm sorry, I don't know. I didn't pay attention." Concern laced his features. "But I can give you a ride back to the hotel, if you want." He set the half-empty beer on the bar. "Just don't tell anyone you found me with a drink."

Fear fluttering around in my chest, I remembered the homing device. I held out my phone for him to see. "That blue dot is Frank's phone. It says he's right here."

The man colored. "That's because he gave me his phone and his wallet earlier, on our way to the golf course. He, uh, he didn't have any pockets. I tried to give them to him when he left, but he told me to take them to the hotel." He held the wallet and phone out to me, a look of dismay on his face. "Ma'am, I swear to God I was going to deliver them tonight."

At this point, I felt Frank deserved to have his wallet stolen, so I couldn't have cared less. But I sighed and told the driver not to worry. "I believe you. I would like a ride back to the hotel, if you don't mind."

Back outside, my head cleared. In the limo, I breathed deeply and rolled my head around, relaxing my muscles. *He has to be at the hotel. He has to be.* To distract myself, I decided to go through my messages, starting with the string of texts. The first four were from Gina:

*Can you give me a call?*

*You have got to call me back, this is important.*

*If you're ignoring me out of spite, you're a terrible friend.*

Then:

*Don't you care about Lucia?*

The last one put me in a whole new panic. What was wrong with Lucia? My hand trembled as I retrieved my voicemail messages.

"Paris, hi, can you call me? Lucia is in the hospital." There was a pause in the message. I could hear Gina sob in the background, just once. Then, in a cracked voice, she said, "Something is wrong with the baby."

That was it. There were a couple of hang ups following the message, but no more information. The last call had been six hours ago and the last text four hours ago. What was happening back home? *Oh, please, please, let the baby be okay.* I prayed feverishly to every entity as I frantically dialed Gina.

The limo rolled up to the Hotel Galvez just as someone answered. I thrust a fistful of cash at the limo driver, but he waved it away and mouthed, *Good luck.* I sprinted into the lobby so I could hear.

"Gina? Gina, is that you? What's going on?"

Her voice dripped with exhaustion. "I've been trying to get a hold of you."

"I know, I know. I'm sorry, we were with the investors, and now Frank is missing . . . It doesn't matter! What's happened?"

"Oh, Paris!" she wailed. "It's awful!" She cried quietly for a minute.

"Gina, you're scaring me." My chest tightened.

"It's the baby. The baby's heart stopped beating." She broke again, weeping.

"The baby is dead?" I whispered.

She didn't answer. I burst into tears.

"Not yet." She sucked in a shuddering breath and blew it out. "Lucia came in for her ultrasound. The baby's heartbeat was under a hundred beats per minute, so they admitted Lucia, to keep an eye on her and run tests.

"I got here as soon as I could. It was awful, Lucia hooked up to a million machines, her face so scared. I was holding her hand when one of the monitors set off an alarm. We both screamed. It was so loud. We could see the rate of the beats dropping. Nurses and doctors rushed in, but there was nothing they could do. And then . . . And then the heartbeat stopped. Just stopped."

Gina breathed in and out again, raggedly. "Eight seconds." Her voice sounded like it had gone through a grater. "The baby's heart restarted on its own, after eight seconds. It was a lifetime. The beat came back strong but has slowed back down a few times since then. Lucia was out of her mind. She's on tranquilizers now."

"So she's okay otherwise? Physically?"

"Yes. They can't find anything wrong with her *or* the baby. Nothing obvious. The neonatal specialist told Lucia to have hope, that maybe the baby just needs a little extra time to build strong organs. But that she should be prepared to lose it." She started crying again. "How do you have hope when you're afraid to close your eyes? That you could wake up to a dead baby in your stomach?"

"I . . . I . . . I don't know what to do. What can I do, Gina?"

"I don't know either."

"I'll get back as soon as I can."

"You can't come right now?"

"Frank has disappeared. As soon I find him, I'll have the jet bring us back. We're scheduled to leave at nine anyway." I looked at my watch. *Jeez, it's two o'clock in the morning.* "It's only a few hours from now."

"I have no one to talk to, Paris. Lucia won't let me tell anyone. She's terrified her parents will find out." She let out a sob. "I'm so scared. I don't want to be here alone."

*You son of a bitch, Frank. I'm going to kill you when I find you.*

"Honey, I love you. I know it's hard, but maybe try to get some sleep, that will help a little. I'll be there as soon as I can."

"Okay," she said, her voice trailing off weakly. "I'll try."

# Chapter 24

Frank was not in the penthouse.

But I did find his crumpled, coffee-stained pants on the floor of his living room. A pair of tighty-whities in a ball next to them.

I dropped, boneless, onto the leather couch, staring into space. *Now what? What can I do?* The only real contact I had in town was Dee, and she was currently being injected with lidocaine in over 40 percent of her body, in order to get stitched up by a physician's assistant. I could either wait here and hope Lucifer made it back to the hotel, or I could call the car service we'd been using and hope one of them was willing to spend the wee hours cruising the mean streets of Galveston with me.

I went into my room, changed into jeans and a hoody, and packed my clothes. Tucking my black dress into the suitcase, I ran my finger over the embroidered peacock one last time. I'd bought this picturing Benji and me at a fancy art gallery opening. The beautiful, beautiful gown was ruined for me. Bad ju ju. *I hate you, Frank.*

I was ready to go. *Maybe I don't have to wait for him.*

No. No, Todd would not be on board with me ditching Frank. His infantile moneymaker was out there, wandering around Galveston high as a kite, and it was my job to find him and get him home. I was going to be in trouble for losing Frank in the first place.

I crossed the hall and knocked again but knew it was futile. After a second, I went in, just to make doubly sure Frank hadn't somehow snuck in and passed out. I was not so lucky.

But just in case he did show up, I packed his clothes and bathroom supplies. I prayed with everything in me that we'd make the scheduled flight home.

He hadn't unpacked in the first place, so I just had to gather up what he'd thrown on the floor. I did notice his swimsuit was missing. Who knew what had happened to that. It was probably lying down by the hotel hot tub. Also missing were deodorant and a toothbrush, which wasn't surprising. I did not touch his lotions, Kleenex box, or the single stiff sock lying on the bed.

*You are disgusting, Frank.*

.....................

I found him at 8:14 in the morning.

I'd spent the night looking for him, finally talking a young Uber driver into driving me around and brainstorming where my boss might have gone. We started at the bars within a few blocks of The Railhead. They were closed, but some had cleanup crews hanging around. No one had seen a middle-aged white man in pajama pants. We widened the search, hitting every dive bar and honky-tonk, but any pajama-clad men they'd seen were the regular homeless people on their stoops.

There was no one at the golf course clubhouse. We stopped at the ER, the police station, and at the oil conglomerates' office building; no one had seen him.

I decided he was most likely at an oil guy's house or with a complete stranger. We drove down a few alleys but I decided enough was enough. If he was unconscious on one of these back streets, it was his own goddamned fault.

By eight o'clock, I was in such a panic I could barely function. I made the poor driver take me back to the hospital one more time. And that was when the admittance nurse told me a John Doe had been brought in, but he was wearing underwear. Only underwear. No orange pajamas. And his hair was blue, not brown.

"Do you have a picture?" I asked her.

She turned her screen to face me. There was Frank. He had a blue Mohawk. And, apparently, someone had given him a pair of underpants.

*I can just walk away now. Pretend I never found him. Go home, quit, find a nice bridge to live under.*

But I couldn't do it. He had no equal in the douche department, but he was hurt. I was the only one there who could help him.

"That's him. Franklin Coyle. Here, I have his wallet with his ID." I handed her his driver's license, tapping the picture. Despite the hair, his puffy, translucent face and squinty eyes were the same.

"What's wrong with him? Can I take him home?"

"I'm afraid he's going to be here for a while. Two broken ribs, a collapsed lung, and a bad concussion."

"Damn it. How did that happen?"

"We don't know. It looks like he was in a fight. He was drunk, incoherent, and then he passed out. It was a taxi driver who brought him in, but the driver said this man flagged him down, practically naked and all beat up."

I sighed. "Do you have the driver's name? I'll make sure he's thanked appropriately. Frank will be grateful." *If only that were true.*

She leaned toward me, whispering. "Between you and me,

he better be very appreciative to that driver. He peed on the man's seat."

My head hurt. "Would you believe it if I told you Frank runs a multibillion-dollar hedge fund? No? I don't really believe it either. God sure is funny, isn't he?"

When I got into his room, Frank's hospital bed was at a slight incline, with a tube running from a port in his chest to a separate, chambered machine.

His head was also bandaged. Electric-blue hair poked up out of the white cloth. He had a black eye. I wished I'd given it to him. He lay there, on a bed, cared for, peaceful, asleep. I tried to get comfortable in a flimsy plastic chair, exhausted and worried out of my mind about Lucia and her baby, and my father. And my raise. And Benji. And, *Oh shit, Liam's birthday party is today* . . . I pushed at the chair arm in frustration, trying to mold it into a bearable shape.

Nine a.m. We'd missed our flight. The company said they could delay for two hours but after that they were rescheduling the plane. Two hours wasn't going to matter. The doctor claimed Frank couldn't leave for at least another twenty-four hours.

Lucia was in her own hospital bed, hours away, intently listening to the heartbeat of her baby wax and wane, with Gina fretting by her side. While there was nothing I could do to solve the problem, I could be there. Show support. Like they'd always done for me. Frank did not deserve the time I was giving him right now. *I hate you, Frank*, I thought for the one millionth time that morning.

His eyes fluttered and then opened. Red slits.

I stood, folded my arms, and glared at him. It wasn't my job to make him feel better.

"What day is it?"

"Sunday."

"Morning or night?"

"Morning. You were only missing for a few hours." I settled back into the bedside chair. "Where'd you go, anyway? Where'd you get the underwear? And what the hell happened to your hair?"

He shut his eyes and fell back asleep.

I went into the hall to call Sonya. Frank's wife was going to be irate that he would not be in attendance at their son's party. What would the neighbors think?

Liam, on the other hand, was still young enough to want his daddy at his birthday party just because he loved him. Given a year or two, he would start to pray his embarrassing father wouldn't show up. Frank had blown what was probably the last time Liam would have loved him, no matter what, and been overjoyed to see him. Was there anyone in Frank's life happy to see him walk in the door? Not anymore.

The call was not pleasant.

"Yes, I know, Sonya, and I'm so sorry. To be honest, I don't know what happened."

"You incompetent little bitch. You had one job. To watch Frank." She hung up.

"Fuck you!" I yelled into the phone. Two orderlies turned around and gave me a dirty look. How come I never got a chance for a comeback?

*That's it. That's the last time someone hangs up on me or walks off before I get to say my piece.*

I'd been trying to decide who to call next, Todd or Benji, flipping through an *Entertainment Weekly* without processing the content, when Frank's phone buzzed. Sonya had sent a text. Actually, it was a video. In the garden behind the Coyle brownstone, the person filming was walking a circle around a messy pile of clothes and small objects, squirting a clear liquid at the heap. I recognized Frank's favorite peach-colored fedora and a green Columbia jacket. Then a barbecue lighter came into the frame, and a merry little flame dancing from the tip was touched to the waiting pile. A streak of fire zigzagged over his belongings, following the path of the lighter fluid. Soon, it was a full-on bonfire, tongues of orange and yellow and black chemical smoke licking the sky.

*Happy Birthday, Liam.*

I hoped Sonya didn't ruin his day, but I guessed that was too much to ask.

I had an idea. According to that month's *EW*, the Biebs was staying at his house in New York, working on a new album. I had Frank's contacts programmed into my phone, thanks to Michelle. I punched in Justin Bieber's name and found his manager. A few phone calls later and she confirmed the rock star would be willing to sing three songs at the party, but it was going to cost Frank.

I gave her Frank's credit card number, happily. "If you can get some backup dancers, Frank will pay for that, too. Just use the card," I said, and hung up.

Then I forwarded Sonya's barbecue video to Todd and explained to him what happened.

He called right away.

"So," the COO said.

"What do you want me to do with him, Todd?"

"What do you mean? Isn't he fine there?"

"Well, Sonya isn't coming to stay with him. She says she hopes he dies. As a matter of fact, she had a number of suggested methods. And I can't stay, Todd. I have an emergency back home."

He cleared his throat. "I suppose you don't see this as an emergency? Did you not agree to take care of Frank and, failing that, now you want to abandon him? What if the press finds him?"

I was surprised at how cold he was. He didn't even ask what my emergency was, just assumed my life was less valuable than Frank's. I stayed quiet. Depression hit me like a truck.

"One last thing," Todd said. "I'm afraid to ask. The investors? How's their temperature today?"

"That is a very good question. It was hard to read them at dinner last night. They think he's funny. It's weird. But by the time we left for the club, I'd guess the guys who didn't come with us were pretty disgusted. Or they were shacking up with the college girls. I don't know. Anyway, I haven't talked to them today. Though I should. To check in on Dee."

"Who's Dee?"

"She's the Texas assistant who Frank kicked and she ended up impaled with broken glass. Which is why I left him to go outside in the first place, to help her into the ambulance."

"Fine. See what kind of damage control you can do while you're there."

"But I don't want to be here. I want to go. Emergency, remember?"

He sighed dramatically. "I'll get back to you. Do what you can in the meantime."

I should have told him about the new credit card charges I'd rung up, but decided that could wait. I wanted him to let me come home.

A minute later, I was at the nurses' station. "I'm sorry to bother you, but my friend Dee was brought in last night. She was cut up by shattered glass at a bar. Is she still here?"

"I'd need her last name." She looked at me suspiciously from behind round glasses.

A younger nurse interrupted. "You know Dee? Yeah, she's in the west wing. Let's see . . . yeah, room 229W."

"How is she?"

The nurse scanned the computer screen. "Her chart hasn't

been updated in a while, but it looks like she's going to be okay. She did have quite a few stitches."

Frank was sleeping, or very convincingly faking it, so I grabbed my tote bag and wandered into the halls. Was I a terrible human being because I felt no pity for the patient? My emotions were all over the place, though the needle spent most of the time in the blues.

The hospital complex was newer, with the main building facing Galveston Bay. There were a lot of windows and cheery paintings, and patients and guests gathered in the many comfortable lounge areas or in the outside sanctuaries. I tried not to eavesdrop but came across a wide variety of people issuing tears, laughter, or hissed arguments.

As I moved down the hall, an old man with wild tufts of white hair burst out of a room and slammed the heavy door; it reverberated as he marched down the hall, shoulders stiff. I felt pain in my gut for him. I had no idea what his situation was, but clearly he was upset. His life had probably been fine one minute, and then, without warning, he was here.

I realized he had come from the hospital chapel. The door was interesting, different. Most of the doors in the hospital were extra-wide pine doors or metal sheets or sliding glass. This one appeared to be a single slab of cedar or fir, something worn and very old. It was rounded at the top, with a slight peak in the middle—an Arabic design, something you'd see in a mosque. The frame was a mosaic of colorful tiles. Each plaque bore an icon or symbol representative of religions from different cultures found around the world.

The Hindu's Wheel of Dharma, the Jew's Star of David, the Islamic star and crescent, the Khanda symbol of Sikhism, the Christian cross, the yin and yang circle found in Asian philosophy, India's Jainism hand representing nonviolence—there were so many, some ancient, some modern. I had only a vague notion of what most of them meant, but I was comforted that they were nestled together, here, a lovely palette of various worlds.

*I hope this is what it's like in the next life, different peoples and belief systems peacefully sharing space. Except Frank. I hope he's chained to an ice floor in the lowest level of hell, with his hair on fire.*

I had my camera with me. *Just can't get enough of doors, I guess.* I shot pictures of the entrance from various angles. *This will tie my collection together,* I thought, a brief moment of happiness settling over me. I finally broke away, taking random pictures of other hospital doors along the way. I was sure I looked weird to the people passing me in the hallways.

When I got to her room, a dozen pillows propped up Dee, a homemade quilt thrown over her bed. It wasn't even ten in the morning and flowers and balloons surrounded her bed.

"Paris!" She offered a huge smile but then winced as a string of sutures on her cheek and another string alongside her eye strained against their knots. She nodded at a woman and a teenage boy beside her.

"Mamma, Jeb, this is Paris. She is the sweet girl from last night I was tellin' y'all about. Paris, this is my mother and my younger brother, Jeb."

We politely shook hands but there was no southern warmth coming my way. I didn't blame them. "So nice to meet you."

They mumbled something and went into the hallway.

I turned to Dee. "Oh, Dee, I am so sorry. I don't even know what to say."

"Ah, heck, it wasn't your fault. Besides, look at all the flowers and candy!"

I laughed. "Good point. Maybe it'll make you feel better to know Frank is also in the hospital." She did a double take. I put my hand on her shoulder. "He'll be fine. Don't spend one second worrying about that jackass. He's got two broken ribs and a punctured lung. Someone beat him up. And gave him a blue Mohawk. All well-deserved."

"A blue Mohawk?!"

"Yeah. I have no idea what happened there."

"Well, that doesn't make me feel better! Poor man. His drinkin' just got away from him. I hope he's got family close by."

"He'll be fine, believe me. Evil never dies." But I had a feeling he'd be convalescing in solitude. Unlike Dee, who clearly was cherished by a number of people.

That made me think of Lucia, who also could have a squad of loved ones around her, if she'd allow it. Was she home yet? How was the baby? Did she have someone besides Gina giving her flowers and helping out? Lucia had friends, but she was not reaching out to them in her time of crisis. I hope she changed her mind. She needed what Dee had here, love and support in bulk. Lucia and her baby deserved that. So did Gina.

Frank did not deserve anything of the kind.

"I should go. I just wanted to check in." I paused. "Also, I should probably find out if your bosses are planning to invest with us after last night. What do you think? Who should I ask?"

"Oh my gawd, are you kidding me right now?" She held her cheek and giggle-grimaced. "Those good ol' boys thought Frank was a hoot. Besides, they were all pretty liquored up by the time we had dinner. Let me tell ya, they can hold their booze. They may not have looked hammered, but they were. I'm sure they won't remember most of his shenanigans."

"Are you *sure* sure?"

"Not a hundred percent, but enough that I'd bet the farm."

I swiped my brow dramatically. "Whew. Okay. Well, that's one less thing to worry about."

I wasn't going to believe it until I saw a check written out to PRCM, but it was enough for me to convince Todd that everything was fine in good ol' Texas and he should let me come home. But I was almost certain Frank was a human being and I couldn't just abandon him, as much as I wanted to. Todd was right about that much.

# Chapter 25

In the end, it was Michelle who solved the problem. Todd had told me I could come home, with Frank in tow, but he had to be stable and I had to do something about his hair.

"He can't be seen like that!" the COO had exclaimed upon viewing a photo of the blue Mohawk. "He looks like he was trapped in a frat house basement!"

"Who knows. Maybe he was," I'd said. Frank had yet to hold a coherent conversation with anyone.

Michelle suggested hiring a concierge physician, a private ambulance to drive us to the airport, and a hairdresser to accompany us home. She also worked out a deal with the pilot so he'd wait for us. Todd was not thrilled at the cost, but I told him I had Frank's private credit card and that Frank was fine with me charging the costs to him. *Which I am sure he'd agree to if he was lucid.*

The medical personnel carefully pushed his gurney across the tarmac to the waiting jet. Anyone watching the bizarre scene would have to assume we were filming a movie. The travelling physician closely monitored the patient and the private ambulance attendees manhandling the tubes and wires coming out of my idiot boss. Frank, in a stupor, looked like Bozo the Clown fresh off a bender. They'd removed his head bandage, which revealed a line of Frankenstein-like staples across the top of his forehead.

Next to me walked a tiny elf of a woman in a long white lab coat. She was from the local high-end salon, supposedly their best colorist. I'd talked her into performing a miracle on our flight to New York, offering a handsome stipend and all the Dom Pérignon and caviar she wanted from the plane's pantry. The pilot even agreed to let her fly back on the private jet, since he had to return to their Galveston base anyway.

As Frank was wheeled past us, she said, "You're kidding me. That guy? Is he unconscious? What happened—" Then she focused on Frank's ridiculous hair. "Oh. Look at that."

She turned to me, wide-eyed. I shrugged and rolled my eyes. "Yep, that's why you're here. Need help carrying your bags?"

Once she was standing over the sedated patient in the cabin of the plane, his table locked down to the floor, the stylist poked at the blue spikes. "Damn. They sure did a number on him." She twisted to face me. "I've only got three hours?"

"Maybe a little longer, but not much."

The physician said sternly, "You better watch those staples. You get anything in the open wound, they'll get infected. Not to mention it would cause Mr. Coyle pain."

"Don't worry about the pain part," I told her.

"Hm. I'm gonna need a step stool."

"The goal here is to make him look as normal as possible."

"Hm."

With the physician watching the hairdresser's every move like a hawk, I sought out the longest couch. I was asleep in under three seconds.

. . . . . . . . . . . . . . . . . . . . .

I woke up forty minutes out from NYC.

Frank was already awake and groggy. He'd made the physician put his hospital bed at an incline so he could see around him and drink some water. His bald head reflected the sun from the window.

The colorist had decided shaving his head was the best option, especially since the Mohawk had been wide in some places, narrow in others, with wandering margins. The dye had left a blue stripe on his scalp, with runlets of indigo staining the back of his neck. It didn't come off with salt scrubs or cleansers, so finally, she'd bleached his skin, leaving an angry red streak down the middle of his head. She assured me once the skin recovered from the chemical burn, he was going to look normal. Or as normal as a bald dude with scraggly eyebrows, pasty skin, and a row of forehead staples could look.

"What happened?" He squinted up at me, the money green of his eyes dimmed to a slate gray. The physician and hairdresser stepped away to give us privacy.

"I don't know, Frank."

"I missed Liam's birthday party, didn't I?" His face drooped, and a tear dropped from his left eye. It was hard to tell if it was genuine regret or a side effect of the morphine.

"Yes. You did. Your wife is not happy." I'd show him the video later. "But I was able to get a hold of Bieber's assistant. Justin made it to the party on time, sang a couple of songs for the kids. Liam probably didn't even notice you were gone."

For most parents, that would sting. Not Frank. Waves of relief swept over his rubbery face. "Oh. Thank you. Thank you, Paris."

I hunched over in my seat, disgusted with the soft, mopey disgrace of a man. Propping my chin in my hands so I wouldn't throttle his fat neck, I said, "You know, Frank, family is forever. Liam is a great kid. I hope he remembers you as a good dad."

He coughed and then winced, putting a hand to his bandaged ribs. "My father was such an asshole. Coyles don't produce functional families. Just money." He hit the button on his dripline for more morphine. Slurring, he said. "I bet your dad was a real doozy. Were you allowed to leave your house in Afghanistan?"

"My family is from Iran, you—" Swallowing it down, I said, "My dad was the best dad ever. He did everything for me."

His eyelids closed; I thought he'd fallen asleep, but then he said, "That's nice. Is he dead?"

I gazed off into the distance. My dad was at home, packing, likely getting ready to live in his car. "He's alive. But now he's about to lose everything he built because I've been spending my time worrying about you firing me instead of helping him."

"Yeah . . ." His voice drifted, far away.

The bitterness and rage billowed. I bent over him, close enough to spit in his face. "People like you, who can't tell the difference between a Persian or an Arab, are ruining my dad. He's no jihadist. He's just a good guy trying to live the American dream."

There was no stuffing my emotions back in the box now, but Frank had closed his eyes again, breathing the deep breaths of sleep. I poked him but he only grunted.

"You're such a pig! Yes, I have dark skin. My dad has dark skin. Does that mean it's okay for him to lose his business? His house!" A torrent of words and feelings and tears spilled out. I wanted to scream, to penetrate Frank's fog, but I don't think it would have mattered. "I could be helping him, but no, I'm here, in a private jet with someone who treats his own kid like a dog, while they foreclose on the house I grew up in."

"I mumble jabba wob . . ." Frank mumbled, surprising me, and then his chin dropped to his chest. He was out.

. . . . . . . . . . . . . . . . . . . . .

Todd and another private ambulance met us on the blacktop in Teterboro. A clammy smog blurred the horizon in every direction. So different than Galveston, which was moist and hot, even in May, and had an ocean that scrubbed the air clean. Our slice of the Atlantic . . . not so much.

The COO approached the slack-faced, drooling CEO. Frank's shaved, blistered head was gray against the white sheet. He did look better than he had three hours ago, though, even with the staples and the chemical burn. Unfortunately, Frank was not the hip guy who could pull off the bald look. At all.

"Excellent work here, Paris."

I did not appreciate Todd's sarcastic, ungrateful tone.

"Asshole," I said behind my teeth. I'd always liked Todd, but this was too much. He'd asked too much, and expected too much, and said too much.

"What was that?" He cupped a hand behind his ear, an impatient grandfather move.

"Nothing," I said, a disgruntled child.

Todd frowned at me before turning away. "You," he said to the waiting medical personnel. "Take him to his house. Paris will go with you."

"I can't," I interrupted. "I have an issue I need to take care of immediately."

"Yes, you do. Frank. Frank is your issue."

He walked away without looking back.

....................

I stood outside the door of room 729, trying to clear my head. It was late afternoon, long after I told Gina I'd be there. Lucia had now been in Mount Sinai for over twenty-four hours, her baby in jeopardy.

Instead of caring for my friends, I'd cared for Frank. What

kind of choice was that? Who did that? My only comfort was that Lucia did have Gina in the midst of her crisis. My dad was also in crisis, but he stubbornly refused to talk to me. Keeping my job and sending him money, especially with the raise, was the only immediate solution I could see. *Okay*, I told myself, *so I wasn't choosing Frank over Lucia, I was choosing to do what I could to help my dad.*

Would my friends buy that?

Peeking through the window outside the room, I could see Lucia sleeping inside. There were machines monitoring her and the baby. Everything seemed calm, the beeps and chimes rhythmic and soft. Gina was sacked out on a padded armchair, head hanging in an awkward position, like a kid asleep in the back seat on a long car ride.

My heart cried out to them, but I was too terrified to go in. What if they didn't understand, if they shouted at me, told me to leave? My heart palpitated, imagining the horrific scene, something out of *The Real Housewives of New Jersey*, Gina throwing a chair at the wall while Lucia wailed "I hate you!" in Italian.

*They need you. You're here now. Stop being such a wuss.*

Gina woke up, caught sight of me, glanced at the sleeping Lucia, and trudged to the door.

I stayed in the hallway. "What can I do?"

"What can you do? First off, change your clothes, girl. You smell like a guido after a night in the clubs." She peered up at me through tired and very judge-y eyes. "Are you wearing a bra? Your bubbies are on high beam."

I buttoned up my cardigan. "Sorry, my bra strap broke. Things got a little crazy. And not in a good way."

"Are you drunk?" She eyed me suspiciously.

"No, I swear." I glanced down. "I mean, I want to be drunk, but come on, I want to help. I want to be here. Do you need me to get anything from your apartment? Please, what can I do?"

"Just slow up for a minute."

Gina and I stood outside Lucia's hospital room, studying the Italian model through the window. She appeared so young, her slight body propped up on the bed. Her eyes were closed, blue veins pulsing behind her eyelids, both hands pressed against her belly, protecting the baby. Her hair was flat and shapeless, and the dark circles under her eyes could easily be mistaken for black eyes. My face scrunched up, trying to hold back tears.

"Every time they think they're going to send her home, the baby's heart rate drops again. If there was anything to be done, we'd be doing it." Gina rested her forehead against the glass. Her dark brown pageboy haircut covered the sides of her face, like a nun's habit. "I'm not much of a praying kind of girl, but my *mama* and my *nona* have a prayer chain in full swing back in Italy. Feel free to tag on to that."

"She's letting you tell people . . . ?"

"No. I wish. I told my family that one of my close friends is about to lose a baby but I didn't give any details." It was hard to understand what she was saying with her nose pressed flat against the glass. Maybe she thought if she pressed hard enough, she'd be back in her own reality, everyone safe and happy. "She made me go home this morning, saying she wanted to be alone for a while. She's been sleeping ever since I got back."

I pressed my forehead to the glass next to her. Sharing space. Breathing air together.

She sighed heavily on the glass and then drew a smiley face in the condensation. "She's my family. I will help her raise that baby. I'll be the perfect auntie. Lucia would do it for me."

Lucia's eyes fluttered open. She groggily peered around, and I watched her focus on the steady heartbeat pulsing on the machine next to her and visibly sigh in relief. Then she caught sight of us at the window and raised a weary hand to wave us inside.

At her side, I hugged her gently. "Oh, Lucia."

"Don't you dare cry." Her voice was raw. "She's a tough little *bambina*."

"You said 'she,' Lucia," Gina whispered, taking her hand.

Lucia smiled, nodding to her. "They did an ultrasound when you were away."

I took her other hand. "They told you the sex?"

She squeezed our hands and laid them on her belly. Warmth seeped into my palm as our fingers tangled together over this new life.

"Say hello to my beautiful baby girl."

"Hello sweet thing," I whispered.

"She's moving already?" Gina's voice was filled with wonder.

Lucia offered a small grin. "No, not yet, but she's alive." Her hands on top of ours, she squeezed again. "*Così molto vivo*. So very much alive."

# Chapter 26

Monday morning, I reported to my desk as if the past weekend hadn't been straight out of a ridiculous, over-dramatic telenovela. Frank was out, back at his home with private care, a pile of burnt clothes, and an unhappy wife. Liam may or may not have been talking to him, thanks to his impromptu birthday concert. Lucia was still in the hospital, the baby's heart rate continuing to dip and soar with no explanation. I didn't want to go, but Lucia insisted both Gina and I go to work. Instead, Gina and I set up a rotating schedule, so one of us was always available.

I'd spent the night at the hospital. Another hospital, another uncomfortable chair, another round of unanswered texts and calls to my dad. I didn't even bother reaching out to Benji. I didn't have the strength to deal with the amount of apologizing ahead of me. And the whole painful ordeal would probably be for nothing—I couldn't see how he was going to forgive me for turning my back on his clients.

A quick early-morning shower at home before heading into PRCM had not made me feel much better. As the elevator doors slid open to reveal our offices, the desire to quit tasted like iron in my mouth. *But I've invested so much time and tears in this stupid company, I refuse to walk away without making something of myself. I will not go backward in the world of finance.* That would help no one at this point.

I called a short meeting with the available PRCM staff on our floor. Todd was not invited. The gray-haired COO was classier and more polite than Frank, but in the end his focus was on the bottom line, not the individuals working for him. I no longer trusted him.

"I'm sure some of you have heard. It's true; Frank broke two ribs and has a collapsed lung. It seems he was mugged. But he's fine now. Todd had him brought home, so he's back in New York, if you feel the need to stop in and check on him."

No one in the room said a word. When the head of Investor Relations coughed, we swiveled in her direction. Andrea, surprised at being in the spotlight, coughed again and then held a tissue to her nose, her French manicure lacking its usual luster. "Just a cold. Sorry."

Nicki snorted and turned to me. "I heard he's come back with a shaved head. Is that true?"

I nodded but didn't offer any more information.

"What happens in Galveston stays in Galveston, huh?" Nicki shook out her long red hair, a skinny bullfighter waving a flag. "It seems like you fell down on the job, if our boss was out on the streets, alone. What were you doing?"

"Nicki, shut up. My God, you are annoying," said Michelle, glaring at the girl over her glasses. "As if you don't know what he's like. Anyway, Paris, tell us about the investors. Are they on board?"

"Frank tried his hardest to tank the deal but, yeah, they are going to go with us, as far as I can tell." I tucked some long strands of hair away, out of my face, thoughtful. "Actually, during the meetings, when he wasn't drinking, he was pretty amazing. I could see why people turn to him. He truly is brilliant."

There were nods and shrugs around the table, among the traders. The young new analyst said, "Everyone knows he's the best. Our college professors lecture on some of his biggest trades. No one can figure out where the market is swinging like he can. Why else stay? It's not because of his office manner."

That turned into a round of "Yeah, remember when he . . ." and a bunch of "Let me be Frank with you," followed by impersonations and hysterical laughter.

The professional men and women in the room were satisfied to be cogs in this particular machine as long as they could make money and let off steam once in a while.

"Remember when he missed his flight in Frankfurt? Did you ever hear that one, Paris?" asked one of the traders, a guy in his thirties who wore golf shirts and was notorious for stealing other people's lunches out of the staff refrigerator. "It's why his last assistant quit."

"You mean Ericka? The executive assistant?"

He nodded. "I don't blame her. Frank called her at one in the morning, screaming that she needed to book him another flight, and then call Lufthansa and have the Frankfurt first class lounge workers fired. He had missed his connection because no one from the lounge had told him his flight was ready. When Ericka called, the attendant was irate—she'd told Frank multiple times they didn't do all-calls. Then Frank missed the alternate flight they'd booked him on—for the very same reason! Instead of figuring it out, he went back to his hotel. He said he wasn't leaving until Ericka flew over and got him onto a plane. She went. And guess what?"

"Oh no."

"That's right. He wasn't there. He'd hitched a ride home on some diamond merchant's jet but didn't bother to leave a message for Ericka. She spent a day searching Frankfurt for him."

"That sounds familiar."

As everyone left the meeting a few minutes later, I asked the four assistants to stay back. Once we were clear of traders and analysts, I rounded on the hatchet-faced redhead.

"I chose not to reprimand you in front of an audience, Nicki, but this is it. Your last warning. I'm your superior, whether you like it or not."

"Oh, what, these guys aren't an audience?" She gestured to Michelle and the two research analysts.

"That's what you have to say for yourself? Not 'I'm sorry,' or 'You're right, I've been out of line'? No, you continue to speak out of turn. This is a place of business. You are supposed to be a professional. I've seen little evidence you can pull that off, but I'm giving you the opportunity to try. But one more catty, mean-girl barb, and you're done."

"You can't—"

"Nicki," said Michelle, sternly. "She can, and she will. Enough now."

I clapped my hands twice, elementary school teacher style, and stood up. "Yes, enough. It's not Michelle's job to reprimand you, either. Right, Michelle?" She was startled at being called out and took a beat to push her glasses up her nose and gather herself, but then she nodded. She'd been cold toward me since I'd arrived that morning, likely still not sure I hadn't somehow screwed her out of an opportunity, but she had seemed to be thawing, once she'd learned how the weekend had played out. I hoped this didn't bring on another ice age.

"I do not want to fight. It's time we got to work."

Michelle nodded again. Nicki huffed, but with the strength of a mouse, a tiny, inconsequential gesture. The other three picked up pens and closed their notebooks; Nicki followed suit. *Good little assistants*, I thought with a warm smile.

"Right." I straightened my shirt and tucked my hair behind my ears, brushing my fingers over my earrings for luck, before standing at the head of the table. "We have the annual investor meeting in a few days. Frank and Andrew and the Investor Relations team are going to need all the help they can get assuring our clients they should keep their millions in our fund. Obviously, the economy is bad, but if word gets out about this past weekend—and it will—Frank will look like a fool. I mean, seriously, who would want to give money to a man who literally loses his pants—and his hair. We need to make sure he, and PRCM, can survive any gossip." I swiveled to give them the eye. "No PRCM equals no jobs for anyone."

I picked up a marker and approached the whiteboard. Over my shoulder, feeling very leader-y, I said, "I've got some thoughts, but I want this to be a cooperative brainstorming session. Let's list the tasks that need to be done before the investors' meeting, and assign them. At the same time, let's list any out-of-the-box suggestions you might have for making Frank palatable, maybe even rock-star-ish, to the investors—"

"Wait!" Nicki said.

I raised my eyebrows at her. "Really?"

She blushed a cherry red, though a slight haughty edge to her voice remained, clearly ingrained since birth. "I didn't mean for that to come out so loud . . . but you're about to use a permanent marker on our whiteboard. That's Todd's pet peeve."

"Oh." *Maybe reward her helpfulness?* "You've been around a long time. Any suggestions off the top of your head?"

She tilted her head to the side, perhaps trying to decide if I was mocking her somehow. "Well . . ." She started slowly, but then gained steam when I grabbed up the proper marker and created notes based on what she said. Even when I thought her suggestions were inane, or I caught her rolling her eyes when asked to clarify, I wrote them down without critique. *'Cuz I'm a big person like that. Right up there with JC on the cross.*

When Frank returned, I'd have the office ready for the meeting and he'd see I was a capable person. There'd be no reason for him to delay mentoring me, as promised.

....................

Later, I returned to my desk to find someone waiting in the reception armchairs.

*Oh no.* "Ms. Jenson! What a pleasure to see you! I don't have you scheduled. How can I help you?"

She frowned and recrossed her leather-clad legs, highlighting a magnificent pair of Jimmy Choos, a style I hadn't seen in any stores yet. Not that I had much time or extra money for shopping.

"Hello, Paris. Actually, my secretary called on Friday and left a message that I would be here this morning. Where is Frank?"

*She remembers my name!* My glee was short-lived, however, when the rest of her comment sank in.

"Friday . . . Unfortunately, I was traveling out of state with Frank on Friday, so I didn't get the message. My assistant must have forgotten to forward it. Frank is out for now."

"Well. That's irritating." She twitched her legs but looked otherwise unperturbed. *One cool customer.* "Frank has papers I need to sign. I'm flying out today."

A trickle of perspiration ran down my back. "If you can tell me what the form is, I can get it for you." I pressed the tips of my fingers to the top of my desk to stop myself from taking a swipe at the sweat pooling in my bra.

"Honey, that's your job, not mine."

"Right. I'll be right back. Can I get you some coffee?"

She shooed me away with a wave of her hand.

I skidded into Frank's office and went through the stacks on his desk, racing through his files. I dialed Michelle from Frank's phone.

"Frank?" She was confused.

"It's Paris." I dropped my voice, panic bringing out an

unattractive screech. "Tris Jenson is here. What was she supposed to sign today? Apparently, she left a message on the office phone on Friday, saying she'd be here."

"Uh . . ."

"Yep, that's not helping."

"I'm scanning through her portfolio to see where Frank is at with her investments. Okay . . . here we go. She needs to sign Form 24A and Form 119. I'm sending them to the printer behind your desk now."

"Thank God for you."

"Do you want me to talk to Nicki about Friday's message?"

She hadn't missed that, either. "No, leave that to me," I said firmly.

I hurried out to Tris. "Here we are. Sorry about the wait."

"Ah, so you've got what I need then?"

"Yes, Frank just needs your signature here, here, and here. Do you need me to go over the content with you?" I held my breath. God, I hoped not. I'd have to call over Michelle and reveal a high level of ignorance. *Yep, good thing I'm sticking with hedge funds. I'm super good at this.*

"No, Frank already ran these by my lawyer. I want to sign and be done with this."

"Of course."

"You never said where Frank is? Why isn't he here?"

I considered how much to reveal. "He was mugged when we were in Texas. He's back, but he has two broken ribs and a collapsed lung. His doctors say he'll be fine, he just needs to rest." I hurried on. "But don't worry, he's working from bed. His investors are his number-one priority, always."

She released a tinkling laugh, like a bell running the scales. "Aren't you a little liar! But good for you, protecting your boss."

I smiled without answering. She signed the papers at my

desk, and I made copies. As my back was turned, I heard her pick up the picture frames from my desk, like last time.

"I see you've added a few shots. This door frame with the symbols is lovely."

My heart swelled. I'd just printed off and framed the hospital chapel photo that morning, when I got to work. I laid the copies in front of her as she returned the photograph to my desk.

"I wasn't kidding before," she said. "I hope you're going to do something with these."

Suddenly I was shy, astounded this woman remembered my photography. "Well, actually, one of them won a big award. Since then, I've done a few professional photo shoots. I like doing it."

Guilt swelled in my chest. I'd also skipped the most important shoot, the one Benji had given me.

Tris gently tilted my chin up with one finger, just as Madame Elena had done, and said in a mom voice, "Girl, you go big or go home." Then she stepped away and collected her bag and a jacket from a side chair.

A Hermes bag. *I bet that is real crocodile. As soon as I stumble into an extra $100,000, I am so buying that bag*, I thought, watching Tris slide her copy of the papers into the amazing satchel.

"I hope the next time I see you, dahling, it's in an ad. In a high-end magazine. Make it happen. No one else will." With that, and a slight wave of her fingers, she glided out of our office.

*So true. No one else will. I freakin' love that lady.* But the warmth in my heart turned to ice crystals when I remembered Nicki. I poked at the intercom. Catching her eye from across the room, I said icily, "Please come to my desk."

The assistant sauntered over and leaned against the tall section. "Yes?" she said in a bored tone.

"Do you mind telling me what happened to the messages from Friday? In particular, Tris Jenson's message?"

"I thought you were in charge of Frank's messages . . ."

"You are perfectly aware you were to be transferring any important voice messages to my cell."

She pouted her lips, letting a concerned and confused expression settle on her face. She must have realized her usual aggression was not the best play, especially after our confrontation that morning. "I, umm, I don't know what . . ."

"I don't believe you."

"I was working with Todd, I didn't realize . . ." She wasn't that good of an actor, her eyes darting around.

"You knew you were in charge of those calls. I'm going to talk to Todd about this, Nicki."

"Go ahead, I didn't do anything wrong." She planted her palms on the counter, leaned into my space, and said, as if to a child, "Frank's messages are your area, everyone knows it. This will be your screwup, not mine."

"Oh, come on." I flipped my hair out of my eyes, the better to glare at her with.

"I would never do something like that." She slit her eyes and hissed, "You can't prove I did anything wrong, accident or not."

"How's that? The task was handed over to you. Even if I'm the only one who knew it . . ." Understanding dawned. I laughed. "You idiot. What, you think you're going to get my job if they think I lost the message?" My laugh started to sound like a machine gun spraying bullets. *Tone it down, Paris.* "Just admit you made a mistake, a big one. Otherwise, it looks like you did it on purpose."

"You think you're so smart. Well, you're not. You can't prove I did anything wrong. Besides, Todd would never fire me."

I slapped my hand down on the desk in front of her and shouted, "I don't need to go through Todd! You're fired!"

She froze, her face chalky white against her red hair. She spit out, "I don't think so. It's your word against mine."

"Exactly. How many friends do you think you have in this office?"

"You cu—" she shrieked.

"What is going on here?"

Neither of us had heard Todd approach. The COO's normally composed features were tight with anger.

Michelle, her blonde ponytail twitching, was right behind him.

"Nicki purposefully erased Frank's phone messages from Friday instead of forwarding them to me," I said.

"If I did, it was an accident, and it was only one," she said with a snap.

Michelle peered around Todd's shoulder and shouted, "Just one! Tris Jenson, of all people! Who do you—"

"Michelle, please." Irritated, Todd turned back to me, glowering. After a second, he slid his gaze to the snotty junior assistant. "Nicki, why don't you work with me today?"

As she sashayed away, Michelle and I exchanged a look of dismay. She may not have liked it when I was allowed to go to Galveston instead of her, but she knew it was Nicki who was the problem in the office, not me. However, Todd seemed oblivious, angry with me instead. My stomach plummeted. Was this really going to somehow turn against me? *So unfair.*

Todd pointed a long, bony finger in my direction. "You. I want to talk to you."

Michelle hovered at the desk, tense with worry. "Todd, I'm not sure you realize—"

He waved her off. "Go on."

I sat, tugging on my earring nervously but also in frustration. *Why am I being singled out here?*

Todd crossed his arms, wrinkling his suit jacket, and lowered his gray eyebrows. "So much drama. We are supposed to be helping Frank, be the quiet machine that keeps him in check. You're usually very good at smoothing the path, Paris. Yes, I do realize you did your best in Texas, and you did it because I asked you to. And maybe I was too hard on you, but I'd expected so much more," he said. "Now, I need to know, are you still on board? Still part of the machine?"

I sighed. "I wasn't trying to cause drama with Frank or with Nicki."

"But it could have been handled better, no?"

I suppressed my instinct to argue. I could sense there was truth to his words. I just wasn't willing to let go of my outrage yet. I no longer trusted the older man in front of me, not since he'd revealed his priorities. He certainly didn't have my back.

"Nicki deserves to be fired," I said. "Her attitude is terrible, but the fact that she put our relationship with Ms. Jenson in jeopardy—"

"I will handle this, Paris. Just stay away from Nicki for now." He straightened his tie, preparing to go. "Like I said, I expect better from you. Get it together."

*I need this job. I need this job*, I repeated to myself. I envisioned my father telling stupid dad jokes to the other homeless people.

I was trying my hardest to appease everyone and yet I was alone. What could I do but try harder?

I smiled with my teeth showing. "I will do better."

"I want to have faith in you, Paris. The investors' meeting is in one week. The report needs to be finished. I will finalize it, no need to bother Frank."

"I need more information—"

"Send me what you have put together, and what you need. I need this to get done right. We don't have room for screwups right now."

*Screwups.* He'd said the last part slowly, laced with meaning.

*So unfair,* I thought again. *My sad little mantra.*

# Chapter 27

An hour later, Gina called. "I'll stay the night with Lucia tonight," she said, "but I'd really like to go home and take a power nap and a shower. Are you cool with that?"

"Of course. I take it that means Lucia and the baby are not stable? Have the doctors said anything more?"

Her voice dropped so low, I could barely hear her. "The same. The doctors are freaking me out, all stern and shit." Then her voice returned to normal, with a forced, chipper tone. "Alrighty, see you soon."

The Uber from PRCM to Mount Sinai didn't take long. Definitely not long enough for me to get over a newfound hatred for Todd. Or to find my dad. Sitting in the back seat of a Corolla, slugging through traffic with a driver fresh from Ukraine and its lack of driving rules, I finally broke down and called Darien. I almost hung up when he answered.

"*Salâm*," he said.

His voice did not bring the pain it had a few months ago. "Darien, it's Paris."

"I thought we weren't talking." He sniffed. "You've not been very nice to me."

*What, are we twelve?* "Have you heard anything about my dad? Would you mind asking your mom if she knows where he is? He won't answer my calls and I'm worried."

"Oh."

"What do you mean, oh?"

"Well, I know he sold the business and he got a crappy return. My mom told me they were foreclosing on the house."

"I had heard that much," I said. "I don't know if he's living on the street or what. Did he get a job?"

"Really, I don't know. But I wouldn't think the foreclosure has gone through yet. That usually takes a little time." Then there was crackling, and I could hear him speaking in the distance to a woman with a babyish voice. She didn't sound happy.

"Look," he said to me after a minute, "I'll ask Mother to check up on him, see what she says. But I have to go for now."

"*Merci*," I said, thanking him as he hung up, grateful he was willing to be a decent human being. Hopefully he was right, that Dad wasn't on the street just yet.

*I need to focus on Lucia, just for now*, I thought as we rolled up to the hospital entrance.

The halls were wide and clean but the smell of antiseptic was layered with the stink of sickness, making me want to throw up. I'd been running around like a chicken with my head cut off, bombarded with stress, and the smells and the fluorescent lights buzzing overhead didn't help.

When I reached Lucia's room, Gina was not there. Instead, an older man and woman dressed conservatively in dark colors and heavy wool were at Lucia's bedside. More accurately, the woman was bowing over Lucia, a rosary dangling from between her pressed palms, reciting what I could only imagine was a prayer, in Italian. A very loud and long prayer, punctuated by rhythmic beeps from the medical equipment. The man stood stiffly at the foot of the bed, his back to me, gripping the metal railing. Lucia, small and childlike, propped up on pillows, noticed me and shook her head slightly. I backed out, shaping a heart symbol with my fingers for her. She twitched her lips, wearily, a ghost of a smile, then turned her gaze back to the chanting woman.

I settled my weight into one of the green, overstuffed chairs in the closest waiting room, glad to rest my tired body. I had to fight to keep my eyes open. Checking my phone, I found that Gina had texted me, to warn me Lucia's parents were there—the Jersey girl hadn't been able to take the haranguing and prayers, so now she was at her apartment, promising to be back in a couple of hours. *Good luck with the nuts*, she texted. *They are in exorcism mode.*

Maybe they were about to go batshit crazy on their daughter, but at least they were there. Even if they were angry, they cared. They weren't ignoring her, like my dad was ignoring me, like Benji was ignoring me . . .

*Dad*, I texted, *if you don't call me back, I'm filing a missing person's report.*

I couldn't decide if I was more worried or mad when I realized I was likely going to have to fly home if I wanted answers. I rubbed at a knot in my neck. Where was home? Why did everyone have to be such a pain in the ass?

*You know what, Benji?* I texted next. *You might be over me, but I was only trying to do what was right for everyone. I went on an errand for my boss so I could keep my job and help my dad. What did you expect me to do differently? You selfish bastard.*

I deleted the last line. Then I typed it back in and hit send.

I heard chuckling from the row of chairs behind me. I glanced over my shoulder, irritated someone was allowed to be in a good mood in a hospital. A pair of beautiful hazel eyes locked on mine. It was Benji, phone in hand. He'd read my message.

"I'm the selfish bastard, huh?" His smile darkened; I could feel the anger dancing through him.

*Oh my God. I finally stand my ground and this is what I get for it.* "What are *you* doing here?"

"Gina told me what's going on with Lucia. She said no one else knows about the baby except you and me, and Lucia could use cheering up. So here I am."

"How noble of you," I snorted. A pain stabbed my chest. He'd come to see Lucia but not me.

"You don't have to be snotty. I like Lucia. I don't know her that well, but I wanted to come, if I could help." He stood up, threw a small teddy bear in my lap. "Anyway, looks like it's time for me to go. That's for Lucia."

"You're willing to hang out with someone who's practically a stranger, but you can't talk to me?"

"Oh, you want to talk? You seem more like you want to yell at me—which I don't deserve, by the way."

"Really? I tried to tell you why I couldn't make it to the job you set up, but you just shut me down."

"Huh. That's funny. I seem to remember texting *you* while you were in Galveston, even after you ditched me at a dinner with your friends and then made it so I had to take your place at the photo shoot—without any warning or real apology. You ghosted me. You either respect me or you don't, Paris. You proved that you don't." He strode toward the doors. "Tell Lucia I'll check in later."

"I didn't ghost you!" I said to his retreating back. But I had. I'd been too cowardly to reach out to him, and then I blamed him for it. I clenched the small teddy bear in my hands, twisting it. A pink bowtie popped off. *I was not made for juggling this many problems at the same time.*

. . . . . . . . . . . . . . . . . . . .

At midnight, I was sitting in the break room at PRCM, eating Nicki's Lean Cuisine lasagna from the staff freezer and smoking a cigarette I'd bummed from Kwan. I'd also helped myself to the good vodka in Frank's office, drinking it from one of his heavy crystal tumblers. *No red plastic Solo cups for me. This ain't no frat party.*

I was slightly drunk. *But, dude, I am on fire.*

I'd gone back to the office. Frank had finally gotten Todd the last of the information on the trades, and Todd had finished a draft of the yearly report. He'd left it on my desk; I was supposed to go over it one more time, looking for typos, and then make copies. I had every intention of finishing before the investors' meeting. Instead, I found evidence that Frank was an embezzler.

I took a long slug of Stoli Elit, which was roughly six hundred and seventy dollars per sip, and fixated on the reports in front of me.

*I knew it.* Frank hadn't given Todd the information on the unlabeled trades. They weren't even mentioned. I had known there was something screwy about how he'd refused to go over the trending activity when I was trying to finish the yearly report. Every time I'd tried to find out which trader was making some of the unlabeled trades, he'd sent me off on stupid errands. Which was why there was so much lime Gatorade in his office.

I had proof Frank was a cheating jackass. I may have been exhausted but I wasn't done celebrating. *I wonder how that Gatorade would taste as a mixer.*

# Chapter 28

My dad finally texted me. I wasn't so sure it was comforting, only more confusing.

*Forgive me,* he texted, *I know you are trying to reach me. I am fine, letting a room from a nice Russian woman in the neighborhood. I have a job now and house will sell next week.*

I immediately tried calling him.

"Hello?"

"Dad! Hi! I've been trying to reach—" My heart sang with relief. I'd only had a couple hours of sleep, and I needed to know what was going on with him before I made any rash decisions about my future with PRCM.

"Hello?" my dad repeated, cutting me off.

"Dad, hi, it's me, Paris, I've been calling—"

"Speak up! I can't hear you!"

I opened my mouth to start screaming into the phone when there was a long beep and then an automated woman's voice saying, "Leave your message now," followed by another beep.

"Damn it, Dad!" I yelled into the speaker. I hung up and threw my phone across the room, where it bounced off the couch. This was not how I wanted to spend my morning.

I screamed in frustration. I needed to know details, if I could save the house or not. Darien's mother had not bothered getting back to me, or even Darien, which wasn't surprising, but it was frustrating.

Gina came out of the bathroom wrapped in a towel, hands on her hips. We'd agreed to meet at my apartment and figure out a game plan. Lucia was going to be occupied for a couple of hours, going through a battery of tests. I needed to work, and so did Gina, but we hated leaving our friend alone. Especially with her parents. They were threatening to remove her from Sinai and take her back to a small, rural hospital outside their hometown. There, they could supervise Lucia and make sure the baby was immediately handed over for adoption, if it lived, and then Lucia was to move in with them. That was their plan. Not Lucia's.

"What are you screaming about?" Gina demanded. "The neighbors are going to call the cops."

"I'm going to be on a first-name basis with them pretty soon, anyway," I grumbled under my breath.

"What? Who? Your neighbors or the cops?"

"Don't worry, I'm not about to get caught subletting. But I might have to move back home anyway. At least, back to Newport."

I went into the kitchen to prepare some oatmeal and dates. *Me and my big mouth. Why did I say anything?*

"What's going on, Paris? Does this have to do with your dad?"

I sighed and threw up my hands. "Yes! Alright? Yes! I know how I can get the money to save his house, if it's not too late. But I'm not sure I have the balls."

"Are you planning on robbing a bank?"

"Listen, I stayed with Frank's freak show because I thought I'd learn something and move on, and then it was only because he promised me a raise. But that's not going to come soon enough. My dad needs my help *now*." My voice was getting louder and louder. "Frank is cray-cray. I can't do this anymore. And I don't have to. I found out something about Frank that I can use against him. I'm going to make him give me the best severance package ever and a fantastic letter of recommendation. He won't have a choice."

"Um, are you talking about blackmail?"

"No . . . well, maybe you could look at it that way, but I'm hoping he's going to do it because he realizes it's the right thing to do. In return, I will promise to keep my mouth shut." Defending my plan made my blood pressure rise.

"So, yeah. That's blackmail. Plus, if Frank broke the law, you're also aiding and abetting if you don't report him. Slippery slope here, Tehrani. I think you need to walk yourself back down the other side."

Why couldn't she see I needed to do this? "You're wrong. That's not what I'm doing."

"Potato, puhtato, Paris. You're playing with semantics. 'Cuz, dude, this *is* blackmail."

"I will make this work, Gina, you'll see. It's either this, or my dad ends up living on the street—"

"Or he could live with you here, maybe a two-bedroom—"

"He would never do that. Besides, he won't even answer his phone anymore. Maybe because he's too embarrassed . . . but I don't know, because he will not fucking tell me! I've got to get a handle on this before it's too late." I felt like my eyes were bulging out of my head from the pressure building up in me. "There's no one else but me that's going to do it."

She held up both hands, placating. "Alright, alright. I hear you. I'm just sayin', your crazy scheme ain't gonna work. This would bite you in the ass in the long run. Also, I don't have a lot of money for bail. We've got a baby to think about." She barked out a laugh. "What an interesting thing to hear myself say."

Gina's cell rang. It was the hospital. After a couple of one-word replies, she hung up.

Her voice was cracked and heavy. "We need to go back. Lucia is asking for us. The baby's heart stopped again and they're afraid she's going to miscarry."

. . . . . . . . . . . . . . . . . . . . .

Lucia's mother met us in the hallway outside her door. She would have been pretty, like an older Sophia Loren, if she wasn't so dour.

"You are not welcome in my daughter's room. This is because of you. Lucia was a good girl. But now . . . *sei una puttana. Partire!*"

I was astonished by the hostility, but Gina seemed ready for it, remaining even-keel in the raging Catholic mama's storm. "I will not leave, and I am no whore. Neither is Lucia. She is a good girl. But she made a mistake. *Non hai mai fatto un errore?*"

"I have not made a mistake such as this. It is a sin!" The mother's smooth face crumpled, crushed under the weight of her fear. "My baby will go to hell now, to burn in fire forever!"

While I could empathize with her worrying about Lucia, I was suddenly very glad I'd not been raised to believe in a hell. There was little room for error with such a belief system. I'd be on my knees in confession every Sunday and still end up roasting in an eternal fire. I wanted to be a good person and do the right thing, but the world didn't always give you a choice.

"We'll go," I said. "But the baby . . . is the baby okay?"

"Pah!" The woman spit to the side. "It would be best if that baby died. But God has seen fit to keep it alive another day."

I sucked in a breath.

"Not it—she." Gina widened her stance and put her balled

fists on her hips. "Lucia is having a daughter. You have a grand-daughter on the way."

Something flitted across the older woman's face, a deep, fleeting sorrow, but it was quickly masked by outrage. She put a finger in Gina's face. "Leave. *Partire.*"

Gina didn't flinch. I was proud of her.

The mother left us in the hall then, going into Lucia's room, where we could see our friend lying on the bed, eyes closed, skin pallid, a doctor assessing the many machines hooked up to her. There were no blaring alarms or hordes of nurses and doctors, though, so it appeared she'd stabilized again. It was hard to picture the young waif striding down a runway, aloof and in control, her confidence making her perfect, willowy frame seem eight feet tall. The poor, barely conscious girl lying in a hospital bed with metal handrails—bars—seemed to be lost to the whims of doctors and parents who would force her to follow their beliefs, no matter who suffered.

I'd often thought about how different my life would be if my mother had lived. Like my father, she would not be like this, so rigid and ugly. My mother would never hurt me in such a way. Nor would my father, not on purpose. *I've been blessed,* I thought.

"That rotten bitch," Gina growled. "I feel terrible she got here before us. Lucia doesn't need her Old Testament bs."

"What *does* she need, though? What can we do?"

"We can be for Lucia, not against her. Offer her love and kindness. Pick up the pieces."

"You're a good person. A good friend."

She grinned. "I just ask myself, 'What would Jesus do?' And, occasionally, I do it. When I'm not too busy being a *puttana.*"

. . . . . . . . . . . . . . . . . . . .

The next few days were hectic, trying to get ready for the investors' meeting and taking turns at the hospital, when Lucia's parents were gone for the night. Lucia didn't want to talk. She slept or quietly stared at the ceiling, her mind far away. One time, though, she broke her silence while I was beside her, looking over some reports.

"I am keeping this baby, Paris. I will not fight this hard for her, only to give her away." She closed her eyes, starting to drift away. "I will be her *mama*."

She must have said the same thing to her parents, because they did not come back the next day. I admired her strength of will. We were in our mid-twenties, having grown up in America, but her parents had not let go the old-world ways. Once again, I gave thanks to my parents, especially to my dad for bringing me here and raising me to be good, but also to be free, to be my own woman. Since moving to New York, I had been doing that. I hoped. Who was I now? I hoped one day I would be as strong as Lucia, as clear and determined as Gina.

And despite what Gina said, I felt the bravest, best decision I could make right then was to take advantage of Frank's crime in order to help my dad. It wasn't like I was hurting anyone.

On the day I planned to confront Frank, the subway ride into work did nothing to calm my nerves. The mother next to me was trying to get a colicky baby to breastfeed, while her two-year-old repeatedly pulled down the mom's shirt and nursing bra on the other side, going for some nipple-time himself. The college student across from us pretended to read something on his iPhone but I was pretty sure he was recording the scene. I glared at him until he turned away.

I picked up a discarded paper. I needed something to look at other than the exhausted mom's boobs. Flipping through the pages, I suddenly sat up, gobsmacked. *What the fuck?* I thought. *This cannot be real.*

There, at the top of the Lifestyle section, was a picture of Darien. Darien and his newest girlfriend. Her family proudly wished to announce to the world their little girl would be marrying my ex-boyfriend at their family synagogue, with a traditional Iranian wedding feast to follow.

The girl looked just like me. Creepy—though the ratio of forehead to face was startling. *Thank God I don't have that huge expanse of real estate to deal with. And I'm pretty sure those are extensions.*

The story was above the fold. Darien must have stumbled into a richer, more Jewish, form of me. They were staring lovingly into each other's eyes, her left hand strategically placed to show off a diamond the size of an orange.

A flash of rage burned through me. I crumpled up the paper fiercely, which drew the attention of the toddler. His eyes were big, instinct likely telling him he was close to a crazy person. He hid under his mom's legs, spying on me from under her skirt.

*Why do I care? I've been avoiding Darien forever now. I don't want him.* I leaned back, rested my head on the wall, and closed my eyes, forcing my fists to unfurl.

*But I do want stability.*

I didn't need to be married. I didn't need anyone to take care of me. But to know that my dad was doing okay, and also to have a loyal companion, someone to share space and events with me, day after day . . . like Benji. I'd tried calling him after our argument at the hospital, to fall on my sword and apologize. I was the one who'd initiated every misunderstanding we'd had. But he must have felt he'd given me enough chances. I hadn't heard back from him. I considered going to his gallery but figured that might just make him more angry, invading his space when he'd made it pretty clear he was tired of my crap.

*But was it crap?* If he'd let me explain, he'd see I'd had good reasons for most of what went wrong. That made another flash of rage sweep through me. *He didn't deserve me anyway. He didn't give me a chance. Screw Benji. And screw Darien.*

By the time I'd made my way into the PRCM building, I'd worked myself up into a fine lather, but I was no longer nervous.

"Hey, Paris. Are you okay?" asked Kwan, coming out from behind the security desk, adjusting the belt under his bulbous stomach. "You look like you could use a smoke."

"Nah, I'm not really a smoker, thanks," I said. He raised an eyebrow at me. We'd been sharing smoke breaks for a couple weeks now. "I was flirting with it for a while, but I'm done." I took a step and then turned back. "But maybe, if you don't care, I could bum one? It's gonna be a long day . . ."

He dug Camels out of a tight back pocket and held one out. "Mr. Coyle is back today. He doesn't look so good. I think you're gonna need this."

*Everyone is worried about my mental health these days but not so much my physical health,* I thought, thanking him and tucking it into my bag.

I sat at my desk, nervous, unsure of my next step. The investors' yearly report was done, the rough draft sitting in a neat stack next to me.

Todd appeared out of thin air. "Paris," he said with a nod of his majestically graying head.

"Oh, hello. Sorry I was late, but my friend is still in the hospital—"

"The report is edited and ready for tomorrow's meeting?" he said, picking up the stack of papers.

"Yes—"

"Good." He flipped through the pages. "I know Frank is in today, but, like I said, no need to bother him with this. I'll take care of it from here."

"But don't you want me to make copies—"

"You're going to have to earn my trust back, Ms. Tehrani. But not with something so important." He nodded toward Frank's door. "Why don't you make sure his refrigerator is stocked?"

As he walked away, through the large, open room filled with light and busy workers, I threw imaginary daggers at his back. I could not understand how Todd, once so compassionate, could turn out to be so . . . Frank-like.

As I bent over to unlock the drawer where I was keeping the incriminating papers, Frank came out of his office. I removed the key casually and sat up.

He was a mess.

A wig sat askew on Frank's head, hiding his baldness and staples. His button-up shirt hung oddly over his wrapped ribs. His black eye had faded to yellow, but his pupils were dilated, only half-hidden behind squinty lids, revealing that he'd likely had a side of Percocet with his breakfast.

"You might want to straighten your hair," I said. I was the one who'd suggested a hairpiece to his butler. He told me Frank had loved the idea so much, he'd had over a dozen delivered to the house and then laid them out on the oversized dining room table like alien dinner guests.

The day's version was a surfer's mop. Frank twisted the part further to the side. He resembled a punk kid on his way into Safeway to steal some Ho Hos. Or Donald Trump on a good hair day.

He stood over me, leaning against the back of my chair. "Listen, I need you to call Zina's. Twice now they have not seated me. Last night I had to sit at the bar like a chump. I live across the street, I eat there all the time. If they want to treat me like a tourist in my own neighborhood, I'm goin' to make sure they are replaced with a restaurant that's friendly.

You know, I want a place where they know my name. Tell them I know the health inspector. They better get their shit together."

I took notes, pretending that was something I would attend to later. The pain meds must have been throwing his bipolar medication out of whack.

"Also, let the research assistants know they're on notice. From now on they are to stay here until seven thirty." He staggered back a step but kept himself upright. I swung my chair around to face him.

"What? They get here at eight a.m."

"I came in last night and there was no one here. That is unacceptable. I can't run a business this way. Someone should be here. What if one of the analysts needs something?"

The analysts rarely stayed past six. If they had work to do, they would do it at home. "Frank, this is going to make everyone very unhappy."

"I don't give a shit about your happiness. They'll be fired if nobody is here."

"So can they at least rotate who stays that late?"

"Fuck no, Paris. This means you, too. You just got a raise, there's no reason for you to leave early."

I stared at him in shock. *This has to be a joke, right? He can't legally make us work twelve hours, can he?*

"And I need you to fire Michelle today."

"No!" I jumped up out of my desk chair. "If you need to fire someone, fire Nicki!"

Frank scrambled back. A number of the traders and analysts were gawking at us. Frank didn't care. He wagged a finger in my face, serious. "You wanted a raise. Well, this is how we're going to make it happen. Michelle makes too much for an assistant, and she's bossy. Now that you're going to be here longer hours, you don't need her help."

"If Michelle's not here, I won't have time to do trades with you . . . Oh. That was never going to happen, was it?"

"We'll never know, will we?" He did an abrupt about-face and then stumbled into his office.

*This is so unfair. To everybody.* The man treated his employees like homeless mutts, creatures to be beaten or exterminated upon a whim. How could he do that to Michelle after her years of dedication and putting up with his craziness? She'd trained everyone in this office.

*You know what? Fuck this. I'm doin' it. Michelle will keep her job. I'm going out in a blaze of glory, and I'm going to make sure Frank Coyle feels the burn.*

He was either going to give me what I deserved or he was in for one hell of a ride at the investors' meeting.

"Frank," I said, following him into his office and shutting the door. "We need to talk."

"No, we don't. Put on your big-girl panties and do your job."

*I'm gonna do just that.* I held out the sheaf of trading reports. "I know what you've been doing."

He glanced at the papers in my hands. "What? Trading? Well, thank God you figured that out. I kinda assumed you already knew."

"I'm talking about the illegal trades."

Frank froze in his chair, his wig sideways. "What are you talking about?"

"Come on," I said, throwing the papers on the desk in front of him. "The unnamed trades? How were you planning on fixing that before the meeting tomorrow? I left them out of the investors' report, but I've got my own report, right here."

"I have no idea what you're talking about, but you are speaking to me in a manner that's dangerously close to getting you fired." He paged through the report.

"You're not going to fire me. I'm quitting." My courage was building, flooding me with endorphins. "Who in their right mind wants to work with you, Frank? You're mean, you don't keep your promises, and you have zero respect for others, including your son. You might not remember much of Galveston. But I do. Every painful second. You're also dishonest. You are going to write me a glowing letter of recommendation, *and* you're going to give me a severance package with one year of my pay, with the raise." I stood tall with righteous indignation. *I should jump up on his desk, make my voice heard.* Quivering with justice, I said, "Or I will stand up at the investors' meeting tomorrow and show them exactly how you used their money for your gain."

"Shut your mouth, Paris." He was quiet. There was no emotion on his doughy face. In a dull voice, he said, "You are to go home and not say a word of this to anyone. Report back to me, in here, at this time tomorrow. Then we'll talk about your goddamn severance package."

Confused by his response, some of the air bled out of my righteousness. "I mean it, Frank. I'm not just sweeping it under the rug."

"You've made that abundantly clear. After all I've done for you." He shook his head in disgust.

I almost lunged across the desk. *All you've done for me!* Instead, I watched as his dignity slipped away with his wig—it slid over one ear and then completely off, landing on the desktop with a *thunk*.

He regarded the wig glumly. "Get out."

I sauntered through his door, my shoulders back and squared, hot and sweaty with my victory and the belief that I was completely justified in my actions. But minutes later, when the elevator doors shut behind me, it wasn't just the quick descent that made my stomach drop.

*What have I done?*

# Chapter 29

The large boardroom was packed. Celebrities as well as the quietly rich lined the rows of padded chairs facing the podium. Todd had given the job of handing out the year-end informational packets to Nicki and the young research assistants. With swollen eyes and slumped shoulders, they worried about their jobs while the clients read about the millions they'd been raking in, thanks to the genius of Andrew and Frank. Really, just Frank.

I'd arrived at his office as instructed, long before the meeting, but waited and waited, with no sign of Frank. I couldn't believe he'd stood me up.

*He must not think I'm serious.*

*Am I serious? I mean, I'm not like a character out of a movie, this is real life . . .*

*Hell yeah, I'm serious. Get it together, girl.*

I sat in the front row, to the side, next to Michelle. She seemed at ease, no idea Frank planned on firing her, too. In my bag, I had my own set of papers—Michelle would be safe, if I had anything to do with it. We were set to start in a few minutes and Frank still had not appeared. *I hope nobody blames that on me.* Todd was also missing, most likely trying to find Frank. Or sober him up.

Andrew was already seated in the front row, wearing a

three-piece suit, crossing and uncrossing his legs, a briefcase at his side. He was like a nervous best man, afraid the groom wasn't going to show. Frank had so much power over other people. I couldn't think of a less-deserving man to be in charge.

As one, the room turned toward a commotion at the door. Frank and Todd appeared to be in a tussle, each trying to get through the door first. Somehow, despite his wounds, Frank broke through, Todd behind him. Frank was wearing a suit and actual dress shoes, but the new bowl-cut wig, something Ringo Starr might have worn, ruined any sense of professionalism he might have wanted to project. That, and wrestling with his COO.

*This man is a child.*

The epiphany hit me, hard, a wallop to the back of my stupid head. *I'm so much a better person than he is.*

I peered around guiltily, and shoved my bag, and the evidence of fraud, under the seat with my foot.

*My God. Blackmail? What was I thinking?* How had I talked myself into believing that committing a felony was a good idea? I was no cheater, and I definitely couldn't live with myself if I went through with it. Frank could do that, but I couldn't.

*Nor will I be able to live with myself if I let this cruel, unjust man take these people's life savings.* Not everyone in the room was grossly wealthy, but even if they were, they'd trusted PRCM to protect their earnings.

So, what was I going to do?

I jumped up and moved quickly to the podium, trying not to think about how my actions would affect my father. My future. I beat Frank and the gray-haired COO to the front of the room by half a second. I could live without a severance package if I knew this criminal was going to jail.

I tapped the microphone to get everyone's attention, though

it was unnecessary, because everyone was already trying to figure out why there was such an odd start to the meeting. My heart raced. I felt sure the mic was picking up the swoosh of the blood storming madly through my veins. Frank stepped up to my right side, too close, while Todd was on my left.

"Hello, everyone," I said nervously. "Welcome to PRCM's yearly recounting of events."

From the front row next to Michelle, Nicki sniggered, her pale lips twisted in an ugly, mocking smile. Michelle elbowed her and then, well aware something unprepared was happening at the front of the room, started clapping, trying to lighten the mood. The room swelled with a round of applause.

Todd said quietly, from between clenched teeth, "You two go sit down, right now."

Frank ignored him, whispering in my other ear, his breath wet. "Paris, you have no idea what's going on. You're going to have to trust me, it's going to be fine. Introduce the CEOs and go sit down. We will talk later."

My boss moved back a step, leaving me to my own devices. Why in any of the hells should I trust Frank? But Todd pressed in closer. In a low, harsh tone, he said, "You keep your fucking mouth shut. Frank is the one who has no idea what's going on. But I do. Don't make this worse for yourself."

I stifled a gasp. Did Todd know what was going on? Why hadn't he done something before now? Why was he protecting Frank? Then it hit me—he thought I was the one who'd been doing something wrong.

A river of panic moved through me. I had no idea what to do. Then I purposefully settled my mind. I was going to have to explain things to Todd before I took any action, so he didn't think I was doing this to cover my own tracks. The wind in my sails evaporated. My plan to shame Frank publically blew away.

"Hello, ladies and gentlemen," I stammered, attempting to cover the awkwardness of the past few minutes. The murmuring trailed off. I took a deep breath, steadying myself. "I'd like to introduce the men who make this happen, who have worked hard to earn your trust. I think you're going to be pleased with the trends over the past year, which you'll find in the packets you hold in your hands. Furthermore, Purple Rock Capital Management is looking at an exciting year on the horizon. Please welcome your COO, Todd Lindstrom, your CEO Andrew Jones, and, of course, the hedge fund maven himself, Franklin Coyle."

I clapped, briefly, stiffly, before walking back to my chair, moving like a marionette.

Andrew remained seated, frowning, a worry line etched deep into his forehead. It was an emotion I'd never seen from him. Frank stepped to the microphone. Todd was just behind him, glaring at me.

*What in the hell is going on?*

Frank lowered the microphone down to his level. His voice boomed across the room. "Hello there!"

Then he held up the report, waved it around. Todd looked like he wanted to grab it from him, but Frank was oblivious. "Welcome to the yearly meeting. If you come across any typos in this document, you can blame it on my assistant." Frank proffered an exaggerated wink in my direction. "English isn't her first language."

*Whaaat? He made me his opening joke!* I sprang up out of my seat.

Gracefully, clear-minded, I turned to the crowd. "There's something you should—"

"Ah, Paris, lighten up. I was just kidding," Frank said over me from the podium. "Ladies and gentlemen, my assistant here has been a lifesaver, in more ways than you know." He gestured for me to take a seat. "For instance, she's the one who brought to my attention that someone in this office was attempting to make illegal trades."

My legs went rubbery. Todd's eyes narrowed at Frank, then me.

I would have fallen to the floor if it hadn't been for Michelle, beside me, guiding me to a seat. But her eyes were drawn elsewhere. Following the gaze of the crowd, I saw Nicki briskly hotfooting it down the side aisle toward the door, red hair flopping with the effort, her eyes round and hollow. The crowd muttered in confusion.

"Nicki, don't bother," Frank said conversationally into the microphone, leaning on the podium, a hand in his pocket. Behind him, Todd's face was etched in shock. He hadn't known this was going to happen. Me, either. *Nicki? No way.* Was she smart enough to have done this? I didn't think so.

*Yet, there she goes.*

Nicki's white face was pinched with terror. But not guilt. She didn't stop. As she reached the doors, they were pushed open from the other side. Two of New York's finest blocked her path.

"Yep, that's your gal," Frank said to the police officers.

"I'm innocent! This is crazy! He's crazy!" Nicki shrieked. The junior assistant's protests became fainter but didn't stop as she was hauled away.

In the sudden dead quiet of the room, Frank shifted his gaze to me. It was hard to read his expression. The long Beatles bangs hung over his eyes, and his shoulders were slumped as usual, his skin grayish. He still looked like the beleaguered middle school science teacher.

Maybe, despite himself, he had taught me something. And saved me from myself.

"What do you have to say now, my little Persian princess?

Your people aren't the only ones who know how to throw a bomb into the room."

His slur crashed around the room and fell at my feet. This time there was no second-guessing my response.

"I quit, you son of a bitch."

The journey to the back of the room, down the long aisle, past our staring investors, took a lifetime. Cement had replaced the blood in my legs, but I held my head high.

# Chapter 30

The peace evaporated as soon as the doors closed behind me.

*What have I done? I'll never get another job in finance. The shadiest bank won't even hire me as a teller, not when Frank's done with me.* I choked, sliding down the wall in the hallway. *Sorry, Dad. I am so sorry.*

I found my cell and punched in his number. I needed to hear his voice now, to know he was going to love me after I'd failed him so miserably.

He answered. For the first time in two weeks, he answered.

"*Parisa!* Oh, my beautiful girl!" And then he burst into tears. "The house . . ." Sobs rolled out of him, crushing my soul.

I started crying, too. "I know. I am so sorry. I tried—"

Through shuddering breaths, he said over me, "How did you do it?"

"I just . . . Do what?"

"You are the most wonderful daughter a man could hope to raise." His gasping subsided.

Even in the worst moments, he was good to me. "Oh, Dad."

"Who else buys a house for their father? Tell me, who?"

"Wha-what did you say?" My dad and I were having two separate conversations. I had no idea what he was talking about.

"I will always be grateful, *Parisa*. Only you know how much this place means to me."

"I think—"

"I could not believe it when the mortgage lender drove up and handed me the title. 'It's yours, Mr. Tehrani,' he says, 'free and clear,' he says. I waited for him to cross the road before I fainted." He spoke at a high speed.

"Wait!" I was so confused.

He finally took a breath and slowed down. "What you have done is a great good."

And then it sank in—he was not distraught. Jubilation laced his voice, pure joy riding his emotions like a cowboy on a galloping horse.

"Someone bought the house?" I asked, trying to understand what was happening.

"What do you mean? The deed is in your name. You bought the house, *Parisa*." Doubt crept into his voice. "Did you not?"

"Dad, go get the paperwork. Find the page where it lists the actual buyer, not the holder of the deed or the title."

Flustered, he finally did it. I could hear him rummaging through drawers. Then he flipped through paper, muttering to himself. "Here it is. But I don't understand. It says the house mortgage was paid off by Franklin Q. Coyle, the Third. Is that not your boss? Why did he do this?"

I had to sit quietly with that for a while.

"I'll call you back later. But everything is okay."

"So, the house, it is ours?"

"I think so. We'll talk in a while. In the meantime, go have a glass of champagne."

"Yes, just so. By the way, my little fairy, how can you tell if an Amish man is drunk?"

"Dad, I don't have time for this . . ."

"He falls off the wagon!"

"Ugh!" But I laughed. "I love you."

So. While I'd been plotting Frank's demise, he'd secretly paid off my father's debt. *Once again, I'm the asshole.*

The only time I'd talked to Frank about the house was when he was drugged, on the plane home from Galveston. Just after I'd told him that I'd sent a rock star to his son's birthday party in his stead and that he was a terrible human being. I sighed heavily. *It's so hard to judge where exactly in Hell Frank belongs when he does things like this. Glad I'm not the one in charge of his soul.*

I peeled myself off the floor outside the boardroom, choosing to be long gone before the meeting ended. I did not have the strength to face anybody, including the racist, misogynistic bastard who saved my family home and kept me from committing a felony.

Back at my desk, I unlocked the desk drawer and hefted out the black binder. The Book of Frank. I tore a sticky note off, wrote a few sentences, and then stuck the note to the front of the binder:

*Frank, I did not fire Michelle. She is the one who created this book. She is the reason your big Texas deal happened. She is the one who knows how everything in this office works, including you. She is fiercely loyal to PRCM, though you don't deserve it. If you don't hire her as your executive assistant, you're an idiot. Be good to her and she'll make sure PRCM runs like a watch.—Paris*

*P.S. You are a jerk. But thank you for keeping me from doing something criminal and stupid. And, I think, maybe, for setting me free? Most importantly, thank you for saving my father's house. You did a good thing there.*

I placed the Book of Frank squarely on his desk, smiling at the spiked aluminum art and the shelf with the shards of blue crystal, taking in the crazy that was Frank one last time.

I might never know for sure why he paid for the house. Or if he'd said those terrible things in order to make me stand up for myself . . . *Nah. He's just a racist. A racist with money to burn.*

Someday, maybe, I'd talk to him about it, but not that night.

Todd was waiting for me at my desk.

"I didn't take anything from his office," I said haughtily. "You can look."

"Paris, I'm sorry."

The nicety was so unexpected, I had to choke back tears.

"Listen," he said, sitting on the edge of an armchair in front of what had been my desk earlier that morning. The office was empty of people. He hadn't brought the police with him. He continued, "This whole debacle came about because of a lack of communication between Frank and I. I knew there was something going on, but I wasn't sure what. My reports weren't matching up. I'd narrowed it down to having to do with you and Nicki, once I realized it wasn't Frank. If he was going to embezzle, he's smart enough to know how to do it in a way none of us would ever find out."

"I get you thinking it was me. But Nicki?" I couldn't decide how to feel, grateful or depressed.

"That was why I had her start working in my office, to split you up, see what happened. It was obvious she couldn't have done anything on her own."

"Todd, I swear to you, I've been trying to talk to Frank about the irregularities for months. I would never do this."

"I know. And if Frank would just pay attention and do his job, he would have seen Nicki's stupid attempts at trying to pull something off right from the start. When Ericka set it up."

"Oh. Ericka." That explained so much.

"His last executive assistant." Todd nodded, then sighed. "Frank certainly gave her enough reason to want to hurt us. She wasn't nearly as smart as she thought she was, though. It was never going to work, but especially when she partnered with Nicki. Who, by the way, has confessed to everything."

"She is one class act."

"Once you showed Frank the report, he figured out exactly what was happening, probably immediately. He truly is a genius. But he's also a moron—Frank decided it would be fun to put on a show for the shareholders instead of talking to me about it first. He's lucky it worked out the way it did." Todd snorted. "They're down there now, patting him on the back, thanking him for all his hard work."

"I'm lucky, too." I opened my tote and removed the pages of evidence I'd printed off, grateful Frank had stopped me from trying to blackmail him. Though I still couldn't believe it wasn't him. I held them out. "You probably don't need these anymore, but they're yours. I'm done."

Todd took the papers. I felt lighter. Jobless, but lighter.

. . . . . . . . . . . . . . . . . . . . .

After Todd left, I stacked the five postcard-sized frames on my desk and laid them gently in my bag. Door photos, reminding me there was always something on the other side.

Kwan greeted me at the elevator in the lobby.

"Ms. Tehrani, I need your badge and your elevator code card." He sounded so serious but then leaned in closer, stress accentuating his whisper. "Paris! What did you do?"

The security guard had offered me a smile and wave every morning. A kind word or gesture every day. I was going to miss him. I slid the badge off my lapel and handed it over with my elevator card. "It's okay, Kwan. I'm not in trouble. It's what I want. Besides, maybe I can quit smoking, now that I'm leaving this place." I gave him a big hug. "And here," I said, handing him a Photography by Paris card, "this is my new business card. If I've left something behind, this has my address."

A woman's silky voice spoke up from behind me. "May I have one of those?"

I whirled around as Kwan tipped his hat. "Ms. Jenson," he said, and then left us.

*Oh.* She'd been at the investors' meeting. She had seen everything.

"You're unemployed." Her bright eyes drilled into me. "What are you going to do now?"

"I . . . That's a good question."

"Oh, for God's sakes, you know the answer, girl."

I straightened my spine, squared my shoulders, and said, "If we're talking about my career, then of course. I'm taking my photography business full-time. And I'm taking the art world by storm."

"Atta girl." She grinned.

"And I'm doing a Kickstarter campaign," I said, spinning the dream into reality. "You, too, can be a part of this, if you so desire . . ." I was smiling, giddy, but serious, speaking from the heart.

"If you want my involvement, let's skip Kickstarter. How about I fund the startup and keep sixty percent of the profits? I happen to have some investment money that was freed up recently."

"Are you saying you're pulling out of PRCM? Because of me?"

"Don't get too far ahead of yourself. Frank Coyle may be a genius, but he's a pig. There are plenty of geniuses out there who are hard workers and decent people. I'm not wasting my time and money on his little endeavor one second longer."

His "little" billion-dollar endeavor—I was never going to move in her circles, be at her level. But I could aim for it.

"If you want in with Photography by Paris, I'll offer you forty percent with your startup coverage," I said. "And you'll sign my company to do the photography for your print ads for a year."

She laid her manicured hand over her chest and laughed, deeply. "Oh, you're good."

We traded cards, shook hands, and then I watched her leave the lobby, moving like a sleek panther sliding into the jungle.

I could be her. I would be her. Strong and confident, moving through a world of her own making with ease, choosing her own path.

I was no longer tethered to my father's dreams of my future in finance. I'd burned that to the ground. But I'd established the first solid foundations of my own business, a commercial photography business. I would prove to my father that my art, my dream, was real and, combined with the business savvy I had learned from him, was going to pay the bills.

And if he couldn't get behind my new plan, well, I'd be disappointed but I was done trying to please others, especially with my life choices. As I reached the exit, Kwan tipped his hat and held the door for me. I floated out.

# *Epilogue*

*A Year Later . . .*

Alessandra looked me in the eyes and smiled, a big, open, friendly smile I couldn't help but return. And then she spewed chunky baby barf across my chest, like a pressure washer, ruining my new silk Dolce & Gabbana shirt. Of course.

"Let me take her. There's a clean shirt in the diaper bag." Gina, grabbing the wiggling five-month-old, glanced at me and said, "You've got vomit in your hair."

I tried not to freak out; it took every ounce of willpower not to strip down to my bra in the middle of Central Park in a disgusted frenzy. Instead, I removed the T-shirt from the diaper bag, an old Pokémon symbol emblazoned on the front, and changed with as much modesty as I could, using my already ruined shirt to remove the biggest chunks from my hair. I was proud of my aplomb, while secretly adding another tally to my "never having a baby" column.

We'd already gone through the stash of costume changes in my photo shoot bag. Regardless, this had been an exquisite fall day, the Indian summer bringing out another round of rose and rhododendron blooms, enhanced by a backdrop of colorful leaves. The sun filtering through the trees, dappling the rocks and grass, made my heart hurt, it was so beautiful.

*Okay.* Being honest, it was really the magic of having friends close on a day like this, everybody working together to make Lucia's sweet child laugh. Shooting picture after picture, endless variations on the family, a mommy, a baby girl, and her auntie.

During the breaks, Gina was texting her boyfriend in Brazil, a timber baron, and Lucia would swap kisses with her newest boyfriend, a librarian from Queens. So, yeah, maybe not the nuclear family described in home ec books from the 1950s, but they made it work.

Gina was baby Alessandra's godmother, and listed as next of kin on the birth certificate; Lucia's parents had turned their backs on her and refused to see their granddaughter. Lucia was devastated but sent them updates and photos, hoping they'd change their mind someday. Once I'd convinced Gina that firebombing the old couple's brownstone probably would not win them over, we made a pact. We were a tribe. The village was going to raise this baby. But I was ready to return to my quiet space for the day.

"I should go. Can you call me an Uber?" I called over to Lucia, who was on her phone, as I finished brushing the puke from my hair.

Someone behind me leaned close and whispered into my ear, "Uber."

I let out a shriek and spun around.

Benji. It was Benji. A camera hung around his neck. His hazel eyes sparkled against his tanned face, his adorable freckles making me want to touch his cheeks. And corduroys clung to his muscled thighs. Not much had changed.

"Get it? I called you 'Uber.'"

"Oh my God, you're making stupid dad jokes."

"Hi, Paris. You look good."

"Hi, Benji. So do you." I tried not to drool. Then I remembered I smelled like vomit.

"You have something in your hair." He reached for me.

"No, no, don't touch it! Alessandra threw up on me."

"Are you talking about her?" Grinning, he threw his thumb back at the five-month-old. "It's baby spit-up. Who cares? You haven't been around a lot of babies, have you?"

As Benji said warm hellos to everyone and then hoisted the baby in the air, rubbing noses with her as he swung her legs out, making Alessandra shriek with laughter, my secret, internal tally experienced a major upheaval. A new column—"Make a baby with this man *now*"—leapt into existence, filled with tally marks.

*I bet we could work out the kinks.*

. . . . . . . . . . . . . . . . . . . . .

"How in the heck can you afford this place?" Benji asked incredulously, turning in a slow circle, admiring my new gallery and adjoining offices on the bottom floor of a large, modern building made from white stone.

I'd left the bubble my dad had created for us with his white picket fence and created my own bubble, in the trendy Picket Building. I knew the minute Tris Jenson's realtor pulled up to the curb in front of the impressive Bronx structure that I was home.

I twirled one of my mother's gold hoop earrings between my fingers, cocked my head thoughtfully, and smiled at him. "Well, I had financial help from a celebrity investor, someone I met while working for Frank. She opened a door for me and I walked through. I decided what my new world was going to look like, and then made it happen."

I slid my finger across one of my favorite photos on the gallery wall, one of the few with a human as the central feature. It was set on the bank of Benji's favorite river. The focus was on my father, his slacks rolled up, and slow, shallow water flowing over his bare feet. He intently studied a river pebble in his hand, bemused and sun-dappled.

"You and my dad taught me about embracing the beauty in simple things. I'm doing that."

As the handsome, kind, and witty man admired my work on the walls, I folded my arms and leaned back, watching him meander among my creations.

*I don't need a man to make me happy.*

Benji flashed me a wide grin and a thumbs-up before moving to the next photo.

*On the other hand, who am I to turn my back on the gift that's come through my door?*

# Acknowledgments

I'd like to thank all my friends that I've had to ditch on numerous occasions for work. To my friends who my boss has insulted, thank you for never fighting back and making a bigger scene. To my friend Mo, thank you for helping me and always being there for me, no matter what. A big thank you to Holly Lörincz for taking an idea I had and bringing it to life, I couldn't ask for a better person to work with. Thank you to Chip Macgregor for guiding me and having my best interests at heart, and Skyhorse for believing in my book and letting me be a part of the decision process. Also, I would like to thank my brother, parents, and my aunt for giving me legal advice. You are the best.

Finally I'd like to thank Mr. Predetti, this book wouldn't have happened if you weren't so understanding.

—L.

Thank you to our editors, Chelsey and Alex. Skyhorse provided a top-notch team. Thank you to Chip MacGregor for being there, always, and bringing this book to fruition and beyond. Thank you to Auggie, who subsisted on pizza for months at a time and didn't complain (much). Finally, thank you to L., who brought me her story and trusted me to write it. You who shall remain nameless have been the perfect partner.

—Holly